MALCOLM

THE REDEMPTION SERIES, BOOK 1

By

INTERNATIONAL
BESTSELLING AUTHOR

S.J. WEST

CONTENTS

COPYRIGHTS

Cover Design: coversbyjuan.com, all rights reserved.
Interior Design & Formatting: Stephany Wallace, all rights reserved.
Proof Reader: Allisyn Ma.

Published by Watchers Publishing January, 2014.
www.Sjwest.com

BOOKS IN THE WATCHER SERIES

Lucifer
Redemption

The Dominion Series
Awakening
Reckoning
Enduring

The Everlasting Fire Series
War Angel
Between Worlds

OTHER BOOKS BY S.J. WEST

The Harvester of Light Trilogy
Harvester
Hope
Dawn

The Vankara Saga
Vankara
Dragon Alliance
War of Atonement

Vampire Conclave Series
Moonshade
Sentinel
Conclave
Requiem

ACKNOWLEDGMENTS

I would like to express my gratitude to the many people who were with me throughout this creative process; to all those who provided support, talked things over, read, wrote, offered comments, allowed me to quote their remarks and assisted in the editing, proofreading and design.

Thanks to Allisyn Ma, my proofreader for helping me find typos, correct commas and tweak the little details that have help this book become my perfect vision. I would like to thank Liana Arus, my beta reader for helping me in the process with invaluable feedback. Thank you to Stephany Wallace for creating the Interior Design of the books and formatting them.

Last and not least: I want to thank my family, who supported and encouraged me in this journey.

I apologize to those who have been with me over the course of the years and whose names I have failed to mention.

PROLOGUE

Andre Greco lifted his hand to knock on the study door, but hesitated because he knew the occupant would not welcome the sad tidings he had to report. With great reluctance, he rapped his knuckles against the dark stained wood and waited.

A minute passed. Then two. Then three. Finally, the answer Andre both dreaded, and felt relief in hearing, came.

"Come in, Andre."

When he opened the door to the study, Andre's eyes were drawn to the lone figure of his leader and best friend standing by the far window in the room. Malcolm's gaze was directed toward the broken world outside. It was a world they had been left to guard but had failed in many ways over the years.

Andre slowly closed the door behind him and stood unmoving, waiting for Malcolm to turn and acknowledge his presence.

As he waited, Andre observed his friend and noted the pained expression that was ever- present on Malcolm's face during the past few years. His friend's shoulders were broad and held straight with a stubborn pride. Malcolm stoutly refused to show the depth of his pain, both physical and emotional, to those around him. And Andre knew the news he brought this night would add to the mountain of guilt Malcolm already held firmly on his shoulders.

"Is the child born?" Malcolm finally asked, breaking the quiet of the room but still not turning his gaze away from the city outside to face Andre.

"Yes," Andre said, taking a slow, steadying breath before continuing. "But Amalie didn't survive very long after giving birth. The pregnancy itself just placed too much of a strain on her body. She lacked the strength in the end to hold onto life."

Andre watched as Malcolm slowly closed his eyes and hung his head, showing the weight of his sorrow. He waited patiently as his friend took a moment to come to terms with the death of someone they had both loved dearly.

"Did she suffer because of that thing?" Malcolm asked in a quiet, tense voice.

"Not in the end," Andre said. "She was able to hold the baby for a few minutes before she passed away. That, more than anything, seemed to help ease her pain."

Malcolm sighed heavily.

"I should have seen what was happening," Malcolm said, shaking his head in dismay. "I should have protected Amalie better."

Andre took a few steps closer to his friend.

"It wasn't your fault, Malcolm. You couldn't have stopped Amalie from following her heart. All of Caylin's descendants have been strong-willed and hardheaded. You did everything you could to warn her about what might happen."

"But it wasn't enough, Andre," Malcolm said, guilt over Amalie's death drenching each of his words.

The pain in Malcolm's voice broke Andre's heart, but he knew there wasn't anything he could do or say to erase the blame Malcolm felt.

Finally, Malcolm turned to Andre to face him fully.

"Take that thing away from here before I do something to it I might regret later, Andre," Malcolm ordered. "Follow the plan we set into motion when we first learned of this damned pregnancy."

"Don't you want to see her before we leave?" Andre asked. "She's still a descendant of Caylin and Aiden's line."

"She is an abomination, and I don't want to have anything to do with her!" Malcolm roared, barely able to keep his temper in check. "Take her to Cirrus and raise her as your own like we planned. In a few generations, I'll take back control of protecting Caylin's heirs. But now, I can't even make myself look at that thing, much less protect it."

"I understand why you hate her, but. ..."

"No," Malcolm said, cutting off Andre's words before letting him finish. Andre noticed Malcolm absently begin to rub the side of his right thigh. "You don't understand everything. I didn't only fail Amalie by not protecting her; I failed Lilly, too, and that haunts me more than anything else. I wasn't able to keep the last promise I made to her. *That* is something that can never be fixed."

"You did your best. Lilly would have understood."

"And when I'm finally able to stand in front of her in Heaven, just how do you suggest I explain this monumental failure to her, Andre?"

Andre was silent, not having a good answer.

Malcolm turned back to face the outside world again.

"You should leave as soon as possible," Malcolm told Andre. "Your titles have been bought and paid for. I've already contacted the Emperor and arranged the marriage between that thing and his son. He's expecting you to arrive in the capital city tonight."

"Are you sure having her marry the crown prince is the right thing to do?" Andre asked, sounding unsure of the decision Malcolm had made about the child's future.

"It will secure her children into a place of honor and safety," Malcolm said. "We've discussed this before, Andre. Don't start questioning the plan now."

"But we've always let the girls choose who they married," Andre argued.

Malcolm snorted. "And look how well that turned out for Amalie. We are not letting that thing choose who she marries. We can't afford another slip-up. Just do what I'm ordering you to do and take that creature to Cirrus!"

Andre sighed. "Do you want me to keep you apprised of her development?"

"No," Malcolm said, lifting his head a notch higher. "I don't want to know anything about her unless it's to report her death."

"Malcolm. ..." Andre said reproachfully.

"I'm sorry," Malcolm said, not really sounding sorry at all. "It's the way I feel, and I won't pretend otherwise. As long as she continues Caylin's line, I don't care what else happens to her, Andre."

"If that's the way you want it, then that's the way it will be."

Malcolm nodded. "Yes, that's the way I want it."

Andre fell silent for a moment, trying to think of a way to change Malcolm's mind, but no solution presented itself.

"I will keep in contact with you while we're in Cirrus," Andre said. "And I've picked a name for her. Would you like to know it?"

"No."

Andre sighed again. "Then I guess I'll see you in a few years, my friend."

Malcolm turned to look at Andre once more.

"I'm sorry to lay the burden of raising her on your shoulders,

Andre, but I simply can't do it. I can't even bring myself to look at her."

"It will be my honor to raise her," Andre told Malcolm. "She isn't the monster you believe her to be, Malcolm. I think she might just surprise you."

Andre had seen the child and knew in one glance how special she was. He also knew no matter what he told Malcolm, it wouldn't be enough to convince his oldest friend that the girl who had been born that night might be the one they had waited for, for over a millennium.

"I'll send a message to you after we arrive in Cirrus," Andre said, "so you'll at least know we made it there safely."

Malcolm nodded, acknowledging that he heard Andre's words.

Andre made his way out of the house to the city street where a horse-drawn carriage waited for him. The night was foggy, like it often was in New Orleans, as he climbed into the carriage. He sat opposite the child and her nanny. The carriage lurched forward as the driver headed toward the only one of a few areas left on Earth where teleporters were permitted. Once there, they would be allowed to teleport up to the cloud city of Cirrus, which was located above what was left of New York City.

"I guess he decided to remain as obstinate as ever," the nanny grumbled, cradling the newborn in the crook of her arm, like the babe she held was the most precious thing on Earth.

"You know how he can be, Millie." Andre sighed.

Millie looked down at the child she held.

"I can't understand why the master would shun such a sweet little nipper," Millie said.

"He has his reasons."

Millie looked over at Andre.

"Have you decided on a name yet?" she asked.

Andre grinned. "Yes, I have."

"Well, don't just sit there grinning like a Cheshire cat," Millie griped. "What is it, for goodness' sake?"

Andre held his arms out to Millie, indicating that he wanted to hold the child before giving her his answer. Almost reluctantly, Millie handed the baby girl to Andre.

When Andre looked down at the child he held, he couldn't help but smile at the little cherub tucked safely in his arms.

"Hello, Annalisse Desiraye Greco," he said to her. "Welcome to the world."

CHAPTER 1

As I stand on the veranda of the home I share with my father, I watch the sun rise over the horizon, bringing with it the start of a brand new day filled with unknown possibilities. Its shimmering rays glance off the transparent protective dome surrounding Cirrus, penetrating just enough to light up the world I live in. I watch the holographic clouds glide by on an artificially created wind, propagating the illusion that they're free-floating. Far off in the distance, I can see the castle of the emperor. Its white stone towers with blue tiled roofs stand out amidst the wispy white clouds, like a dream from a simpler time in Earth's history. I know it will be my home soon, but the mere thought of living within its walls tightens the ever-present knot in the pit of my stomach.

I love the man I will have to marry, but not in the way a wife should love a husband. Newly crowned Emperor Augustus Charles Ronaldo Amador has been my childhood friend almost since the moment I was born. I was told that, on the night of my birth, we met and were betrothed to one another within hours of my entry into this world. I grew up knowing that I will marry

Auggie on my twenty-first birthday and eventually become Empress Annalisse Desiraye Amador. On that day, I will fulfill a long-ago arrangement made to place me on the throne of Cirrus to rule by Auggie's side.

But it isn't what I want to do. I don't want to become Empress of Cirrus. I don't want to become Auggie's wife. Yet what I want to do isn't within the realm of possibilities.

"A penny for your thoughts."

I turn around and find Auggie leaning up against one of the four white marble pillars that lead into my private chambers.

I've always found Auggie attractive with his wavy, shoulder-length blond hair and barely-there mustache and beard. His clear blue eyes hold a tenderness for me and a certain amount of pity. He's dressed in one of his white collarless suits, and I know today must be one of the few days in his life he has all to himself.

Auggie pushes off the pillar and saunters over to me.

"Auggie," I say, "do you think I'll ever find someone to love me?"

"I love you," he replies, smiling at me with unending gentleness.

"You love me like a sister," I say, and I bow my head because I feel sad all of a sudden. "That's not the type of love I'm talking about."

Auggie places a gentle hand under my chin and makes me look back up at him.

"He's out there somewhere, longing to meet you as much as you are him," he says to me. "And when you finally find one another, God help anyone who tries to come between the two of you."

I tilt my head to the side as I continue to look up at my best friend. "Why would you say that?"

"Because I know you," Auggie says with a proud smile. "You

would tear anyone to pieces if it meant protecting someone you love."

"I would do anything for him," I say, completely meaning my words with all my heart, "and everything."

"Keep your faith, Anna," Auggie tells me. "Keep believing he's out there. Don't give up on him just yet. Maybe he'll sweep you off your feet, and your father will have no other option but to break our marriage contract."

"Do you think he would?" I ask, sounding overly hopeful, even to myself.

Auggie raises a perfectly groomed eyebrow at me. "Well, that's a fine how do you do, Lady Anna. Do you want to cast your betrothed to the side so quickly? I am emperor, you know. Being my wife does come with *some* perks."

"But not true love," I say to him, not in argument but sorrow.

My heart feels incomplete, and Auggie isn't the man who is supposed to fill the gaping hole within its chambers. No man I've met during my years in Cirrus has been a match to my soul. I know without a shadow of a doubt that if I had crossed paths with my soul mate, I would have felt it instantly. The earth beneath my feet would have moved, and my heart would have quaked from just being in his mere presence.

I run my hands up Auggie's chest and behind his neck.

"Kiss me, Auggie," I almost beg.

Auggie smiles at me and wordlessly relents to my request.

When our lips meet, I feel comfort in the warmth of my best friend's mouth against mine, but little else. Auggie eventually pulls away, causing me to sigh my disappointment yet again, not feeling an ounce of passion or excitement from the joining of our lips.

"Nothing, I take it?" Auggie asks, already knowing what it is I'm hoping to feel because we've tried this little experiment at least a hundred times now.

"Nothing," I confirm. "How about you?"

"Nothing, I'm afraid." Auggie sighs his own regret. "Who would believe the two most attractive people in Cirrus feel absolutely no passion for one another?"

"Well, if people knew where your true predilections lie, they would understand," I tease. "How *is* Gladson, by the way?"

"He's fine," Auggie answers with a hint of a blush at the mention of the man who holds his heart in secret. "I wish we didn't have to hide behind closed doors, though. It just seems ridiculous to be emperor yet have to hide from the rest of the world the fact that I love someone of the same sex."

"I'm sorry, Auggie. Maybe one day you won't have to hide your love for one another."

"Well, it won't be while my mother still lives. That much I know for sure. I don't suppose you have a message for me from him?"

The look of hope on Auggie's face makes my answer even harder to give.

"No, he hasn't sent a message for you. I'm sorry."

With the mention of the dowager empress, the knot in my stomach tightens even further.

"I have my lesson with your mother this morning after breakfast," I tell Auggie, sounding about as enthusiastic as I feel. "Not exactly the highlight of my day."

Auggie chuckles.

"She likes you," he reassures me. "Or she can at least stand you, which is a lot more than I can say for anyone else in Cirrus besides me. If she didn't like you just a little, she wouldn't be spending so much time to prepare you to take her place after we're married."

"I can't believe the wedding is only a few days away. It seems like it's too soon. I don't feel ready."

Auggie places his hands on my shoulders and looks me in the eyes.

"You are ready," he tells me, filled with more confidence than I feel. "You will be the greatest empress Cirrus has ever had. We were both born to rule, Anna. And maybe together we can change things for the better."

"Is Gladson filling your head with propaganda again?" I whisper, never quite trusting that the dowager empress doesn't have us under constant surveillance.

"Do you disagree with his propaganda?" Auggie whispers back, telling me that he's not quite sure if our conversation is being listened to either.

"You know I don't," I say. "I see no reason for us to keep the down-worlders in the dark anymore. It's not right that we should have free reign over so much technology while we keep them living in a world only run by steam-powered engines. It's barbaric."

"Yes, but it's the law," Auggie reminds me. "It's been the law for over two hundred years. And Cirrus isn't the only monarchy that does it. Every cloud city in the world does it."

"That doesn't make it right," I say. "It's the thirty-first century, Auggie. We should be more civilized than this. Yet we've basically enslaved the down-worlders to make them grow our crops, raise our livestock, and harvest what few natural resources we have left on this planet. It's no wonder so many of them enter their names into the lottery to go off-world to work. At least on the other planets they have access to our advancements. I still don't understand how we got to this point."

"You know the history as well as I," Auggie says. "After the Great War, those who could afford it built the cloud cities and brought up only those who were the best and brightest of the down-worlders. Then when the down-worlders almost annihilated each other and destroyed every city on the surface with their class wars, we helped them pick up the pieces. In a way, by keeping their access to technology to a minimum, we're protecting them from themselves."

"Do you really believe that?" I ask. "Do you think they would go to war again if they had our technology?"

Auggie shrugs. "I'm not sure. I would hope not, but I can't see into the future either. No one can."

"Gladson believes we shouldn't be separated from them anymore."

Auggie smiles. "He thinks we're becoming too inbred up here with our self-enforced isolation. I can't say I disagree with him. It's one of the reasons you were chosen to be my wife. You had one of the purest genetic codes our physicians had ever seen in an up-worlder or down-worlder. In essence, you are genetically perfect in every way. Plus, your father offered such a large dowry for the privilege, that my father couldn't refuse."

"Anna! Anna!"

I look back over to the pillars leading to my chambers and see my little dog, Vala, come at a run toward us. I pull back from Auggie as Vala launches herself into my arms.

"They're coming!" Vala tells me, turning her little head to look at Auggie and then back up at me again.

"I guess that's my cue to leave," Auggie says, leaning down to kiss me lightly on the lips. "I'll see you later this evening at the Tribute Ball."

"Yes, I'll see you there."

Auggie looks down at his left palm where a holographic display lights up. He presses one of the options and teleports, setting off a quick flash of light with his departure.

I look down at Vala, my ever-loyal robotic Pomeranian, and wonder what it would feel like to hold a real dog instead of one made out of synthetic parts. She looks and feels like a dog, or so I have been told, but she has no heartbeat. Blood doesn't course through her veins, just some sort of fluid to mimic the warmth of a living creature. Her orange fur is silky soft to the touch, but I have no idea how it compares to real fur. Real animals aren't allowed in the cloud cities due to population control and cleanliness issues.

Vala is more advanced than most of the pets in Cirrus, though. She's one of the rare sentient robots that have an organic computer for a brain, which learns from her life experiences. Honestly, she's more real to me than most of the people I know.

With Vala in my arms, I walk across the veranda, past the gossamer white curtains hanging to act as a visual barrier between the outside world and my chambers. Since the temperature inside the dome protecting Cirrus remains a constant seventy degrees, it's nice to have free access to the breeze outside ... even if it is an artificial one.

Someone knocks on the door to my sitting room from the hallway.

"Come in," I say, already knowing who will be walking in at this time of day.

My lady servants, Vivian and Eliza, walk into the room, with the woman who helped raise me coming in last and closing the door behind her. I see that Eliza is holding a silver tray covered with a white silk napkin, and I cringe inwardly because I know what it means.

"Now, Vivian, you go lay out something appropriate for Lady Anna to wear for her lesson with the dowager empress. Eliza and I will handle her treatment," Millie says, her natural bossiness in full effect as she places fisted hands against the girth of her waist.

Vivian, a tall redhead with ivory skin, and a complexion so clear you would have thought her face was carved out of stone, crosses her arms in front of her and rolls her eyes at Millie.

"We've been Anna's ladies for five years now, Millie," she says irritably. "Why do you keep thinking you need to tell us what needs to be done?"

"Because that's what I do," Millie says matter-of-factly, nodding her head and causing a stray strand of her gray hair to escape from underneath her white dust cap. "I make sure Lady Anna and Lord Andre get what they need when they need it. Now shoo," Millie says, waving her hands at Vivian. "Go do your job while we do ours."

"Surely it can't be treatment time again so soon," I complain. "I could have sworn we just did this a few days ago."

"We did, my lady," Millie says, sympathetic to my plight. "Seven days ago today, to be precise. You know the empress insists you have them once a week."

On the day of my thirteenth birthday, the empress sent over the first batch of my "treatments." Every seven days since then, I've been required to have the strange green liquid injected into my body. My father tried to find out what the liquid was, but all the empress would say is that it is totally harmless and meant to protect me. If I didn't have the injections, she threatened to have my marriage contract to Auggie terminated on the grounds of non-compliance.

The strange substance couldn't be administered like most drugs with a normal transdermal patch either. For some reason, it had to be injected into my body by using old-fashioned needles.

I sit down on the white couch in my room and hold out my arms to the two women.

"Do it," I say, looking away as they each take a syringe from the silver tray Eliza brought into the room.

"I'm so sorry, Lady Anna," Eliza says as I feel the needles pierce the skin in the crook of my arms.

"There," Millie says, being the first to take her needle out, "all done."

Eliza soon follows, and I hear the clatter as they lay their respective syringes back onto the silver tray. Vala whines and comes to sit on my lap by way of comfort. I pick her up and hold her close to my chest as I stand to walk into my bedroom. I find Vivian laying out a mint green chiffon dress for me to wear to breakfast and ultimately to my lesson with the dowager empress.

The fashion in Cirrus is simple and elegant. Those in the other cloud cities adopted their own sense of style, and the Cirruns chose one that resembled that of ancient Greece, at least for the women. The men generally wore suits of a simple collarless design, much like the one Auggie wore when he came to see me that morning.

After I'm dressed and Millie fixes my waist-length brown hair into a thick ponytail braid, they escort me up to the roof where I have eaten breakfast with my father every morning of my life, as far as I am aware.

If ever there was a man who looks the part of a Lord, it's my papa. Every unmarried woman in Cirrus has made a play for him, from what Millie has told me. But my father tells me I am the only person his heart will ever truly belong to. His love for me is absolute, and I've never doubted that for one second. It isn't because he tells me he loves me every day of my life either. It is because I can see his love for me in the little things he does for me. As a child growing up, he took me almost everywhere he went and spent endless hours making sure I was as well-educated as anyone in Cirrus—more so than most. He seemed to know something about everything, and I thrived in the knowledge that he thinks I am someone worth spending his time with.

I know any man I eventually give my heart to will have a high standard to meet if they want to even come close to being the man my papa is to me. Not even Auggie can compare to Lord Andre Greco.

My father is dressed in a white suit similar to the one Auggie wore. He's facing away from the crystal elevator when I step off, seemingly lost in his own thoughts. The click of my glass slippers against the marble tile on the roof alerts him to my approach, and he turns to face me. A smile of pure joy lights his features as he looks at me, rivaling the brightness of the morning sun still rising in the background. Even without the sun at his back, my papa glows to my eyes. He always has. When I asked him why he looked like he had an ever-present light shining down on him when no one else did, he told me it was because I could see his complete devotion to me. As a child, I simply found the notion mystical. As an adult, I have to wonder what the true reason is.

"Good morning, cherub," he says to me as I walk up to him.

I shake my head, but can't help the smile that stretches my lips.

"Every time you call me that, I feel like I'm three years old again, Papa."

I kiss my father on both cheeks as he continues to beam with pride as he looks at me.

"And every time I look at you, I see that little three-year-old smiling back at me."

"Stop it, Papa. You're going to make me cry."

My father holds out an arm to me and escorts me to the granite table that is permanently situated underneath an ever-growing arbor of purple wisteria.

"I hope to never be someone who makes you cry," my papa says as he pulls out my chair. "I live to only make you happy."

"And spoiled," I laugh as he sits down beside me.

"Well," he says, smiling guiltily, "there's that, too. But not so spoiled that you aren't grateful for the things you have or the people in your life."

Millie and Vivian bring us our plates laden with breakfast while Eliza fills the crystal goblets in front of us with water.

"Papa," I say hesitantly, because I've broached the subject I'm about to bring up before but received negative results. "Are you sure you won't come live with me and Auggie after we marry? I don't like thinking of you staying here all alone."

"I'll be fine," he says to me with a reassuring smile. "You don't need your father so close when you're just starting your married life."

"You know as well as I that married life with Auggie won't exactly be normal," I say, knowing my father already understands the chaste marriage Auggie and I will end up having. "Plus, I might need your help dealing with the dowager empress."

My papa laughs out loud, the fine lines at the corners of his eyes becoming more pronounced.

"Handling her is something I have no doubt you will be able to do, Anna. You've already proven that on a few occasions now. You happen to be in the auspicious position of having her actually like you because of it. I don't foresee you having any trouble with her, especially after you take her place as empress. But. ..."

I look over at my papa and see a concerned look cloud his handsome features.

"But what? What's wrong?" I ask.

"You know if you didn't want to go through with the marriage, I would take you away from here," he tells me. "I know places in the down-world that not even the empress knows about."

"That wouldn't be any sort of life for either one of us," I tell him gently. "I may not be in love with Auggie, but I do love him. We'll have a good life together, Papa. Don't worry about me. I'll be fine."

"But finding true love is something you'll have to give up as his wife."

"I'm not sure that's even possible for me anyway," I admit. "I'm almost twenty-one, Papa. I've pretty much met every man within marrying age in Cirrus and haven't felt that sort of connection with any of them. I'm luckier than most. At least I'll be marrying my best friend and not someone who is forced on me like some of the other girls here. And I'll be empress soon. How many girls are granted a privilege like that? Maybe I can dedicate my life to helping others and actually do some good with the power I'll have."

"At the cost of your own happiness?"

"Who says I won't be happy? I can find happiness in the work I'll be able to do. So, please, don't worry about me."

My father sighs, and I know worrying about me is not something he can just turn off. I love him for his concern over my happiness, but I came to terms with the path of my life a long time ago. Auggie and I can support one another and find ways to satisfy any urges we might harbor for others in a private way. I'm not sure if I'll ever find the person who is meant to fill the gaping hole in my heart, but I won't give up on finding him just because I'm married either. The marriage between Auggie and me is simply one arranged for convenience.

If my soul mate truly does exist, I have no doubt we will find one another one day.

And when we do, God help anyone who tries to keep us apart.

...

CHAPTER 2

Just as my father and I are finishing breakfast, I catch a flash of light out of the corner of my eye. Two of the empress' personal guards have teleported to the roof and wait at their regular positions near the crystal elevator to act as my escorts to the palace.

"I guess it's time for me to go to the castle for my lesson," I say, wiping my mouth on my napkin before laying it on the table beside my plate.

"You shouldn't have too many more of these lessons to endure after you become empress," my father says sympathetically, knowing how much I dread my time alone with the dowager empress.

"I have a feeling, even after the crown is put on my head, Auggie's mother will find a reason to continue them." I sigh. "I don't think giving up so much power will be easy for her."

"She's known this day is coming for a while."

"But if Auggie's father hadn't died two months ago, she would have remained empress for many more years. Now with Auggie on the throne, she has to give all of that up a lot sooner than she ever thought."

"It's the way the law is here. Only a man can hold the throne. She understands that."

"I'm not sure I could be as gracious," I admit, actually finding a reason to pity Auggie's mother. "She's only in her mid-forties, like you. She's a little young to be going into retirement."

"Maybe she'll find a new husband and have someone else to concentrate her attentions on."

"We can only *hope* for such a miracle to happen," Millie says as she comes to take my empty plate away.

I can't help but giggle at Millie's impudence as I stand from my chair. I lean down and kiss my papa on the cheek.

"Let me know when you return," my father says to me. "I always like to know you've made it back in one piece after a visit with that woman."

"I will," I promise before walking over to the guards.

"Good morning, gentlemen," I say.

"Good morning, Lady Annalisse," the guard named Christopher says rather stiffly as they both bow to me.

The other guard, Clark, remains silent. I don't think he's ever uttered a word to me in the almost eight years since my lessons with the empress began.

I stand in between them, and they each place a hand on my shoulders before teleporting me to the palace.

For whatever reason, the empress didn't allow me to be fitted with the teleportation conduit that every royal was given when they turned eighteen. Regular citizens of Cirrus had to use one of the many teleportation terminals available within the city, but they were only allowed to travel between other terminals strategically placed within the city, never to the exact location they wanted to go.

The guards teleport me straight into the empress' private sitting room, where she's waiting for me, and then teleport themselves out almost immediately. I wish I had the same opportunity of escape.

"Good morning, Annalisse," she says to me as I walk over to the glass table where she's sitting.

"Good morning, Empress Catherine," I reply, taking my seat opposite her at the table, wondering what my lesson will be about today.

As I look across the table at Auggie's mother, I marvel at her strength and beauty. It was well-known that the empress and emperor had been madly in love with each other. They were almost always together except for the times when the emperor liked to go down-world to hunt. It was on one of those hunting expeditions that he apparently fell off his horse and broke his neck, ending his life prematurely.

The empress still wore black to mark the memory of her husband's passing, stoutly showing the world that she remained in mourning over the loss of her beloved. It made me wonder if she felt like the twenty-five years she shared with her husband was worth all the heartache she was now enduring. I would have to imagine that it was. There's nothing I wouldn't give to feel that kind of connection with someone, even if it meant losing them in the end.

"Since you'll be attending your first Tribute Ball tonight," she says, "I thought it might be a good idea to refresh your memory on why we have it and the duties of our overlords on the surface."

"Of course," I say, even though I don't understand why the empress feels the need.

She should know by now that my memory is perfect. I never forget anything, which comes in handy when you're trying to learn the ins and outs of ruling an empire.

"Now," the empress says, "what is the purpose of the Tribute Ball?"

"To have the overlords come to Cirrus and pay their tribute to the royal family."

"And why is this important?"

"To remind the people of Cirrus that our life in the city is only sustainable because of the work the overlords do for us in the down-world."

The empress raises a delicate eyebrow at me. "And the other reason?"

"To remind the overlords that they may run things in the down-world, but they are only allowed the privilege through our good graces."

Empress Catherine smiles, pleased with my answer. She leans toward the glass table between us and runs one well-manicured hand across its surface, bringing up the holographic images of four men.

"Now," she says, taking on the voice of a teacher, "can you name the five overlords who run things for our family and what it is that each of them is in charge of?"

"Yes," I say, leaning toward the table also and looking at the rotating images of the overlords, pointing to each one as I name them. "David Dean is in charge of agriculture. Matthew Knowles is in charge of livestock. Sean Rhodes is responsible for the mining of raw minerals. Paul Kennedy oversees the manufacturing of goods. And. ..." I look up at the empress. "Why is it that we've never had an image of the fifth overlord?"

"Because he's obstinate," the empress snorts derisively, "and doesn't like to have his image rendered."

"But you're his ruler. Why not just force him to do it?"

Empress Catherine laughs. "It's obvious you've never met the man. You know who he is and what he does, though, right?"

I nod. "Yes. His name is Malcolm Devereaux, and he's in charge of commerce between our down-world and that of the other cloud cities. It's one of the most lucrative overlord positions, which means all of the other overlords want it."

"Correct."

"I still don't understand why you don't have an image of him," I say.

The empress tilts her head as she looks at me. "And I'm surprised your father hasn't shown you one already."

This time, it's my turn to tilt my head in bewilderment.

"Why would my father have an image of him?"

"They're best friends, dear heart," the empress tells me, watching for my reaction. "Or at least they were at the time of your birth. Malcolm was the one who paid your dowry and the titles you and your father hold now."

I take in a sharp breath at this unexpected news.

"I don't understand," I say, quickly recovering. "Why haven't I been told this before?"

The empress shrugs her thin shoulders. "I assumed your father would have told you at some point. But I can see from the look on your face that he hasn't. I was hoping you could tell me why Malcolm has always refused to come up here to pay his tribute in person."

I shake my head. "I have no idea. I don't know anything about him except that he's one of the overlords."

"Hmm," the empress says, studying me closely as if she's expecting me to slip up in a lie. "I suppose you really don't know anything. However, I have a feeling you might get your own answers when you return home."

"My father probably had a good reason to keep this informa-tion from me," I say in his defense. "But yes, I will ask when I get home, just because I don't keep secrets from him. I'll also let him know what you've told me."

The empress smiles tight-lipped at me as she brings up a map of North America.

"Now," she says, "can you draw the borders of each overlord's territories for me on this map?"

The rest of my lesson with the empress goes by smoothly. I do wonder why my father never mentioned that Malcolm Devereaux —the most powerful down-world overlord—was, at one time at least, his best friend and our benefactor. I knew it took a lot of money for a down-worlder to buy even a single title of lord or lady-ship in Cirrus. I couldn't imagine what this Malcolm Devereaux had paid out to buy titles for both me *and* my father. Plus, he apparently paid a large enough dowry for me to become Auggie's wife that not even the emperor could decline.

Who was he to my father? Why did he care what happened to me?

Just as my lesson with the empress ends, Auggie enters the room.

"Ahh, I thought I might find the two of you in here," he says, knowing full well we would be in here at this time of day. "I thought I would escort Anna home if she's through with her lesson."

"Of course, my love," the empress says to her only child. "The two of you should spend as much time together as possible in the coming week. You'll be man and wife soon."

Auggie pulls out my chair for me, and I stand, feeling relieved that he's come to rescue me from his mother.

"I couldn't agree with you more, Mother, which is why I will be spending the afternoon at her home, if that's all right with you."

"Of course, Augustus. You're emperor, after all. You don't need my permission anymore."

"Old habits die hard, I suppose," Auggie says, holding out his arm for me to take. "Are you ready to go back home, my lady?"

I simply nod, because I feel sure that if I voice my answer, my eagerness to be as far away as possible from the empress will be transparent.

"I'll see you later this evening at the ball, Annalisse," the empress says, just before Auggie teleports me to the veranda outside my chambers.

"I suppose you won't be spending the afternoon with me, but with someone else?" I say knowingly to Auggie.

Auggie grins. "Yes, I was able to arrange a certain meeting with someone of special interest. I also wanted to tell you that I have a surprise for you."

"What kind of surprise?" I ask, my interest piqued.

"If I told you, then it wouldn't be a surprise anymore," Auggie says indulgently. "It will arrive here before the ball, and that's all you're getting out of me, Lady Anna."

Auggie holds his chin up stubbornly, like a child refusing to give anything else away about his special secret.

"Then I'll wait patiently for my surprise," I say, leaning up and kissing him on the cheek. "Say hello to Gladson for me," I whisper before turning to walk into my chambers.

Just before I pass through the curtains into my rooms, I turn to look at Auggie one last time. I notice a glimmer of light right behind him but can't quite make out what it is before he teleports away. The glimmer vanishes with him, and I simply chalk it up to being the effects of the sun's glare. Yet it seemed to have a physical form. I shake my head, realizing my eyes must have been playing tricks on me, and go seek out the person who can answer the many questions I have after my lesson with the empress.

I find my father in the training room, practicing his sword fighting with the holographic sparring partner we nicknamed Rob.

I stand to the side of the wooden platform and watch my papa as he maneuvers Rob into a defensive position with his swordplay until Rob ends up on the floor and says he yields. My father extends his hand down to Rob and helps him stand up.

"Thank you, Rob," my papa says before looking over at me with a mischievous smile, "but I think I have a flesh-and-blood opponent now. You may leave."

"As you wish, Lord Andre," Rob says before vanishing from sight.

My father walks over to me, twirling his sword effortlessly in his hand.

"Up for a little practice?" my father asks with a taunting grin.

"Are you that anxious to be beaten by me again?" I say, unable to suppress a smile of my own.

"Now, is that any way to talk to your father, Lady Anna?" he asks jokingly. "Or are you afraid I might actually defeat you this time?"

I look down at my dress. "I'm not exactly dressed for a sparring match."

"You never know what you might be wearing if you're attacked unawares," he says, turning serious. "You need to be prepared no matter the occasion, Anna. What you're wearing shouldn't matter."

"Fair enough," I reply, stepping onto the platform. "Sword," I say, holding out my hand and having one materialize in it. It's only a hologram of one because real weapons aren't allowed in Cirrus, but it mimics the weight and feel of a real sword adequately enough.

My father and I stand across from one another and bow before we take up our fighting stances. Swordplay with my father is something we've done ever since I was able to hold a sword. It is something we do to relieve stress and something we easily bonded over.

My papa said I was a natural with a sword and that he had never seen anyone who could swing it so effortlessly. I suppose my unnatural strength gave me an advantage, too.

When I was six years old, I learned my strength was greater than that of anyone in Cirrus when I accidentally pushed one of the walls in my room down because I was throwing a temper tantrum over not being allowed to go down-world with my father. It scared me when it happened. My father explained to me that I wasn't like other children and that I had to be careful with the strength I possessed. At such an early age, I didn't quite understand why I was so strong. I still don't. It is just a fact of my life, and I have come to accept that I am different from other people. I just don't know why. I assumed my father would fill in the details at some point, but apparently that point simply hasn't come yet.

My father and I cross swords, and I take the first swing.

"Why didn't you ever tell me Malcolm Devereaux was the one who paid for our titles and my dowry?" I ask, catching my father off guard to the point that he almost drops his weapon.

He soon recovers and doubles his attack against me.

"It wasn't something you needed to know," he tells me, the ferocity of his attack forcing me to back up.

My father is strong, but he could never match my strength no matter how hard he tried.

I twirl around him, making him falter and twist his torso in an awkward position to block my next strike.

"Did the empress tell you that today?" my father asks, knowing the information had to come from someone.

"Yes," I say, ducking a swipe of his sword at my head. "She told me everything."

"I seriously doubt that," my father says knowingly, "because even she doesn't know the whole story."

This brought me up short, and the tip of my father's holographic sword pierced my mid-gut.

"Ha! I finally won!" he declares triumphantly.

"I'm not sure that one counts," I say, stepping up to him. If anyone had been watching, it would have looked like I was impaling myself further onto his blade.

"Who is this Malcolm Devereaux to you?" I ask. "Why would he care about my future? Does he plan to extort special favors from me once I'm on the throne?"

"Of course not," my father says, sounding completely appalled that I would even think of such a thing.

"Then, why? Why would someone like him spend so much money to make sure I was placed in a position of power?"

"Because we both wanted to make sure you were safe," my father says. "Swords, disengage."

Our swords disappear, and we just stand there facing one another.

I can tell by the set of my father's jaw that he doesn't want to talk about the particulars of his relationship with Overlord Devereaux, but I want answers.

"If he's such a good friend of yours," I say, "why hasn't he ever visited us here? As far as I know, he's never set foot in Cirrus."

"He doesn't like to involve himself in the politics up here. Honestly, I don't blame him. If conditions were better, I would have rather raised you on the surface. But life is easier up here, a fact you yourself reminded me of just this morning at breakfast."

"Do you have an image of him?" I ask. "The empress doesn't have one. She said he doesn't like having his image rendered."

"No, I don't have one of him."

"Do you talk to him very often?"

"I talk to him once a year."

"Why only once a year?"

"It's the arrangement we made to commemorate the death of your mother."

I pause in my interrogation because I know what that means.

"You talk on my birthday? He knew my mother? How?"

"Malcolm was friends with your mother's family. He was devastated when Amalie passed away. He always felt responsible for her death."

"Why would he feel guilt over that? She died in childbirth."

My father shakes his head at me. "Can you just leave it at what I said? Why are you asking so many questions, Anna?"

"I just want to know more about him," I say. "And I want to know why I had to hear about his connection to our family from the empress instead of you. You should have been the one to tell me, Papa, not her."

My father nods. "I agree. You should have heard it from me, but I honestly didn't think it would matter, and I'm not sure why the empress told you in the first place."

"She doesn't seem to know much about Overlord Devereaux either. Maybe she thought I could provide her with more information since you obviously have a close connection to him."

"Well, the less she knows, the better. Malcolm likes his privacy. As long as he pays the tribute she extorts from the overlords each year, I don't see why she should care."

"Extorts?" I ask, slightly confused by his use of the term. "You don't think they should pay tribute to the royal family?"

"Not when it amounts to fifty percent of their earnings."

"It's that much?" I ask, having never known the taxes imposed on the down-worlders were so exorbitant. "How can they afford to give so much?"

"They don't have a choice." My father sighs. "Maybe when you and Auggie take the throne, you'll be able to find a way to make their tributes more reasonable."

"Then this Malcolm *does* want something in return for putting me on the throne."

"No. He wants you safe, Anna," my father says, and I know he's telling the truth because I've always been able to tell when someone is lying to me. "He doesn't want a thing from you."

Okay, that was actually a small lie, but I don't call my father out on it. I feel as though I've probably questioned him enough for one day.

However, I did learn one thing.

Overlord Devereaux did want something from me. I just didn't know what.

CHAPTER 3

The Tribute Ball is usually the pinnacle event amongst the royals of Cirrus. However, this year it would be eclipsed by the celebration ceremonies surrounding my marriage to Auggie. Nevertheless, everyone was looking forward to it. This year, I would be allowed to attend my very first one. Most royals were able to attend by the age of eighteen, but the empress decided I shouldn't go until I was twenty-one. Since my birthday was only a week away, she relented to my father's plea that I be allowed to attend with him this year. He argued that if I was to oversee it the following year, I needed to bear witness for myself what the protocol of accepting tributes from the overlords was.

"I can tell you why she doesn't want you there," Millie grunts as she brushes out my hair, preparing to braid it for an intricate bun she plans to style it in. "She knows you will be the most beautiful woman there instead of her."

"Oh, Millie," I say, rolling my eyes at her in the mirror of my vanity. "I seriously doubt the empress considers anyone her equal in the beauty department."

"True enough," Millie agrees with a hearty laugh. "That woman is about as vain as they come. Watch your back, my sweet. I have a feeling the empress doesn't relish giving up her throne just yet."

I feel my brow furrow. "Do you think she would do something to prevent my marriage to Auggie?"

"That, I don't know," Millie says with a worried frown of her own. "All I do know is that women like her don't like being cast aside so easily. She's been the belle of the ball for a long time now. I can't say I blame her for not wanting to give it all away because of some silly law that says only men can rule Cirrus. If you want to know the truth, I've heard she's basically been running things since she married the emperor to give him free reign to go play whenever he wanted."

"Unfortunately, it was his playing that got him killed," I say.

"Just be careful," Millie advises. "Remember to watch your back when you're around the empress. She didn't get to where she is without being smart and cunning. Did you know she was once a down-worlder?"

"No," I admit, "I had no idea."

"Her father won a lottery to go off-world and apparently made enough money to buy her a title. From what I heard, she had her eyes set on the throne from the moment she got here."

"Everyone says she and the emperor were actually one of the few royal couples who loved one another."

"Oh, I don't doubt that," Millie says. "But love can come because of different reasons. I think she loved the idea of being empress more than she actually loved the emperor. That much power can make anyone imagine that they're in love with the person who gave it to them."

"I've never felt threatened by her," I say. "I don't think she would harm me."

"She never thought you would be taking her place this soon either. I seriously doubt that woman thought she would have to give up her power for another twenty years or more."

"I didn't either, if you want to know the truth. If I could, I would let her keep it."

"No, my sweet; it's time for a change around here, and I think you and Auggie are just the ones to bring it," Millie says resolutely.

"Don't let anyone else hear you say that," I say in a low voice, "or you'll be brought up on heresy charges, Millie."

"Humph, I'd like to see them try."

Vivian and Eliza walk into my bedroom then, and my conversation with Millie is put to an end by their presence.

Vivian has a dress I've never seen before draped across her outstretched arms.

"This just came from the emperor," Vivian says, obviously in awe of the extravagant gift the emperor has sent me.

"Hold it up and let me see," I tell her.

Vivian holds the dark purple dress against her torso and twirls around like she's the one who will be wearing the gown. I see a look of envy cross her face just before she meets my eyes in the mirror. I have always had a feeling Vivian thinks herself too good to just be a lady's servant, but that's the way her life has turned out, and there isn't much that can be done about it.

When I view the beauty of the gown in the reflection of my mirror, I see why she's in awe of it.

Not only is the gown made of the finest silk, but it's decorated with a myriad of small diamonds, making it sparkle in the light of the room. It's sure to draw a lot of attention at the ball. If the diamonds don't get me noticed, the plunging neckline most definitely will.

"What was Auggie thinking, sending me a dress like that to wear?" I ask, turning in my chair to look at the gown fully.

"I'm not sure, my lady," Eliza says, walking over to me, "but this message was sent with the dress."

Eliza hands me a small neural patch. I take the translucent square and place it behind my right ear. Auggie appears to me by way of a neurally-transmitted hologram that only I can see and hear.

"Since five men you haven't met yet are coming to the ball," Auggie says, hands clasped behind his back and looking extremely excited about his gift, "I thought this dress might make you stand out to them. Not that you wouldn't have stood out anyway with your beauty, but they would literally have to be blind not to notice you in this dress tonight. Good luck!"

I giggle and shake my head at Auggie's master plan. Only the man I am marrying would try to play matchmaker for his future wife. In my heart, I wish Auggie and I had been able to break through the friendship barrier to truly become husband and wife in every way, but neither of us felt that particular attraction for one another. We simply weren't meant to love each other romantically.

"Well, we'll have to change the color of your eye shadow now," Millie says, picking up the makeup wand, which looks like a simple silver tube, from my vanity. "Close your eyes, Lady Anna."

I close my eyes and know that Millie is waving the wand down my face once again to change the green eye shadow she applied earlier to purple to match the dress.

"There. All done," Millie tells me as I open my eyes and see her set the wand back on the table. "Now, let's finish your hair, and you'll be ready to go to the ball with your father."

Once my hair is perfectly coifed to Millie's rigid standard of perfection, Vivian and Eliza dress me in the gown Auggie sent.

Afterwards, I seek out my father in his study to let him know I'm ready to make my first appearance at a royal function.

When I walk into the room, I find him sitting behind his old-fashioned, wooden desk. Papa is the only person in Cirrus who still prefers wood over the polymerized desks most people use, which can transform into any shape with a simple verbal command. I think he likes the feel of the solid, textured surface of the wood against his hands, instead of the smooth surface of the polymer desks. He said once that his desk reminded him of a simpler age, but I had no idea why he was so attached to a time period he had never himself seen.

My father looks up from his holographic interface terminal and smiles proudly when he sees me.

"New dress?" he asks, knowing full well that it is.

"A present from Auggie," I tell him.

"Is he trying to show you off or find you a lover?"

"Both, I think."

My papa stands from his chair and walks over to me.

"Well, I can't say I approve of either," he tells me. "However, I can't say I totally disapprove. All I want is for you to be happy, Anna. I think that's all a parent can ever want for their child."

"I'm not sure I'll ever be as happy as I have been here with you, Papa."

My father cups my face in his hands.

"Then I will do my best to make sure you are happy wherever you go. And I've decided that, if it will make you happy, I will move into the palace with you after your marriage."

My heart feels like it's going to burst with joy at this news, and I feel like a burden has been lifted from my shoulders. I throw myself into my papa's arms.

"That's the best wedding gift you could have given me," I tell him, hugging him around the neck tightly, but not using all of my strength because I don't want to hurt him. "Thank you, Papa."

"Don't thank me just yet," he says to me. "If I see the empress mistreating you, I won't be able to keep my mouth shut."

"I wouldn't expect you to," I say, pulling away from him slightly so I can look into his deep blue eyes. "You don't have to worry; I won't let her abuse me. You have my word on that. You raised me too well. I won't let anyone do that to me and get away with it."

My papa laughs. "Good. I'm glad I succeeded in raising you with enough self-esteem to make sure no one, not even your mother-in-law, has the power or right to treat you harshly."

I hug my papa one more time because he's made me the happiest person in the world with his willingness to move into the palace with me. I know what a sacrifice he's making. He'll always be under the scrutiny of the empress now. But I know together, we can handle anything she throws our way.

My father teleports us to the entrance of the palace's ballroom. I've been in the ballroom before, of course, though never for a formal function. Auggie and I used to play in the large, cavernous room when we were children. With the floating lights fully lit, the gold walls and mirrors in the room glimmer, telling of the wealth of the family who owns it.

As we approach the entrance, the herald, dressed in a red velvet jacket and matching pants, bows to us and turns to those already present in the room.

"Presenting Lord Andre Romanoff Greco and his daughter, Lady Annalisse Desiraye Greco—the future empress of Cirrus!"

I cringe inwardly at the last part of the herald's announcement, wondering what Auggie's mother must think of such an introduction. It wasn't just the words the herald said, but the way he said them with such conviction and eagerness. I have to assume she isn't exactly happy that some of her subjects are fervently awaiting the day she will have to abdicate her throne.

As my father and I walk down the staircase into the ballroom, arm in arm, I search through those in attendance, hoping to find at least one friendly face within the sea of people staring back at me. Unfortunately, I don't see anyone I would readily call my friend. There are a lot of acquaintances present, but no one I would label as an ally to me. In all honesty, the only person in the world I consider to be a true friend to me, besides my papa and Millie, is Auggie. Strangely enough, he's nowhere to be seen.

My father walks me up to the dais, where the empress is sitting on her red velvet and hammered-gold throne, looking regal, as a monarch should, in her black gown. Her back is ramrod straight as she oversees the proceedings. The throne beside her is empty of its occupant, and I wonder where Auggie is. I know he can lose track of time when he's with Gladson, but surely he didn't get so caught up in his lover that he forgot about the ball.

"Good evening, Andre," the empress says as my father bows and I curtsy to the empress. "Annalisse, you look very lovely this evening, my dear."

"Thank you, Your Majesty."

"I hope you enjoy your first ball."

"I'm sure I will, Your Majesty."

My father bows once more to the empress, and then turns me away from her scrutiny, so that those behind us can show their respects to the reigning sovereign of Cirrus.

"Would you like a drink?" my father asks me, escorting me to the table set up with ever-filling glasses of champagne.

"If I ever needed a glass of champagne, it would be now," I say with a sigh.

"You shouldn't let her bother you so," my papa says.

"Do you think one person should have so much power all by themselves?" I ask him. "It doesn't seem quite right, does it?"

"You know, the cloud cities did try to put together ruling

parties like they had in the old days, but they bickered so much amongst themselves that nothing ever got done. So it was decided then that having one ruling family, as long as they were just and fair, caused less conflict."

"And what if the ruler isn't just or fair?"

"Then I think you know what happens," my papa says with a raise of his eyebrows.

My father didn't have to say more, especially considering the company we were in at the moment. Most of the royals benefitted from the profits the Amadors took in from the overlords. None of them would complain that the down-worlders were being mistreated. In fact, they probably thought the people who lived on the surface were lucky we didn't just annihilate them on the spot. We could, though. We could easily destroy them with one push of a button and scour the surface clean of their existence.

However, as this gathering was supposed to show, we needed the down-worlders. We needed the goods and services they provided us. Without them, we would be nothing, and I feared many of the citizens of Cirrus had forgotten that simple fact. One world didn't function without the other. It was a symbiotic relationship, even if one of the parties took more than their fair share.

Not long after our arrival, the trumpeters blow their horns, causing me to jump slightly from the unexpected explosion of sound.

"What was that for?" I ask my father.

"It's time for the overlords to be presented and bring in their tribute," he tells me.

All heads turn to the top of the staircase, where the entrance to the room is.

There stands a man I recognize. It's David Dean, the overlord of agriculture. He is tall, lean, and handsome, with shoulder-length brown hair and a look of superiority about him that isn't exactly overbearing, just visible.

He descends the staircase and walks up to the empress.

"Overlord Dean," Empress Catherine says, bowing her head slightly in greeting as he bows deeply to her. "We welcome you to Cirrus."

"Thank you, Your Majesty," Overlord Dean says. "I am grateful to be here and to offer you my tribute."

A royal page walks up to Overlord Dean and takes a memo card from him. The page inserts the card into a device he holds, which I know will upload the monetary value of the card into the royal treasury. The amount of the tribute is displayed on a holographic board on the wall behind the empress. It will show everyone present how much each of the overlord's tributes are.

All four of the overlords enter into the room, one by one, and offer their tribute to the empress. It's not until the last tribute is to be given that my interest piques. I direct my gaze to the top of the stairs with bated breath, wondering if Overlord Devereaux will actually show up this year. Since this is the first Tribute Ball I've attended, I'm not sure what will happen if he doesn't.

A man appears at the top of the landing and I gasp. I don't gasp because the earth beneath my feet moves or because my heart quakes. I lose my breath because the man at the top of the stairs is glowing to my eyes, just like my father does.

I turn my head to look at my father and find him already staring at me, like he is watching for my reaction to the man.

Before I can ask my papa who the man is, the herald calls out, "As representative for Overlord Devereaux, Emissary Jered Alburn will be presenting tribute."

I look back at the man as he makes his way down the staircase.

He's handsome in a dashing sort of way, with brown hair and eyes. I notice him scanning the crowd before him as he descends the staircase, until his gaze rests on me. He smiles. It's the type of smile my father has given me countless times, one of unabashed pride.

Why would he feel anything for me, much less pride? And why is he glowing just like my father?

As he stands in front of the empress, he bows to her deeply.

"Emissary Alburn," Empress Catherine says, "it's lovely to see you again. I hope your overlord is well."

"Overlord Devereaux sends his deepest regrets that he can't be here in person, Your Majesty," Jered says. "He hopes the tribute he has sent will make up for it."

The royal page walks up to Jered and takes his memo card. After the page inserts the card into his device and the amount of the tribute is uploaded onto the holographic display, I can hear the faint gasps of the crowd around me. The sum overshadows all of the other tributes paid that night. You would have to add up all of the other overlords' tributes and multiply that sum by ten just to come close to what Overlord Devereaux made for the royal family in the past year.

"My, my," the empress says, looking and sounding happier than I've ever seen her. "Overlord Devereaux has obviously been very busy this year. Please give him our best regards and gratitude when you return home."

Jered bows to the empress once more.

"I will, Your Majesty."

Empress Catherine stands from her throne to address the crowd.

"Now that the tributes have been made, please enjoy the revelry for the rest of the evening," she announces, clapping her hands twice, signaling the musicians situated on the balcony behind her throne to begin playing a waltz.

I keep my eyes on Jered and ask my father, "Why does he look like you to me?"

I don't want to ask why a man I've never met before is glowing in mixed company, but I have a feeling my father will know exactly what it is I'm asking without me having to spell it out for him.

"Because he's as devoted to you as I am," my father answers.

I tear my eyes away from Jered and look at my papa.

"Who is he to me?" I ask.

"Someone who would lay down his life to protect you," my papa tells me in a whisper. "Just as I would."

"Andre."

I look away from my papa and find Jered standing in front of us, extending his hand to my father.

My papa shakes the other man's hand vigorously. "Jered, my old friend, it's good to see you again. Once a year just doesn't seem like it's enough."

Jered's gaze turns to me, and he smiles kindly.

"You're even lovelier than the images your father has sent of you over the years, Anna," Jered says, leaning in and kissing me on the cheek like we've known each other forever.

I don't take offense to the rather intimate act. For some reason, it feels natural coming from him, like he's a long-lost uncle or old friend.

"Thank you," I say to the compliment.

As I look into Jered's kind, brown eyes, I see a love there that I don't quite understand. It isn't the love of a man for a woman, but one I've seen in my father's eyes—like I'm his daughter, too.

"Have we ever met before, Mr. Alburn?"

"Once," he says, "but it was on the day you were born, which means you wouldn't have a memory of our meeting. And, please, call me Jered."

"You knew my mother?"

Sadness enters Jered's eyes, briefly eclipsing his happiness to see me.

"Yes, I knew Amalie quite well. Her passing was a great loss to all of us."

"Us?" I ask, finding this an odd thing for him to say. "You and my father, you mean?"

Jered glances in my father's direction, like maybe he's said too much.

Before I can get any sort of clarification, the trumpets blare again, causing the revelry in the room to come to a complete standstill.

"Ladies and gentleman," the herald says, "Emperor Augustus Charles Ronaldo Amador."

I look to the top of the staircase and see Auggie standing there, looking out at the crowd below him. He's dressed in a white suit, with a long topcoat embroidered with an ivy design in gold thread around the edges. He looks every bit the part of an emperor, but ... something doesn't seem quite right about the smile on his face. Auggie has never been one to seek out attention, yet the swagger with which he walks down the stairs—like he knows he's the most powerful person in the room—and the spread of his lips into a smile that shows his pleasure in such a fact, tells me something is wrong with my best friend.

"It can't be," I hear my papa say almost angrily beside me.

"We have to get her out of here," Jered whispers to my father, an urgent quality to his voice.

I know he's talking about me, but I don't know why he thinks I need to leave just because Auggie has arrived.

Before either of them can say more, Auggie walks up to me and holds out his hand.

"Care for a dance with your soon-to-be-husband, Lady Annalisse?"

If the eyes are truly windows into our souls, I instantly wonder what has become of the pure, joyous spirit belonging to my best friend.

Auggie grabs my hand roughly without waiting for my answer and practically drags me onto the dance floor. He waves an imperious hand to the band on the balcony, signaling them to play a song.

Auggie forcefully pulls my body up against his. His frame is pressing so hard into mine it's almost painful. He begins to twirl me around the ballroom floor, but it feels like it's more for punishment than fun.

"Auggie, what's wrong?" I demand. "Why are you doing this?"

Auggie just smiles at me and says nothing.

Abruptly, Auggie comes to a complete stop on the dance floor and lifts his hand again, which causes the band to stop playing. He quickly releases me from his hold, like he doesn't want to have anything else to do with me.

"Ladies and gentleman," Auggie says before turning to look at his mother, "and Empress Catherine, my dearest mother, I regret to inform you that we have a traitor within our midst!"

A murmur of excitement weaves through the crowd.

Auggie begins to walk around me as he glowers, causing me to panic slightly as I become the center of attention.

"I'm afraid my dear betrothed has been conspiring against the crown with a known rebel named Gladson Gray," Auggie accuses.

As I look around at the other guests, I can see them whispering to each other with shock in their eyes at the accusation.

"Are you sure, Augustus?" I hear Empress Catherine say behind me, sounding a little too thrilled by the news.

Auggie stops in front of me and looks me straight in the eyes.

"I'm afraid so, Mother. It seems that our beloved Lady Annalisse has been receiving messages from him for over a year now. It saddens me to have to report this, but since our marriage is only a few days away, I feel relieved to have been given this knowledge now rather than later. Who knows what kind of havoc she might have instigated if she were crowned empress?"

"What evidence do you have?" my papa demands of Auggie, coming to stand out from the crowd of onlookers to challenge Auggie's accusations.

Auggie turns to face my father.

"The only proof that I need," Auggie tells him, lifting his hand again toward the stairs.

My gaze drifts up the staircase, and I see Vivian standing there, holding a box I had hidden under my bed that contains the messages Gladson sent to Auggie through me.

"Your servant came to me and told me of your traitorous ways," Auggie says, turning to me again, smiling devilishly. "It's all the proof I need."

"Guards!" Empress Catherine calls out. "Seize Lady Annalisse and take her to a holding cell!"

I look to my papa and see the helpless panic on his face. Jered comes to stand beside him and whispers something in his ear.

I look back to Auggie but don't recognize the sneering man standing in front of me.

As two guards grab my arms, I close my eyes and pray that I'll soon awaken from the nightmare my life has suddenly become.

CHAPTER 4

As I pace back and forth in my prison cell, I begin to understand why so many people who are held captive for years on end lose their sanity. The four walls surrounding me are white. The floor is white. The ceiling is white. There is nothing to sit on except for the floor, which is kept at such a cold temperature that standing is preferable for the most part.

I have no way to judge time except for counting the meals that are teleported into my cell. If I assume they are feeding me three times a day, then I've been trapped inside these walls for at least two days.

As I make what has to be the thousandth lap around the perimeter of my prison, my mind races with thoughts about what might be happening on the outside. I have no doubt my father is trying to arrange my release, but I know he will fail. My Auggie isn't my Auggie anymore. I don't know what's wrong with him, but I do know the man who accused me of treason isn't the boy I grew up with. He is not my best and most trusted friend any longer.

I'd heard rumors that a technology existed which allowed you to change yourself into whatever human form you wanted. However, that type of science was outlawed because ... well ... no one wanted someone else to have the ability to look exactly like them. It didn't mean someone couldn't gain access to the technology, though. There were always black marketers who could procure whatever you wanted as long as you had the money to pay for their services.

With no warning, my father suddenly appears in the middle of the room. I go to him but know it isn't really the flesh-and-blood him, just a holographic projection.

"Anna, don't say anything," my father warns me, not only with his voice but his eyes as well. "They're only allowing me to speak to you for a few moments to explain things."

I see my papa's eyes dart around him, and I know he isn't alone in whatever room he's in. He's being watched, and his words will be chosen carefully.

"I'm sorry you were accused for a crime that I committed."

"Papa. ..." I say, about to ask him why he's confessing to something he didn't even know about. No one knew about the messages I received from Gladson for Auggie except the three of us.

My father holds up a hand to signal me to not say anything more.

"I should have told you about my dealings with the rebels, but I knew how loyal you were to Empress Catherine and Emperor Augustus," he continues.

I stand there speechless, but let him continue to spin his false confession.

"The emperor and empress have accepted my declaration of guilt and have agreed to release you, my little cherub. They have also agreed to keep to the marriage contract, even in the face of my betrayal."

"What will happen to you?" I ask, needing to know this above all else.

"The emperor knows how close you and I are," my father says. "He has agreed to not execute me, since he knows how much it would upset you. I guess you can consider his compromise a wedding gift to you. Instead, I will be sent to our farthest settlement off-world. It will take me half of my remaining lifetime to get there. So even if I tried to come back, I would die before I ever reached Earth again. I'm so sorry that this has to happen, Anna, but I want you to know that I will always love you and carry you in my heart until the day I die."

My eyes well with tears, and I feel the sting of my heartache leech the last bit of hope I have left for a happy life. Even though my father will remain alive on a distant planet, which I'm grateful for, he might as well be dead to me. Our life together has come to an end, and I'm not sure where to go from here. I will have no one left to lean on. I'll be all alone.

"I won't be allowed to contact you again until I've reached my destination," he tells me, his voice breaking over our loss of one another. "I hope you will trust in your instincts since I will no longer be around to help guide you, my little girl. The best advice I can give you is to seek out your true friends and always remember to be mindful of things around you. Take nothing for granted, Anna. I love you, my little cherub, and I wish you the happiest of lives."

I reach out a hand to my father, but his hologram disappears, taking him away from me forever.

I bury my face in my hands and begin to cry uncontrollably. I drop to my knees on the cold prison floor, bereft of hope. It takes me a few minutes to pull myself together, but one thought creeps into my consciousness, sustaining my sanity.

I need to find out where *my* Auggie is. If I can do that, maybe I can piece back together the shattered remains of what was once a happy life.

As I wipe away my tears of self-pity, filled with a new determination and purpose to save not only my father, but my best friend as well, two guards teleport into my cell. They are the same two guards who have always escorted me to my lessons with the empress.

"We've been ordered to take you home, Lady Annalisse," Christopher says as he and Clark walk up to me.

I stand to my feet as they touch my shoulders and transport me to the front entrance of my home. Without another word, they teleport away, leaving me completely alone. I open the front door and walk in.

"Millie!" I call out, closing the door behind me and walking toward the living room to search for her. "Millie!" I call again, even more desperately, but still receive no answer.

"Anna! Anna!"

Vala comes barreling down the stairs from the second floor and launches herself into my arms.

"Vala, where is Millie?"

"Some of the palace guards came and took her, Vivian, and Eliza away two days ago," she tells me. "I've been here alone ever since. What's happening, Anna? What's wrong?"

I tell Vala what transpired at the ball and whisper to her the sacrifice my papa made to secure my freedom.

Vala whines. "Lord Andre is gone? Forever?"

"Not if I have anything to say about it," I whisper in her ear.

Vala's little brow furrows, and her eyes look troubled.

"What's wrong?" I ask her.

"Nothing. I just miss Lord Andre. Do you think we could go to his study?"

I don't voice my suspicion that Vala is up to something. I

simply nod and walk up the staircase to seek out my father's sanctuary.

Once I close the door to his study, Vala leaps out of my arms and scampers over to the desk. I walk over to watch as she pulls out one of the bottom drawers. Inside the drawer is a device I've only heard about but know to be outlawed because it essentially blocks out any surveillance the royal family has in place.

Vala jumps into the drawer and presses one tiny paw on the single red button at the top of the device.

"Now we can talk without anyone listening," Vala says, jumping out of the drawer and sitting on the floor in front of me. "Lord Andre told me that if anything ever happened to him, I should tell you to tear his desk apart."

"Why?" I ask, knowing how much my father treasured his link to the past.

"He didn't say," Vala tells me, "but I think you should do it, Anna."

I lean down and take the blocking device out of the drawer and set it on the glass table behind the desk. Vala runs over to the middle of the room to get out of my way. As I glide a hand across the surface of one of my father's prized possessions, I grab the lip of the top and yank the thick, heavy wood off easily, setting it aside behind me.

When I look back at the desk, I notice something wrapped in a silver reflective bag within the empty void at the front of it. I walk around to the front of the desk and grab the bag, immediately feeling the weight of something heavy inside.

I lay the bag on the floor and kneel down beside it. Vala walks over to me and sits down.

"Open it," she urges.

The seam is sealed with a magnetic closure, which is the way most garments are sealed. I was told things known as zippers and buttons were used at one time.

I pull the seam apart and stare at the contents of the bag.

There is a broadsword and a small black box. I pick up the box and open it. Laying within its interior is a translucent neural memo. I grab it and immediately place it behind my right ear. A hologram of my father materializes in front of me, and a fount of tears immediately clouds my vision.

"Anna," my papa says, "if you are watching this message, it means something has happened to me and Vala has told you to seek out the items in my desk. There is so much I need to tell you, my little cherub, but what you need to know should be told to you in person, not through a simple holographic message. Plus, I have no way of knowing if this message will be found by you or someone else, and the information you need is far too important to be discovered by a third party. I have no doubt that once my best friend learns of what has happened to me, he will come here and take care of you. He is not someone you have met before, and I must warn you that he is a stubborn man. No matter what he says or how he acts toward you, know that he will protect you with his life. We have been the guardians of your family for a very long time. He will not forsake you just because of his personal feelings. I love you, my dearest Anna. No matter what has befallen me, I want you to always remember that I treasure the time I've been able to spend with you. I knew from the moment I held you in my arms after you were born that you were meant for greatness. You are going to change the world, my little cherub. I have complete faith that you will live up to your birthright. I am so proud to be known as your father, and so thankful to have been given the opportunity to watch you grow and mature into the beautiful, self-confident woman you are today. Keep safe, my love. And always remember that your papa is proud of you and loves you more than anything or anyone else in this world."

I sit motionless on the floor as tears trail down my face. I play the message again and again because it's the only link I have left to my father.

Finally, I look back inside the bag and pull out the sword.

It's not a hologram. It's real. I'm not sure how my papa was able to smuggle a weapon into Cirrus, but somehow he did. And he thought it important enough to leave for me to find.

As I heft the hilt in my hand, the silver blade suddenly ignites with red-orange flames, mesmerizing me with their flickering brightness.

"Whoa," Vala says, her dark, little, hazel-colored eyes shining from the flames as she stares at the sword in my hand. "What kind of sword is that, Anna?"

I shake my head. "I have no idea, Vala. No idea at all."

CHAPTER 5

A day passes. Then two. Still no word comes about Millie's and Eliza's whereabouts. I have no way to find out where they are or why they're still being held. In truth, I welcome the silence in the house. It lets me focus on what I need to do next. I decide that if I'm ever going to find a way to bring my father back, I will have to wait until after my marriage to the emperor. On the day of our wedding, I will also be crowned empress and have far more power than I do now.

I can't call the person masquerading as the Emperor Auggie because he *isn't* my best friend. He is an imposter. Of that I have no doubt whatsoever. I'm not sure how long it will take or what I will have to do to prove that fact to everyone else, but I feel certain the truth will reveal itself in time. I simply have to be patient and choose my actions carefully, because I am also certain the dowager empress will be watching my every move. I will have to hide my real agenda from them both if I am ever going to get my family back together.

Two days before my marriage to the emperor, the usurper

shows up in my home completely unannounced. I am playing with Vala in my sitting room when he suddenly appears in front of me. I find his unexpected appearance odd because I didn't see the flash of light that usually coincides with someone teleporting. It was more like he just materialized out of nowhere.

"Good evening, Annalisse," he says, his eyes roaming over every inch of my body with undisguised carnal interest—further proof to me that the person standing before me is not Auggie.

"Good evening," I reply as Vala sits up on my lap, staring at the emperor like she'll pounce on him if he dares try to touch me.

The emperor looks around my sitting room like he is seeing it for the very first time, taking in every detail before returning his gaze to me.

"It's a pity, you know," he says with a heavy sigh of regret.

He doesn't complete his thought, and I know exactly what he wants.

"What's a pity?" I ask, providing the slight prod he seems to need to finish what he was about to say.

"It's a pity how your life has turned out," he finishes. "You were given everything a person needs to survive in this world, yet look where you are. Forced into a marriage you don't want. Exiled from your father and friends. It just seems rather pathetic, considering all the effort that went into placing you where you are now."

"What are you talking about?" I ask.

The emperor makes a clicking sound with his tongue, like he's chastising me for something I said.

"Come, come, Annalisse. I think we both know what's going on here. You don't have to hide your knowledge from me. You know what I am."

"I know you're an imposter," I say vehemently, not being able to control my temper. "Where is Auggie?"

The person masquerading as my friend narrows his eyes at me, looking slightly confused.

"Don't you know?" he asks.

"How am I supposed to know what you did with him?" I demand. "Where is he?"

I watch as the man's expression transforms into one of sudden realization. He begins to laugh. It's not a joyous sound, but one filled with scorn.

"I can't believe they didn't tell you anything!" he howls, completely amused by my ignorance of what's really going on.

"Then why don't you enlighten me," I say, becoming annoyed at his mocking. "If you're so smart, why don't you share your vast store of knowledge with me?"

The man is finally able to bring his mirth under control and looks at me with no pretense of friendliness. He hates me; that much is certain. I just don't know why he hates me.

"What fun would that be?" he asks. "Why would I give up the upper hand I have over you? Plus, you really don't need to know anyway. You won't be alive long enough to do anything with the knowledge."

My body tenses, and Vala begins to growl.

"You leave her alone," Vala threatens.

The emperor chuckles.

"I've lived longer than this world has been in existence, my little robot friend," he says to Vala in disgust. "It will take more than you to end my life. Of that, you can rest assured."

Even though he didn't want to give up any information that would help me, he just did.

"How can you be older than the Earth?" I ask, hoping to coerce him into opening up a dialogue. "I think you're lying."

"How limited your mind is," the man says condescendingly. "I can't believe Andre raised you to think so inside the box. There are powers within this world that are beyond your limited imagination. And I'm one of them."

"Prove it," I say. "Just what kind of powers do you presume to have that would amaze my limited intellect?"

The man stares at me, and I can see that he's trying to decide whether or not to entertain my request. Before I know it, a whip made of what looks like lightning appears in his right hand, crackling with a supernatural power. He lifts his hand and slashes the portrait of my mother that has always hung over the fireplace in my sitting room, cutting it in half and causing it to catch on fire.

I feel my heart race but try to hold back my fear. Fear isn't an emotion I want to show the creature standing in front of me.

"What are you?" I ask in a whisper.

"I hate to sound cliché, but I'm your worst nightmare."

"Why do you hate me so much?"

"Oh, where to start?" He chuckles. His gaze is drawn to what remains of my mother's portrait. "We could start with her, I guess."

"You knew my mother?"

"I've known your family since the beginning of it," he tells me, sounding sickened by the fact of the association. "You come from a long line of thorns in my side."

"Sounds like I would have liked them," I taunt.

"Well, you will be happy to know that little smart-ass mouth of yours was inherited honestly," the man snorts derisively. "However, the knowledge won't do you much good, I'm afraid. You won't live long enough to have time to really think about it."

"Are you going to kill me?"

"Absolutely not," he says, looking offended by such a notion. "I wouldn't want to dirty the emperor's hands with such a task."

"Where is Auggie?" I ask again, hoping his arrogance will prod him into flaunting the truth in my face.

"Standing right before you," the man says with a devilish grin.

"You are not Auggie."

"But I am in his body."

"How?"

"I took it."

"How do you just take over a body? Are you remotely controlling him somehow?"

The man laughs and shakes his head at me like I'm the most ignorant person on the planet.

"No, I forced his soul out, so mine could wear his skin."

"Who are you?" I demand.

"Allow me to introduce myself," the man says, bowing to me exaggeratedly. "I am the archangel Levi, one of the seven princes of Hell, at your service, my lady."

My father had, of course, shared his religious beliefs with me, but I didn't remember him ever mentioning Hell having princes.

"Where is Auggie's soul?"

"I guess that depends on how well-behaved a boy he was while he was still alive. However, my guess would be Heaven, since he seemed to be such a do-gooder."

"Then he's dead?" I ask, my voice breaking uncontrollably over my loss.

"Afraid so."

I take a moment to absorb this fact, pushing back my emotions for now, because if I let them surface, they will incapacitate me, and right now, I know I will need all of my senses to outwit the creature standing before me.

"Why do you hate me so much?" I ask. "Why do you hate my family?"

"As I said, your predecessors have been a thorn in my side for many, *many* years. It seems like each generation is worse than the last. If I kill you, I can end your line and be done with you once and for all. I've simply been waiting for the right time before revealing myself again. It's been a thousand years since I took a mortal's form. After I heard about your birth, I knew the time had finally arrived for me to come back."

"Why me?" I ask. "What makes me so special?"

"Because of who your father is."

"Do you have a grudge against my father's family, too? Is that why you banished him off-world?"

Levi looks at me like I've completely lost my mind.

"Don't you know who your *real* father is? They didn't keep that from you, too, did they? Unbelievable! They've just made this far too easy for me."

I feel my breath catch in my throat but force myself to ask, "My real father?"

Levi chuckles. "I hate to be the one to inform you. ... No, scratch that. ... I'm pleased to be the one who informs you, dear Annalisse, that Andre Greco is not your real father—not the one who spewed into your mother and knocked her up with you anyway."

"You're lying," I say, my jaw clenching in anger. "You're just saying that to upset me. It won't work. I know who my father is."

Levi shrugs his shoulders. "Believe what you want, my little dove. But it seems like I'm the only one in your life thus far who is willing to tell you the unvarnished truth."

"My papa would have told me he wasn't my real father if that was the truth," I say confidently. "I know he would have."

"No," Levi says, "I don't think he would, because your real father is simply too terrible to admit to. Not even Andre could come to terms with the person your mother chose to spread her legs for."

"Stop talking about my mother like she was some kind of whore!" I yell, feeling my temper reach the point of no return.

"Oh," Levi says, holding a hand up to his mouth, acting like maybe he accidentally said too much, "should I just let you remain deluded about the purity of your dear mumsie? Or do you want to know the truth of your parentage, Lady Annalisse?"

I swallow hard because I want to know the truth, but I'm almost scared to hear it. So far, I haven't detected a lie from Levi. I decide to gather what information I can from him and worry about the implications later.

"Who is my real father?"

Levi opens his mouth, but his attention is drawn to something behind me by the entrance to the veranda.

"Ahh," Levi says, "I was wondering if you had forgotten our little plan, Amon."

I turn around in my seat on the couch and see a man standing by one of the pillars on the veranda, dressed in a black suit and holding a sword in his right hand.

"No, I didn't forget," the man named Amon says, staring at me like he hates me as much as Levi does. "I've waited too long for this moment to forget about it."

"Well, then," Levi says, looking back to me. "I'm afraid this conversation will have to come to an end, just as your life soon will. I would love to stay and watch, but the empress is a needy little bitch. I swear I don't know how this Auggie ever put up with her sniveling demands. All she does is nag, nag, nag. I'm afraid I'll have to find a way to dispose of her soon, just to preserve my sanity. Good-bye, Annalisse. I wish I could say it has been a pleasure meeting you, but that would most certainly be a lie."

As soon as Levi teleports out of my sitting room, Amon appears in front of me.

I duck his first swing of the sword, meant to take off my head, and roll onto the floor away from him. Vala launches herself at Amon, teeth bared and mouth open to take a bite out of his face, but he easily swats her away with his free hand, causing her to fly up against the door in the room and fall to the floor, unmoving.

Her sacrifice gives me just enough time to get to my feet and run to my room, but Amon teleports right behind me and grabs a fistful of my hair, yanking me back against him.

"There's nowhere you can hide!" he yells at me, viciously pulling on my hair until I'm lying on my back on the floor.

He lifts the sword above his head, holding the hilt with both hands, the blade angled down toward my midsection.

It's then that I do something I've never done before.

I teleport myself to safety, out onto the veranda.

I don't have time to wonder how I did it, because Amon teleports outside, too.

He sneers at me as he runs toward me.

I need a weapon. I need the sword my father left for me. And I need it now!

I hear a whining sound behind me like something is flying through the air at high velocity. I spin around just as I see the sword I had hidden underneath my bed come zooming toward me. I hold out a hand, and the sword's hilt lands in my palm like it knew exactly where it needed to be.

I hear Amon grunt behind me and know instinctively that he's swinging his sword at me. I kneel down as his blade slices through the air with a whistling noise, where my head would have been if I hadn't knelt with split-second precision.

I immediately stand to my feet and thrust my sword at him, only to have him block my blade with his own. As the edges of our blades meet, my sword bursts into red-orange flames, which seems to make Amon fall back in surprise.

It's all the advantage I need.

I swing my sword at him relentlessly, never letting up until I have him backed up to the railing of the veranda. He's strong, but

I'm stronger, a fact he doesn't seem to realize until it's too late. I suddenly see my opening and slide the flaming blade of my sword straight into his gut. Amon falls to his knees before me, yet doesn't seem ready to give up so easily. He lifts his sword and swings it at me desperately. I'm able to dodge his attack by teleporting behind him. He yanks my blade out of his torso, just as my hands burst into blue flames. I wrap my fingers tightly around his neck.

I want him to die, not only to save my own life but to make him pay for what's happened to Auggie and my father. If I can't wreak my vengeance on Levi, Amon will do.

With one thought, I wish him dead, gone from this life forever.

Amon screams just before he disintegrates into what looks like black ash at my feet.

A pain stronger than any I have ever felt sears through the lower portion of my back, causing me to double over from the torture and fall to the ground. I scream as it lights every nerve in my body on fire with no end in sight.

I'm not sure how long I lay there, writhing in agony. It's not until a cool, gentle hand cups one side of my burning, tear-stained face that I feel even a modicum of relief. The pain is so excruciating and debilitating, I can't even force my eyes open when I feel strong arms lift me up from the ground and cradle me against a bare, brawny chest. I lay my head against the man's shoulder, welcoming the comfort I feel, because I simply don't have the strength to do anything else.

"I've got you, Anna," I hear the man say to me. The timbre of his voice is deep and soothing to my soul. "I've got you."

CHAPTER 6

I hear the heels of the man's shoes click against the granite of the veranda and then move on to the softer-sounding marble in my sitting room. He finally lays me down on what feels like my bed, but even the softness of it causes me unending agony when my back touches it. The man seems to understand where it is I'm hurt and turns me onto my side instead.

"Hold still," he instructs gently, and it's only then that I realize I'm crying so hard that my whole body is shaking uncontrollably.

I feel him pull apart the magnetic closure on the back of my dress and hear him take in a sharp breath.

"What the hell. ..." I hear him say in a startled voice, obviously not understanding whatever it is he's found on my back.

I can't ask what's wrong because I can barely draw in a breath, much less speak.

I feel the tips of his fingers glide down the center of my spine, bringing with them a much-needed coolness to my flesh. His touch brings me relief, and I'm finally able to take a deep, shuddering breath. His fingers circle something at the base of my back, causing me to wince involuntarily because the skin there is so tender.

"Sorry," he says, and I feel him pull his hand away.

"No," I beg, "don't stop. Your touch is the only thing making the pain bearable."

His fingers return, and he gently strokes my back up and down, wiping away my hurt with each pass over my skin. Minutes pass, and the pain finally becomes manageable enough for me to stop squeezing my eyes shut, so I can open them again.

"Thank you," I breathe, relishing the feel of his skin against mine, a sensation I've never experienced before with a man.

"I'm not sure I'm really helping that much," he says, sounding doubtful that his simple ministrations are doing anything to assist in the healing process.

"You're helping more than you know," I tell him, closing my eyes once again, but not because of the pain this time. I'm simply enjoying the feel of his touch and don't want him to stop.

A few more minutes pass, and the pain completely ebbs away. Yet I can't quite bring myself to ask the stranger to stop gliding his fingers up and down my back. I feel slightly ashamed, knowing that he's only doing it to bring me comfort, and I'm taking advantage of his generosity. I know if I tell him the pain is gone, he'll take his hand away, and that isn't something I'm ready for just yet.

"Are you sure this is helping?" he asks again, sounding doubly uncertain that his actions are serving any real purpose.

I open my eyes and let out a resigned sigh because I know I'll need to tell him to stop. I wait just one more selfish minute before saying anything.

"You can stop now," I tell him and feel him instantly pull his hand away, like he was simply waiting for me to give him permission to stop touching me. "Could you close the back of my dress for me?" I ask, finding a small way to make him touch me again, however briefly.

He does as I ask, and I feel his fingers momentarily graze across my back as he brings the seams of my dress close enough together for them to grab hold of one another.

I immediately roll over onto my back and look up at the man sitting next to me.

The earth beneath me moves and my heart quakes.

I find it hard to breathe because the beauty of the man I'm looking at is beyond any I've ever seen before.

His long black hair is slightly wavy and hangs down just past his shoulders. His features are so perfectly symmetrical that they look like they were chiseled by the hand of God Himself. He's shirtless, and I don't even bother to pretend to avert my eyes out of propriety as I look at the length of him, wondering how I could have not noticed a man like him in Cirrus before.

"Who are you?" I ask. "How did you know I was in trouble? Where did you come from?"

His soulful blue eyes stare at me for what seems like forever. He looks confused by me, like there's something about me that he wasn't expecting to see. Before I can ask another question, he stands and turns his back to me, walking a few feet away while running his fingers through his hair, as though he's thinking about something that troubles him.

I sit up and watch him as he stands completely still. I can't help but admire his well-formed muscular back, and I again wonder how I could have missed meeting a man like him in Cirrus.

Finally, as if making up his mind about whether or not he intends to give me answers to my questions, he turns around. The look on his face isn't one of confusion anymore, but grim determination.

"My name is Malcolm Devereaux. I'm not completely sure

how I knew you were in trouble, and I come from a city known in the down-world as New Orleans."

"I know you. Well, I know of you," I amend. "You're one of the overlords on the surface. Did you actually come to the Tribute Ball this year? Was I already in prison when you arrived there?"

It was the only thing that made sense to me. Why else would he have been here in Cirrus this evening?

"No," Malcolm says to me, looking uncertain as to whether he wants to explain things further. "I did not attend the Tribute Ball."

"Then why were you in Cirrus tonight?"

"I wasn't."

I sit there and just stare at him, waiting for a better explanation, but he doesn't seem to want to elaborate any further on what he just said.

I need an explanation. I need answers, and I need them now.

"Then how did you get here?" I ask again, pressing for an answer.

He stands there silently, as if he's carefully weighing his next words.

"I can do something called phasing," he finally admits.

"Phasing?" I ask, never having heard the term before. "Is that a special type of teleportation?"

"In a way," he says, "but I do it on my own without needing to use a teleportation device."

I sit there and think about the events of the night. When Levi suddenly appeared in my sitting room, I noticed then how he teleported in without the flash of light usually associated with teleportation. Then, when I was fighting Amon, he was able to do the same thing.

I was, too. ...

"Can I phase?" I ask, watching Malcolm's expression, because if there is one thing that I will know, it's if he tries to lie to me.

"Yes," he says without hesitation. "You can phase, Anna."

"How?" I ask. "How does it work?"

"We're able to fold space and travel between two points that we've been to before," he says. His brow furrows like this fact worries him for some reason.

"What's wrong?" I ask.

"It's just that," Malcolm says, his eyes drifting around my room as he looks at things, "I've never been to Cirrus before, but somehow I was able to come to you when you needed me."

"How did you even know I was in trouble?" I ask again, wanting to understand just what our connection is to one another.

Malcolm is silent as he looks back at me. I'm not sure he's going to answer until I see his lips part and he whispers, "I felt your pain."

This time, I'm the one who is silent, because I'm not sure what that means.

"You felt my pain?" I ask, just to clarify.

Malcolm doesn't move or say anything else. He simply stands there wordlessly, either unable or unwilling to tell me more. My guess is the latter.

"Are you the one my father told me about in his last message to me? Were the two of you best friends at one time?"

"We have been friends for a very long time," Malcolm tells me.

I reach behind my right ear and pull off the neural memo patch there. I swing my legs off the bed and walk over to Malcolm. I hold out one of the last gifts from my papa to him.

"He would probably want you to see his last message to me then," I tell him.

Malcolm looks hesitant to take the patch from me. Finally he holds his hand out, and I tilt mine to drop the patch into the palm of his hand. He places it behind his right ear and plays the message. Once it's over, he dislodges the patch and hands it back to me.

"Can you tell me what happened here tonight?" Malcolm asks. "I need to know exactly what occurred and how you were injured."

"I was sitting in the front room with. ..."

It's only then that I remember Vala.

I quickly dash out of the room without explanation and run to where her little body is still lying motionless by the door to my chambers. I kneel down beside her small form and pick her up. I rush into a room off of the sitting room.

"Lights!" I call out frantically, illuminating my study as I walk over to my desk.

I sit down behind it and say, "Tools."

The silver tools I've used to repair Vala over the years suddenly materialize on the surface of my black desk. I lay Vala down in front of me and pull apart the seam on the underside of her belly, praying whatever Amon damaged when he threw her against the door is easily repairable.

I'm faintly aware of Malcolm leaning up against the entrance of the room, watching me intently. I look up briefly from my task and feel my heart race when our eyes meet.

"You look like you've done that before," he comments, sounding somewhat impressed with my mechanical skills.

"I have," I say, returning my attention to Vala, determined to fix her quickly. "I just hope it doesn't take me long to figure out what's wrong. Vala has an organic brain. Like anything living, the longer her brain is starved of nutrients, the more damage it'll sustain."

Malcolm pushes off the door frame and saunters over to me. I notice a slight catch in his gait, like he's favoring his right leg for some reason, but don't make mention of it.

He comes up behind me and props his hands on the desk on either side of me. I feel his warm breath against the crook of my neck as he leans in to study the inner workings of Vala's design.

"Impressive," he says, sounding in awe of my little friend. "Andre must have spent a great deal of money to give you such a gift."

"Papa has always been generous to me," I reply, trying to keep my mind focused on the task at hand and not the man standing unnervingly close behind me, studying my every move.

"There it is," he tells me. "That tube was just dislodged from its connector."

I see what he's talking about and quickly reconnect the tube.

"Thank you," I tell him, feeling relief that the solution was a simple one.

I close the seam of Vala's belly and push the reboot button in a secret compartment on her chest.

Her eyes slowly blink open. She rolls herself over into a sitting position and looks up at me.

"What happened?" Vala asks, sounding a little on the woozy side.

"You were injured trying to protect me," I tell her, admonishing her slightly for such an act. Vala might only be as big as both my hands put together, but in her mind, she imagines herself the size of a mastiff.

Vala's little eyes open wider, and I see her gaze travel to Malcolm, who is still standing behind me.

"Who are you?" she asks him.

"I'm Malcolm," I hear him say, sounding slightly amused that he's being questioned by a dog, even if it is a sentient robot.

Vala hops up on all four paws and assumes a fighting stance as she growls, "Friend or foe?"

Malcolm chuckles, and the sound of his mirth lightens my heart.

"Hopefully a friend," he replies.

"Definitely a friend," I tell Vala, chancing a glance behind me to Malcolm.

The smile on Malcolm's face vanishes when he notices me looking at him. I get the feeling he's not sure if I'm exactly friend-worthy material. There is distrust in his eyes as he looks at me that I can't quite understand. Even though he's a complete stranger, I feel like I can trust him more than anyone else who has ever been in my life, besides my papa. Yet it's apparent he doesn't feel the same way about me.

Vala seems satisfied with our answers and lies back down, crossing her front paws before her and resting her head on top of them.

"I need to sleep for a little while, Anna," Vala says, sounding tired. "I need to heal a bit more."

Before I know it, Vala has fallen asleep.

I turn in my chair and look back up at Malcolm.

"I'm sorry. I didn't finish answering your question about what happened earlier. We can go into the sitting room, and I can tell you everything that I know."

Malcolm nods like this idea is agreeable to him. He waits for me to stand and walk toward the outer room before following behind me.

As I walk, I wonder why, if Malcolm is truly my father's best friend, he doesn't completely trust me. And how can someone barely in his thirties be someone my father has known for "a very long time"?

Things simply aren't adding up, but I hope Malcolm will help me unravel what is really going on.

CHAPTER 7

I sit down on the couch and expect Malcolm to sit beside me, but he chooses to stand in the exact same spot Levi had earlier. His eyes travel to the ruined portrait of my mother, which is hanging by burnt threads from its damaged frame over the fireplace. A shadow of sadness covers his face, making me wonder just how well he knew my parents.

Malcolm drags his eyes away from my mother's picture and looks at me.

"Anna, I need you to tell me exactly what happened here tonight," he says, crossing his arms in front of his bare chest, standing with his legs slightly apart.

I have to take a deep breath just to steady the rapid beating of my heart at the sight of him. I look down at my hands clasped in my lap in order to give myself some extra time to compose my thoughts before answering.

"I was sitting right here with Vala when the emperor tele-ported into the room," I tell him, looking back up at him. "But I've known since I was arrested that he isn't my Auggie anymore.

During the conversation, I forced him to tell me who he really is and learned that he's actually an archangel named Levi, living inside Auggie's body," I say, feeling the heartache over Auggie's loss threatening to overwhelm me. I will myself to keep my sorrow buried for now. I can't break down because, if I do, I might never recover. I need to tell Malcolm everything first. Maybe then we can figure out what needs to be done next and how to get my father back from his exile before he reaches the point of no return. I've already lost my closest and dearest friend. I can't live with the loss of my papa, too.

"I was already aware that Levi had taken control of the emperor's body," Malcolm informs me.

"How?" I ask in shock.

"The night you were arrested at the ball, Jered came to me and told me."

"Is there any way to get Auggie back?" I ask in desperation but know in my heart that Levi was telling me the truth when he said Auggie's soul had moved on. I know I'm grasping at straws, but it's the only hope I have of saving my friend.

Malcolm stares at me, looking confused by my question.

"Why?" he asks.

"Why what?" I counter.

"Why would you make an effort to do such a thing?"

"Because I love him," I say without hesitation. "Auggie's my best friend. If there's any chance I can save him, I have to take it. I'll do whatever it takes to get him back."

Malcolm remains silent for a while before finally saying, "You can't save your friend. He's dead, Anna. His soul has moved on, and it can't be retrieved."

The resolute way in which Malcolm says these words to me crumbles the little bit of hope I had left in my heart of saving a person who had been in my life for as long as I can remember. The realization that Auggie is truly gone hasn't quite sunk in, and I don't fully permit it to. I'll allow the dam holding back my sorrow to collapse later. Right now, I need to stay focused and figure out if there is any way to save the other man in my life.

"What about my father?" I ask, straining to gain a small bit of hope that at least one person I love can be saved. "Is there anything you can do to bring him back?"

Even before Malcolm verbally gives me an answer, I already suspect it will be "no." The way his brow furrows at the question and the troubled look that enters his eyes tells me everything.

"I can't find Andre," Malcolm says, like he's admitting to a failure.

"What do you mean you can't find him?" I ask. "He's on a ship to one of the outer worlds."

Malcolm's brow furrows even deeper as he says, "No, he's not."

I sit there for a moment, letting this new information sink in.

"Then where is he?" I demand. "Where is my papa?"

Malcolm shakes his head slowly and keeps his eyes completely focused on me.

"I don't know, Anna," he admits. "Like I said, I can't find him."

"That doesn't make any sense," I say, trying to find reason in something that has none. "He can't have just vanished into thin air. There has to be a trail we can follow to figure out where he is."

"Either Levi has him hidden very well or. ..." Malcolm lets the words hang in the air with ominous portent.

"No," I say resolutely, refusing the idea Malcolm is trying to plant. "My father isn't dead. I would know it if he were."

"How exactly would you know something like that?" Malcolm asks, not even trying to hide the fact that he doubts my words.

"I just would," I say defensively. "I would know if he was dead. I would feel it in my heart, and I don't. So get that look off your face and help me figure out a way to find my father!"

My words seem to penetrate through Malcolm's stubbornness because the creases across his forehead disappear, and he looks at me in surprise. I get the feeling he isn't used to being yelled at.

"For argument's sake, let's assume that he *is* still alive," Malcolm says, still sounding doubtful that I'm right. "Levi has him hidden extremely well. It'll take some time and cunning to find out where he's being held. I have people searching for him, but even they don't have access to some areas. So, in the meantime, let's get back to what happened here tonight. What exactly did Levi say to you?"

"He told me he was an archangel and one of the seven princes of Hell," I say. "Then he made some disparaging remarks about my mother's virtue and told me I came from a long line of smart-mouthed thorns in his side."

Malcolm chuckles. "Truer words have never been spoken."

"He also said. ..." I can't quite bring myself to say the words because then they would become all too real. But I have to have it confirmed. I have to know the absolute truth. "He also said that Papa isn't my real father."

I watch for Malcolm's reaction to this statement, but his expression remains the same, giving nothing away. Instead, he asks me a question.

"Did you believe him?"

"I don't care what he said," I say adamantly. "Andre Greco is my father. Even if he isn't my biological one, he is my papa in every other way that matters."

"Then I wouldn't worry about what Levi said to you," Malcolm replies, seeming to want to dismiss the subject of my true parentage for now. "What else happened?"

"Someone named Amon came and we fought," I tell him. "I stabbed him with the sword my father left me, and then I phased behind him, grabbed him by the neck, and. ..."

I pause for a moment to collect my thoughts, not completely sure how to explain what happened next.

"And you turned him into black ash," Malcolm says quietly, finishing my sentence for me.

I nod slowly. "Yes," I say, "but how did you know that?"

Malcolm doesn't answer right away, and I see the confused look return to his eyes.

"I didn't think it would be you," he finally says. "Andre never had a doubt you were the one. He seemed to know the moment he first held you in his arms. That's why he smuggled the sword up here. He knew you would need it one day to protect yourself from Amon."

"You talk like the two of you already knew what would happen here tonight," I say. "How is that possible? How did I turn Amon into ash?"

"I guess I should have known, too," Malcolm says, his eyes becoming unfocused, almost like he's talking to himself and completely dismissing me from his mind. "I should have known the moment you were conceived that only a child from Lilly's line and his could produce someone who can actually kill an archangel. I just let my hatred cloud my judgment." Malcolm's eyes refocus on me. "Andre loved you from the moment you were born, and because of that love, he was able to see who you truly are. I should have listened to him, but I don't think I was meant to be a part of your life until now."

"Why?" I ask, needing to know why his thoughts were leading him to that conclusion.

Malcolm stares at me, and I can tell by the tense way his jaw is set that I won't get an answer.

"There are things you need to know about yourself," he says instead, "things about the history of your family, your lineage. I know Andre purposely withheld the information from you. I think he secretly hoped that you weren't the one we've been waiting for. He loved you so much he even gave up his immortality because just the thought of living longer than you caused him too much pain."

"Immortality?" I ask. "But that was outlawed years ago when it was decided no generation should outlive the next."

"I'm not talking about immortality gained through science," Malcolm says patiently. "I'm talking about the immortality of angels."

I let what Malcolm tells me sink in for a moment, but then it all makes sense.

"That's why you look so young, yet you've been friends with my papa for a long time. Did you know my mother, too?"

"I've known your family since it began," Malcolm tells me. "Andre, Jered, a few others, and I have been waiting almost a thousand years for you to be born, Anna. Now that we know for certain that you are the one we've been waiting for, we can finish the task we were asked to undertake and finally be released from a promise made a long time ago."

"A task? What task?"

"Have you ever read the Book of Revelation in the Bible?"

I nod. "Yes."

"In it, seven seals are opened and they bring about the end of the world. You were born to stop the seals from ever being opened here in this reality."

"This reality?" I ask, getting more confused by the second. "You say that like there's more than one."

"There are a multitude of different realities," Malcolm says. "The one we live in is what we call the Origin. All of the other realities stem off of this one. Any major or cataclysmic event that takes place here will trickle down to all of the other realities. If the seals are opened here in the Origin, they will destroy not only this reality but all realities."

"How am I supposed to stop the seals from being opened?" I ask, still confused by how I, of all people, can prevent such a thing from happening.

"Each of the seven princes of Hell has one of the seals," Malcolm says. "They stole them after the war in Heaven. You were made to retrieve those seals from them."

"How?" I ask, still not understanding.

Malcolm takes two steps closer to me and holds out his hand.

I don't hesitate to place my hand into his. I immediately feel the same peace and warmth from his touch that I felt earlier when he was caressing my back. I stand up from the couch and follow his lead back into my bedroom. If any other man would have done such a thing, I probably would have worried that his intentions weren't noble, but with Malcolm, I feel no need to worry and secretly hope that his intentions *aren't* noble ones. I suppose I should feel ashamed of myself for hoping for such a thing, but I don't. It just seems like a natural thing to want with Malcolm, like needing air to breathe.

Unfortunately, Malcolm leads me to the reflective wall in my room and not my bed. He turns me around, so that my back is facing it. He lets go of my hand, and I immediately feel a loss from the absence of his touch.

"I need to undo your dress in the back to show you something," he warns, walking behind me and gently grasping the top of my dress there to pull the seam apart and bare my back.

He separates the seam until it reaches the small of my back, while I hold up the front so the dress doesn't fall off. I look over my shoulder and see that he's staring at something on that portion of my body with a troubled frown on his face.

"What's there?" I ask, concerned by his expression and

remembering the pain I felt earlier when he caressed that same exact spot.

Malcolm looks up at me before stepping to my right side and allowing me to see the reflection of my back in the mirror.

At the very base of my spine, I see a circular raised mark—almost like a brand burned into my skin. The symbol is strange, like nothing I've ever seen before. Yet I immediately know what it says.

"Conflict," I say, reading the word aloud.

"It's one of the seven seals," Malcolm tells me. "It was the one Amon had."

I stare at the seal burnt into my flesh. "How did I get it? Was it transferred to me when I killed him?"

"That's what I'm assuming," Malcolm says. "We were told that you would be able to recover the seals from the princes, but we didn't know how exactly until now. After you've retrieved them all, you can take them back to where they belong."

"Which is where exactly?"

"Heaven."

I stop looking at my reflection and turn my full attention back to Malcolm. "Don't you have to be dead to go to Heaven?"

"Not the women from your family line. You inherited the ability to phase into Heaven whenever you want."

"Why would anyone want to do that?" I ask.

"Most don't," Malcolm admits. "For the living, Heaven isn't a place where they feel comfortable because they're not meant to be there. But I think once you recover the rest of the seals from the other princes, you'll need to go there and return them to God."

I stare at Malcolm, because I can't seem to make myself stop staring at him. I feel an uncontrollable urge to just throw myself into his arms and kiss him until he makes me stop, but I restrain myself because that isn't the proper way a lady should behave around a gentleman, especially one she's just met. Yet my heart feels tethered to Malcolm in a way I don't absolutely understand. The gaping hole that has always been there is filled now, and I finally feel complete.

It's only the wariness in Malcolm's eyes as he looks back at me that tarnishes the moment. For some reason, he doesn't seem to trust me, and I can't fathom the reason why. In my fairytale dreams about meeting my soul mate, I always envisioned him wanting me as much as I want him. Yet I get the feeling Malcolm may not feel the same way I do. Could I have just been deluding myself into thinking true love was instantaneous for both parties? Would Malcolm ever be able to return my feelings, or was I doomed to a one-sided attraction that would never be requited?

Malcolm clears his throat and walks behind me again to close the seam of my dress for me.

I feel the tips of his fingers glide across my back as he brings the two pieces of fabric together. I expect him to walk back in front of me, but he doesn't. He stays behind me and remains silent, unmoving. I give him a few seconds more to walk away. When he remains in the same position, I slowly turn around to look at him.

Again, he has a puzzled look on his face. When our eyes meet, I can see that he wants to say something to me. His lips part slightly, like he's about to speak, but then he presses them back together firmly, and his jaw muscles tense.

"What should we do next?" I whisper to him, still feeling perplexed by the events of the evening and completely clueless what our next move should be.

"You need to go through with your marriage to the emperor," Malcolm says, catching me off guard.

"Have you lost your mind?" I demand. "I can't marry that thing!"

"If you want to have a chance at finding Andre, you need to do what I say, Anna. As empress, you'll have more power and privileges. If you truly want to save Andre, that's what you're going to have to do."

"I'll do it for my father," I say. "But that thing will never be my husband."

"It's a marriage of convenience," Malcolm agrees, "not one of the heart, and that's the only one that counts in God's eyes."

"Will you be staying here?" I ask, hoping Malcolm will remain close to my side. "Will you stay in Cirrus to help me?"

"I need to return to my home and make a few arrangements first," Malcolm says. "But I promise to be back in time for the party tomorrow night at the palace."

Until that moment, I had completely forgotten about the ball at the palace. It's tradition in Cirrus for the bride and groom to host a gathering of friends and family the night before their wedding. It's definitely not something I'm looking forward to.

"Anna, you can count on me to help you fulfill your destiny," Malcolm tells me with hesitation in his voice. "But you need to know that I'm only doing it because of a vow I made to someone very dear to me. I promised her that I would see this mission through to the end, and I don't intend to break my pledge to her."

"Who did you make that promise to?" I ask.

Malcolm hesitates. Finally he says, "To the woman who has always been dearest to my heart. For her, I will help you."

My heart sinks into the pit of my stomach. How can Malcolm already be in love with someone else when I feel so certain we are meant for one another?

"Try to get some rest, Anna," Malcolm says. "I'll see you tomorrow."

Malcolm phases and leaves me feeling more alone than I have ever felt in my entire life. As I look at the spot he phased from, I see a room through what looks like a shimmering hole floating in midair. I stare through the hole to this other world, until it finally disappears.

With a heavy heart, I go to my bed and lie down. As I lay there, the events of the day come crashing into me like a boulder barreling down from the top of a mountain, crushing my soul with grief over the loss of Auggie, uncertainty over my father's fate, and pain over the knowledge that the man I thought was the match to my soul has already given his heart to someone else.

CHAPTER 8

Just as sleep loosens its fervent grasp on my consciousness the next morning, I hear a melodic tune I haven't heard in years, but I immediately recognize the voice of the person singing it.

I open my eyes and find Millie sitting on the side of my bed, gently brushing my hair out of my face and tucking it behind my exposed ear.

I instantly sit up, and we wrap our arms around one another.

"Where have you been?" I ask, feeling a rush of relief to have one of my friends return to my side.

"They kept Eliza and me in a cell until this morning," Millie says, hugging me tightly to her. "We weren't told why they were keeping us, though. What's happened, my sweet? Where is your father?"

I pull back from Millie and tell her everything that happened, from the time I was arrested at the Tribute Ball until the moment Malcolm left me the night before.

"Master Devereaux was here?" Millie asks in astonishment.

"Well, I never thought that man would ever step a foot into Cirrus."

"You know Malcolm?" I ask. "How?"

"I was the head of his household in New Orleans, before I came to Cirrus with your father the night you were born. I haven't seen him since then, though. I wish I had been here to speak with him."

"Well, like I said, he told me he needed to make some arrangements back home and then he's supposed to come back to Cirrus. He promised me he would be here in time for the party tonight."

"If that's what Master Devereaux promised, then that's exactly what he will do. He never breaks a vow if it's within his power to keep it."

"Millie," I say, hesitant to voice my next words but needing answers to questions I didn't feel comfortable asking Malcolm directly, "Malcolm said that he made a promise to a woman who is dearest to his heart to help me stop the seven princes. Do you know who she is? Have you ever met her?"

"I'm not completely sure I should talk about her," Millie replies, looking reluctant to say anything beyond this simple statement.

"Please, Millie, who is she?" I beg, needing to know the name of the woman Malcolm seems to have so much respect and love for.

"She was one of your original ancestors," Millie finally says. "That's about all I feel comfortable saying, my sweet. If Master Devereaux found out that I talked about her with you, I'm not sure he would like it very much. Plus, I would feel as though I was breaking his confidence in what he shared about her with me."

"She was one of my ancestors?" I ask, feeling confused all of a sudden. "So, she's dead?"

"He buried her a long time ago, from what I gather," Millie

tells me. "But her loss still haunts him to this day. I think he's simply been waiting all these years to fulfill his promise to her before welcoming death for himself."

"Death?" I ask, feeling panic set in. "After he helps me reclaim the seven seals, do you think he'll kill himself just to be with her again?"

Millie shrugs her shoulders. "I can't say. All I know is that he loved her more than anything in this world, and even after she died, he couldn't bring himself to stop loving her. I think the promise he made to her is the only thing that's been keeping him going all these years. It must be such a relief to him now, to finally know Lord Andre has been right all these years about you being the one they've been waiting for. Your father knew you were special from the first moment he held you in his arms, but Master Devereaux would never admit it."

"Why?" I ask. "Is there something about me that he doesn't like?"

Millie is silent, and her eyes drift to her hands in her lap as she wrings them nervously.

"I'm not sure I'm the person who should be answering these questions," she finally says. "I think your father would want to do that himself."

"He's not here, Millie, and you are," I reason, needing the answers she seems reluctant to give. "Please, if there's a reason Malcolm doesn't like me, I *need* to know it."

Millie looks up at me with a question of her own on her face. She hesitates to ask, but finally she does.

"Why is it so important for you to know, my sweet? Why does the opinion of a man you just met matter so much to you?"

I shake my head slightly. "You'll probably think I'm crazy if I tell you why."

Millie places a gentle hand on top of one of mine resting on my lap.

"I won't think you're crazy," she says. "Tell me."

"I've waited so long for someone to make me feel the way he did last night," I say, feeling a desperate need to share my feelings about Malcolm with someone. "I always imagined when I met my soul mate that I would feel the earth beneath me move and my heart tremble just from being in his presence. When I looked at Malcolm for the first time, I felt those two things happen, Millie. But. ..."

I find it hard to go on and admit the rest. Millie gently squeezes the hand she still holds.

"But what?"

"But I don't think he felt the same things I did. He acted more like he was simply here to fulfill a duty."

Millie sighs. "Well, there is one thing that you absolutely need to know about Master Devereaux. He is the most stubborn man I have ever met in my life! And from what you told me, I wouldn't discount his feelings for you just yet."

"Why?" I ask. "What did I tell you that makes you think that?"

"Your father has shared a lot of stories with me over the years," Millie begins. "I think he wanted me to know about your family's past in case something ever happened to him and he wasn't able to tell you himself. I remember one particular story about an ancestor of yours named Jess. She fell in love with a Watcher. ..."

"Wait," I say, interrupting her. "What's a Watcher?"

"They were a group of angels sent to Earth a very long time ago," Millie tells me. "Your father and Master Malcolm are Watchers. Though, from what I understand, there are only a handful of them left here on Earth now. Most of them asked to become mortal after they found their soul mates. When the Watchers were first sent to Earth, they were only meant to act as teachers to mankind, but all of them ended up falling in love and marrying human women. Most of them even had children with them. Since they broke God's one and only rule, He cursed them and their children as punishment. The Watchers became something known as vampires and were cursed with an insatiable need for human blood, and their children were doomed to live as werewolves, which means they lived in their human form during the day and were transformed into wolves at night. It was only through the bravery of your ancestor, the one Master Malcolm's heart still pines for, that some of the Watchers were able to regain who they were and earn their forgiveness from God.

"Now, as I was saying, one of your ancestors, whose name was Jess, fell in love with a Watcher named Mason. From the story about them that your father told me, Mason was able to feel Jess's pain whenever she was hurt or extremely upset and could phase to her exact location because they were soul mates. God opened up that special connection between them. That sounds precisely like what Master Malcolm was able to do last night when you were hurt, my sweet. He said he felt your pain, correct?"

I nod, gaining hope from Millie's story. "Yes."

"Also, if you add in the fact that he's never been to Cirrus before, which is an essential part of phasing, what other explanation is there but that he is indeed your soul mate? He knew you were in trouble, and he came to you. I'm not sure it can get any clearer than that, even to someone as stubborn as him."

"Why would he try to deny this connection between us?" I ask, not understanding why he would want to reject his feelings for me if he felt the same way I did.

"Odds are the old codger still holds a grudge against your biological father," Millie snorts. "It was the reason Master Malcolm asked Lord Andre to raise you instead of doing the job himself."

"Did you know my biological father?" I ask, feeling curiosity get the best of me. "Who was he?"

Millie shakes her head resolutely. "Now, *that* I absolutely *cannot* tell you."

"Why?" I ask.

"Because your father made me promise that I would never talk about him to you until he had the opportunity to do it himself first. Since we don't know what's become of Lord Andre, I have to keep to my faith that the two of you will be reunited again one day soon. When you are, you can ask him whatever questions you might have yourself."

"Can you at least tell me why Malcolm seems to hate this man so much?"

Millie hesitates but gives me at least this much information: "I don't know the whole story, but I do know that he hurt Master Malcolm a long time ago. That's all I know about it. Neither Master Malcolm nor Lord Andre wanted to talk about the incident much."

"Did ... did my real father love my mother?"

Millie smiles forlornly, like the memory is a bittersweet one for her. "I believe he loved her very much. Your mother was exactly what he needed, because she was able to teach him the most important lesson of all: how to love again. Their union was doomed from the start, I think, but you couldn't tell either one of them that. Master Malcolm tried to separate them after he learned about their relationship, but neither of them paid any mind to his words of caution. All they could think about was each other. It was almost like the outside world didn't exist for them when they were together. I was so happy for your mother. I just wish the happiness could have lasted."

"Why did she die giving birth to me?" I ask. "With our technology, people don't normally die from that sort of thing anymore.

It should have been preventable."

"The pregnancy itself was simply too hard on her body. Your mother refused to have anything placed inside her that might harm you. From the moment you were conceived, you became more important to her than her own life. Your biological father and Master Malcolm tried to persuade her to seek medical attention, but Amalie was just as stubborn as the two of them. She believed that if it was meant for her to survive the pregnancy, then she would without any outside help."

"Why did a normal pregnancy kill her?" I ask. "I still don't understand."

"I think you and I both know that you are not like everyone else," Millie says gently.

I sit there for a moment, letting my thoughts run their natural course.

"I killed her, didn't I?" I ask, my voice breaking over the knowledge that I truly did cause my mother's death.

"It wasn't your fault," Millie says with such tenderness I have to believe her. "You were conceived out of pure love, my sweet. I don't think you can ask for a better reason to be born into this world than that."

"Was my father a Watcher, too?" I ask.

"No, he was definitely *not* a Watcher."

"Then why am I able to phase?"

"That ability comes from both your mother and your father. They could both do it."

"Then my father was an angel of some sort?"

"Yes, but that's all I can say," Millie says stubbornly. "I would really rather wait for Lord Andre or Master Devereaux to explain him to you."

"Did you like him?" I ask, wanting to know more about this mystery man I shared half my genetic code with.

"I liked him well enough when he was with your mother," Millie says, acting like this small admission is as far as she is willing to go in saying she approved of my biological father. "He was a totally different man when he was with her. I think if anyone was surprised by their love for one another, it was him. Your mother had to work extra hard to make him realize he had feelings for her. He was quite obstinate in the beginning, but Amalie was always one to get what she wanted, and she wanted him. She broke down his walls and made him realize there was a small part of his soul that belonged only to her."

I feel sure my mother passed down her tenacity to me. This thought more than anything else gives me hope that I will be able to make Malcolm accept his feelings for me. After Millie told me about the connection between my ancestors, Jess and Mason, I had no lingering uncertainty that Malcolm was made for me, and I was born for him.

I simply had to make him realize it, too.

And there wasn't a doubt in my mind that I would be able to do it.

CHAPTER 9

"Oh, Lady Anna," Eliza croons as she walks around me, examining every angle of the gown I'm wearing to the party celebrating my marriage to the emperor the next day. "I don't think I've ever seen you look lovelier. There's an inner glow about you tonight. Did something good happen during all the bad while we were away?"

Millie and I decided to keep Eliza in the dark about all the secrets I had just unearthed concerning my family history. The less she knows, hopefully the less danger she will be in.

"Thank you, Eliza," I tell her. "I think I'm just excited about the party."

It wasn't a lie, just a truncated version of the truth.

If I were to tell her the truth, I would have to admit that my heart is yearning to see a certain someone make his appearance at the wedding celebration. Not only would it be the first time anyone in Cirrus besides Millie and I gained the privilege of seeing Malcolm in the flesh, but it would also be my next chance to be near him again. It hadn't even been a day since we last saw each other, but even that short span of time was simply too long for my heart's way of thinking.

"I'll go get your coat for you," Eliza tells me as she walks out of the front room and back into my bedroom.

"You *are* glowing," Millie says to me knowingly, "and I think I only need one guess as to why."

"Do you think I'm being silly, Millie?" I whisper. "Is it crazy to feel the way I do for someone I've only just met? Someone ... I don't really know? It doesn't make any logical sense, does it?"

"Whoever said love had to be logical?" Millie whispers back. "I was with Master Devereaux for as long as I've been with you. If there was ever a man who needed someone to love him unconditionally, it's him. His life has been a hard one, and I think he's due a great deal of happiness. If you are the one meant to bring joy back into his life, I say jump on that man and ride off into the sunset together."

I giggle. "Millie, I didn't know you were such a romantic."

"When it comes to two people I care dearly about, I will do whatever it takes to make sure their lives are happy ones."

I hold my hand out to Millie, and she grabs it.

"Now, just remember," Millie tells me, "he is as stubborn as this day has been long for you. But don't let him get away with it. Don't let him use it as a shield to protect himself from you. Do whatever it takes to make him face his feelings. I'll wager he'll fight against falling in love with you. Don't you dare let him do that and ruin both of your lives."

"You sound so certain that he feels the same way I do."

Millie nods her head. "I am. I know it in my heart just like you do. It just makes sense that you would be the one who was made for him. Of all the people I have been privileged to know in this world, you, my sweet, are the best of them all. I've watched you grow from a newborn babe into the strong, beautiful woman standing before me. If anyone can handle Master Devereaux, it's you, Anna Desiraye Greco. Of that I have no doubt whatsoever."

I squeeze Millie's hand to silently tell her thank you for her encouraging words as Eliza walks back into the room with my fur coat.

For the wedding celebration, Empress Catherine decided to lower the temperature inside the dome and produce an artificial snow. In the down-world, it was just approaching winter. It was one of the few times Cirrus tried to mimic the weather of those less fortunate. We would not have to endure the harshness of it for more than a day, though. Unfortunately, those below us would have to struggle through the cold temperatures for a few months.

Ever since the last Great War, temperatures had steadily become extreme on the surface. Summers were excruciatingly hot, and winters were unbearably cold. I was told it had something to do with the ozone layer protecting the surface. Apparently after being exposed to so much radiation from the bombings during the war, it had been thinned out to a point where keeping the temperature regulated on the surface was almost impossible. As far as I know, our scientists are still trying to figure out a way to repair the damage that has been done, but no solution seems to be a permanent one.

Eliza drapes my fur coat over my shoulders. It's not fur from an actual animal. That was outlawed years ago. Now we have the ability to produce fur which looks and feels like the real thing, without the barbaric mutilation of animals just for their pelts. The furs of this particular coat are a blending of warm color tones: auburn, gray, and beige.

Millie helps me pull my long hair over the back collar of the coat. She decided I should keep my hair simple for this ball. It is split down the natural part on top of my head and completely straight, which means it hangs down just past my waist.

"I can't believe you get to ride in the royal carriage," Eliza says excitedly, showing far more enthusiasm than me about the event.

"I would rather not have to," I say, dreading the ride to the palace through town.

I was told everyone in Cirrus who wasn't invited to the palace would be watching me make my way to the castle. Being gawked at by strangers isn't exactly something I am looking forward to.

"Empress Catherine simply wants to show you off," Millie tells me, straightening the collar of my coat until it's flush against my neck. "The people of Cirrus love you, my sweet, and that woman knows it. If it appears that you accept the royal family as your own, I believe she hopes to earn favor amongst the populace. Just think of it as a little act of goodwill between you and your future mother-in-law. Now, put on that lovely smile of yours and get ready to wave to the people you intend to help one day."

"I hope to help us all, Millie," I whisper.

Millie winks at me and turns to head toward the door.

Once we're outside, a footman helps me into the crystal carriage. It reminds me a lot of a fairytale one in an old-fashioned story about a girl named Cinderella that Millie used to read to me when I was a child. Two holographic white horses with light blue plumes on their heads are controlled by a holographic driver to perpetuate the illusion that the carriage is being drawn through town by old-fashioned means. It's all illusion and fantasy, but I suppose people need to imagine the unreal sometimes.

It seems as though everyone in Cirrus is gathered along the side of the street between my home and the palace that evening. They wave to me and cheer me on as I pass them by. Some even yell that they love me. It's all exceedingly strange. I've done nothing to warrant such devotion, yet I seem to have become a beacon of hope for those in Cirrus. It makes me wonder how those on the surface view me. Do they see me as their best chance at a better life once

I'm crowned empress? Have they placed all of their hopes and dreams on my ascension to the throne, or do they believe I'll be just like Empress Catherine and turn a deaf ear to their pleas?

The more I think about what it means to be empress, the more my stomach churns with nervousness. I want to help as many people as I can, but will I be able to? Since Levi is one of the holders of a seal, I know I will most likely have to kill him one day to retrieve it. At least I assume I'll need to kill him. Could there be a way to retrieve the seals without having to murder all seven of the princes of Hell? I don't relish killing, but I know I'll do it if I have to. It seems like there should be a less brutal way of taking the seals back.

Once my conveyance finally reaches the palace, I am escorted to the ballroom. I stand at the top of the stairs and survey the crowd of people below, desperately seeking out the one face I most want to see. But Malcolm is nowhere to be seen.

As the herald announces my arrival, the servant who escorted me helps me take off my coat.

"Lady Annalisse Desiraye Greco," the herald announces to all present, causing everyone in the room to look up at me, "future empress of Cirrus and bride-to-be to Emperor Augustus Amador."

As I walk down the staircase, I see that Empress Catherine and Levi are sitting on their thrones on the dais. My eyes are immediately drawn to Catherine because I notice something doesn't look quite right about her. Her eyes hold a frantic quality, and her face doesn't look entirely right either. Something is definitely wrong with the empress.

Levi's eyes travel the length of me, and I feel myself involuntarily shiver at the undisguised lust he shows. It makes recognizing the charlatan he is easy enough, though. I don't have to keep reminding myself that, even though he looks like Auggie, he isn't my best friend anymore. It sickens me to know the beautiful spirit who was my best friend has lost his life to something so despicable. I vow to make Levi pay for ending the life of someone I loved before it was his time to leave this world.

I walk up to the dais and curtsy.

"There's no need for you to lower your head in our presence, Lady Anna," Levi says. "You will be crowned empress in the morning. In fact," Levi looks over at Empress Catherine, "don't you think it's time you stopped pretending you have any real power anymore, Mother? My future wife is more than competent to take your place."

I look to Empress Catherine. Her eyes meet mine, and for the first time in my life, I see fear on the empress's face.

"Of course, Augustus," Empress Catherine says, standing from her throne but not looking the least bit sorry to leave it, "whatever you want. You're ruler here now, not me."

"I'm glad we've finally come to that understanding." Levi snickers as he watches the empress stand from a throne she proudly sat on for most of her life.

After the empress descends the steps of the dais, she walks over to me.

"I wish you the best of luck during your reign," she tells me, leaning in to kiss one cheek.

"Be careful," she whispers in my right ear, before moving to kiss my left cheek and saying, "that is not my son."

Empress Catherine takes a step back from me, and I see why her face looked odd when I entered the room.

Just underneath her makeup, I can see a faint patch of blue and purple below a slightly swollen left cheekbone.

I don't need to ask who did it to her because the answer is obvious.

"I will take care of Cirrus and its people," I tell her, hoping she knows she is included in my remark.

Empress Catherine smiles faintly before walking away to mingle with the guests.

"Come, Lady Anna," Levi commands, like I'm some sort of animal that needs to be led on a leash, "take your place by my side as future ruler of Cirrus."

I walk up the steps of the dais and sit on the throne beside Levi. As I look out at the crowd, I notice they all seem to be dissecting my every move. I have a feeling their scrutiny will be something I have to live with for as long as I reign over Cirrus.

Levi leans toward me and whispers, "Tell me, Lady Anna, how did you survive Amon's visit to you last night? I didn't expect you to see the light of another day, much less make it to this little soiree of ours. What happened after I left the two of you alone?"

"I killed him," I say bluntly, but in a low voice, not even bothering to sugarcoat my words as I look Levi in the eyes.

His surprise is ... amusing. The widening of his eyes and the way his jaw slackens wordlessly makes me smile. I want to hurt him. I want to scare him so badly that he doesn't have time to think straight.

"Where is my father?" I demand while I have him off guard.

Levi stares at me for a moment then narrows his eyes. "I think you're lying. Not even your real father can kill an archangel."

I hold my hand out to Levi.

"Care to test me?" I taunt.

Levi looks at my outstretched hand like it's a snake about to bite him.

"I don't have to test you," he says, not sounding quite so sure about his safety around me anymore and shrinking back into his throne, "because you have to be lying."

"Where is my father?" I demand again angrily, trying my best to keep my voice low in front of mixed company.

Levi smirks. "Why would I tell you where I've hidden Andre? It's the only thing I have to use as leverage against you."

"Then he's alive?" I ask, holding my breath because the next words that come out of Levi's mouth will either be the truth or a lie.

"Yes," Levi says. "He's alive."

The heaviness inside my chest partially lifts, and I breathe out a sigh of relief.

"Can I see him?" I ask, being careful not to let my question sound like I'm begging. I won't willingly grovel at Levi's feet if I can help it.

"No," he says without hesitation, "not unless you are a good little girl who does as she is told. Then I might think about letting you see him. As it is, I've decided to let you live. You might be useful to me in other ways."

I look back out at the crowd and feel heaviness return to my heart. Levi knows he has me now. I won't do anything to jeopardize my father's life. I'll act the way he wants me to act until the time comes when he will pay for what he's done.

There is a slight commotion at the top of the staircase leading into the ballroom. I look up and feel my pulse begin to quicken, like my heart is about to grow legs and run up the stairs without me.

Malcolm has arrived.

His long black hair is pulled back into a ponytail, which only accentuates the striking bone structure of his face. He's dressed in a black suit with a one-inch collar around the neckline, which is what almost every man in the room is wearing, except on him it actually looks dashing. There is a small silver pin on the collar, slightly off-center from the middle of his neck. At this distance, I can't quite make out what it is.

"Your ... M-M-Majesty," the herald says, fumbling slightly with his words and looking as shocked as everyone else in the room. "I humbly present Overlord Malcolm Xavier Devereaux."

I'm not sure there's a person present who doesn't gasp and immediately turn their eyes to the top of the staircase.

"I can't believe that fool is actually here," I hear Levi say beside me, but even his derisive words can't make me turn my gaze away from Malcolm as he descends the staircase.

If anyone looked the part of an emperor or a king, it is Malcolm. With just one glance at the crowd of people below him, Malcolm immediately takes command of the room. I am concentrating on his face so intently that I almost miss the wolf-head cane he's using to walk down the stairs with. It's an odd-looking cane with two silver wing-shaped adornments a few inches below the wolf's head on the shaft. The hitch in his gait isn't extremely pronounced, and he seems to be using the cane as more of a prop than a real aid in his walking.

Once he's at the base of the stairs, his eyes drift to the dais and to me.

I can't prevent the smile that lights up my face any more than I can stop the beating of my heart.

Malcolm makes his way across the ballroom floor to me; our eyes lock and, for me at least, it feels like we are the only two people in the room.

"You'd better be careful," Levi whispers to me, leaning in close to my ear. "His heart has always belonged to someone else, my poor little dove. And not even your beauty will be able to tear his loyalty away from her memory."

Levi's words penetrate through my happiness, tainting it. I look over at him.

"What was her name?" I ask him.

"Why don't you ask lover boy for yourself?" Levi sneers, sliding back into his throne as he watches Malcolm's continued progression toward us with undisguised hate.

As Malcolm reaches us, Levi says in a rather haughty voice, "Overlord Devereaux, to what do we owe this rather unexpected visit? I believe this is the first time you've been to Cirrus, correct?"

Malcolm doesn't bow to us like most people would when first greeting royalty. Instead, he simply stands before us at his full height, with his cane held off to the side of him, and stares at Levi like he's indulging a child's question.

"It's not every day your ruler gets married," Malcolm says pleasantly. "I thought I would come up to give the two of you my blessing on your imminent nuptials. I'm happy to see that the money I earned for you this past year with my hard work has been useful in providing the means with which to throw yourselves such a lavish party. I'm sure the wedding will be just as extravagant and costly."

I hear a few snickers in the crowd, but they are short-lived.

"Yes," Levi says while plastering a smile on his face, "thank you so much for paying your tribute this year. I daresay it was quite a large sum. Tell me, Overlord Devereaux, just how is it that you make so much money for us?"

"Hard work," Malcolm answers. "You should try it sometime."

Levi smiles grimly. "How is life on the surface these days?"

"As well as can be expected with what we have to deal with."

"So I suppose you don't have parties as extravagant as ours?" Levi asks.

"I live a rather frugal life," Malcolm replies. "I don't need much to live on in the down-world. However, even a meager means down there can make you a king."

"A king?" Levi repeats mockingly. "Is that what you think of yourself? Do you feel as though you are the king of the down-worlders?"

Levi laughs, but no one else joins him.

"Your words," Malcolm says with a small smile as Levi's laughter dies, "not mine."

I can feel Levi seething with hatred beside me, but he keeps his temper in check. He begins to chuckle again, but there's no mirth behind the sound.

"Have you met my future wife yet?" Levi asks, standing from his throne, grabbing my hand and jerking me out of the seat of my own throne, forcing me to stand up beside him.

I see Malcolm's jaw tense and eyes narrow on Levi. If someone could die from just a look, I would imagine Malcolm's stare at Levi at that moment would have accomplished such a task.

"Her name is Lady Annalisse, if you didn't already know," Levi says. "And tomorrow, she will be my wife in every way that counts between a man and a woman."

Levi's words aren't lost on me, and I know exactly what he's insinuating. I hear a few of the women in the crowd giggle because they know what he's talking about, too. My cheeks grow warm, and I hate the fact that Levi's lewd remark has made me blush uncontrollably.

Malcolm remains silent, but I can see the muscles of his jaws tighten even further. Finally he looks above us to the band on the balcony and tilts his head to them. It seems to act as a signal, because they immediately take up their instruments and start playing a waltz.

"May I have the honor of dancing the first dance of the evening with your fiancée?" Malcolm asks Levi.

Levi smiles politely, but you can see it's just for show.

"Of course," Levi says. "I would hate to deprive you of such a privilege while she's still intact."

Levi practically throws my hand away from his, and I immediately turn toward the stairs to walk off the dais and put as much distance between him and me that I can. I'm so focused on getting away from Levi that I don't notice Malcolm has moved until I'm at the bottom step and see him standing there, waiting for me.

He holds out his hand to me, and I gladly slip mine into his. He throws his cane to a man in the crowd, and it's only then that I notice Jered is present.

"Keep that for a moment, please," Malcolm tells Jered before he pulls me into his arms and gently presses me up against his torso. He twirls me around the ballroom floor, making the people there move out of our way whether they want to or not.

"He has my father," I tell Malcolm as we dance across the floor. The blaring music from the band helps hide my words. "But he won't tell me where he is."

"Of course he won't," Malcolm says in disgust. "He'll use Andre's safety against you for as long as he can. That's the sort of creature he is."

"I won't let him touch me," I say with grim determination. "I'll kill him before I let him do that to me."

A faint smile tugs at the corners of Malcolm's lips. "I'm glad to hear it."

We continue to dance, and I can't help but stare up at Malcolm. I don't care if everyone in the room is watching us. I don't care if they see how I feel about the man holding me in his arms. If there is one thing my father taught me, it is to stay true to myself and my feelings for others. He always said that love for others isn't something you should try to hide. You should never feel ashamed for caring about other people, just because some think it's inappropriate. I feel sure that anyone who sees me looking at Malcolm will instantly know that he's captured my heart in the palm of his hands, and he is the only one who can decide its fate.

My eyes are drawn to the silver pin I saw earlier on the short collar of Malcolm's black jacket. I recognize it as a flower, a lily.

"Is that a family heirloom?" I ask him, keeping my gaze centered on the pin.

"Yes," Malcolm answers, not seeming to want to talk about its significance.

"Did someone you love give it to you?"

"Yes."

I don't press for more details. It's obvious he doesn't want to elaborate on his answers.

I decide not to let the moment be ruined and simply enjoy the feeling of being in Malcolm's arms. Joy in life is fleeting, and I intend to soak up every last second I can steal with Malcolm, because I have no way of knowing how many of these moments I will get. As I let my gaze drift up from the pin on his collar to his face, I catch him staring down at me with the same look of confusion he had the night before.

Why do I confuse him? Why won't he simply let me in?

CHAPTER 10

As the waltz comes to an end, I feel myself involuntarily grip Malcolm's hand and shoulder tightly, not wanting to let him go just yet.

"Anna," Malcolm says in a slightly strained voice, "you're hurting me."

I instantly loosen my grasp. I look up into his clear blue eyes and see the light of amusement dance there as he looks down at me.

"I'm sorry," I tell him. "I usually have better control over that part of myself. Are you all right?"

"I'm fine," he says with a small smile tugging at the corners of his lips. "I just forgot how strong you girls could be. You're stronger than any of us, you know."

"We all were?"

Malcolm nods. "Yes."

"Was she as strong as me?" I ask.

"She ... who?"

"The one you said was dearest to your heart. The one you made the promise to about helping me. ..."

Malcolm's face becomes completely expressionless, like a mask has descended, covering his features to hide his true emotions from me.

"She was strong in a lot of ways, but physical strength wasn't one of them."

"What was her name?"

Malcolm stares down at me, and I don't think he's going to answer, but he finally does.

"Lilly," he whispers.

The music comes to an end, and Malcolm steps back, dropping my hand so suddenly it's like he can't wait to get as far away from me as possible.

Malcolm bows to me deeply at the waist and says, "Thank you for the dance, Lady Anna. I hope you enjoy the rest of your evening."

I watch with a despondent heart as Malcolm turns and walks back toward Jered. Jered hands him back his cane and leans in as Malcolm whispers something to him. I see Jered nod his head and immediately turn his gaze toward me. Malcolm walks into the crowd, and I lose sight of him as he's swallowed up by those curious to know more about him and those who hope to gain his favor.

I return my gaze to Jered and see a kind, gentle smile grace his face.

"May I have the next dance, Lady Anna?" he asks, bowing to me at the waist as the band begins to play the next song and people venture onto the dance floor.

"Yes," I say, "of course you can, Emissary Alburn."

Jered takes me into his arms, but he holds our bodies conspicuously well apart from one another.

As we begin to dance, he says, "We're still looking for your father, Anna. Don't give up on him just yet."

"I have no intention of giving up," I assure him. "Finding him is the only reason I'm letting that thing over there live."

Jered chuckles, but it's low enough to not attract unwanted attention. "Andre always knew you were the one we had been waiting for. It took me a few years to believe him, but it just seemed like everything started to fall into place after you were born. I became so convinced that I helped him smuggle the sword up here."

I look up at Jered in surprise. "I thought he might have just used some mercenaries to get it into the city."

"No," Jered says, smiling down at me kindly. "He wouldn't have taken that sort of chance with it. I phased it up here on your sixteenth birthday. We knew the time was approaching when you would need it."

"How did you know that?" I ask. "Malcolm hasn't told me how you all seem to know so much about what's supposed to happen."

"It's a long story," Jered says, "a far longer one than this dance will permit for me to tell you, I'm afraid. It should really wait for a time when either Malcolm or I can tell it to you in its entirety. Is there anything else I can answer for you?"

"Why does Malcolm still love someone who's dead?"

Jered nods his head knowingly. "I guess you know a little bit about Lilly then."

"Yes, very little." I sigh. "Why hasn't he let her go? She must have died a long time ago."

"It was a very long time ago," Jered confirms. "But, as angels, our memory of things can live on forever. What has been almost a thousand years to the world only seems like a blip in the passage of time to us. His memory of her is as fresh as it ever was."

"How am I supposed to compete with that?" I ask aloud, but the question is really for me, not Jered.

"My advice to you is to not compete with it," Jered tells me.

"Then I should just give up before I even try to make him forget her?"

"That will never happen. Malcolm will *never* forget Lilly. And he would hate you if you tried to make him choose between you and her."

I fall silent for a while before asking, "Then what can I do?"

Jered smiles sympathetically and says, "Let him come to realize how he feels about you on his own. Don't rush him. It'll take some time for him to finally let someone else into his heart."

"Is there enough room in there for two people?" I ask. "Even if one of them is a ghost?"

"I believe so," Jered says in such a way that I can't help but believe him.

We dance for a bit in silence before I have to ask, "So ... you think Malcolm has feelings for me?"

Jered tilts his head as he looks down at me, almost like he doesn't understand my question.

"Don't you feel it?" he asks.

"Feel what, exactly?"

"The connection," he says, almost in awe. "I've always been told that when soul mates meet they feel an instant connection to one another."

"Of course I feel it," I tell him, almost wishing I didn't. "But I'm not sure if he feels it, too."

"Oh, he does," Jered says with complete confidence. "I can tell. Plus, he knew you were in trouble last night. There's no explaining that away, no matter how hard he tries to rationalize it."

"Does he feel like he's being unfaithful to her?" I ask, trying to understand Malcolm a little better. "Is that why he's trying to deny what he feels for me?"

"It's a possibility." Jered sighs. "I think it was hard for him to understand the fact that Lilly was never his to have because his love for her was so strong. But Lilly married her soul mate and had a daughter named Caylin. They are your ancestors and the origin of your family line."

"Why has Malcolm held onto his love for Lilly for so long if he knows she found her soul mate while she was alive?"

"You would have to ask him that question," Jered says tenderly, obviously seeing my distress over the situation. "I don't pretend to know the inner workings of Malcolm's thought processes. However, I have high hopes for you, Anna Greco. I have a feeling you were born into this world not only to take back the seals from the princes but for other greatness as well, including bringing Malcolm a well-deserved happy ending."

"I would rather think of it as a happy beginning," I say.

Jered's smile grows wider. "And so it shall be."

The song comes to an end, and I regret having to stop dancing with Jered. I have a feeling he won't only be an ally in my fight against the princes of Hell, but also a friend. If there is one thing I need more of in this world, it is true friendship.

I spend most of the evening greeting others in the room, perpetuating the pretense that all is right in my world and that I'm looking forward to my wedding to the emperor the next day. I catch glimpses of Malcolm in the crowd, mingling with the citizens of Cirrus. However his contingent of followers seems to mostly consist of those of the female gender. One woman in particular, Lady Sophia, seems to have taken Malcolm under her wing and assumes the responsibility of introducing him to the guests in the room. Lady Sophia's reputation is anything but pristine. It's well-known that she takes on a new lover whenever someone strikes her fancy, and it seems as though she has already chosen her next target.

Malcolm doesn't seem to mind Lady Sophia's rather ardent attention either. He does nothing to stop her possessive hold of his arm as she leads him from person to person around the room. Eventually I have to turn away from the sight of them together because it causes my heart too much pain.

"You look a little green," I hear someone say beside me.

I look over and see Levi smiling at me, no doubt relishing my torment.

"Jealousy doesn't become you, Lady Anna." He smirks. "I'm not sure what you expected of Malcolm, but fidelity has never been his strong suit."

"He's just never had the right person to love him," I say in Malcolm's defense.

"I suppose you think you're that person?" Levi scoffs. "Good luck getting him to forget Lilly. Don't look so surprised, Anna. I know a lot more about Malcolm than you do. If you think you can win that big oaf's heart, think again. No one, and I mean no one, will ever be as special to him as she was. You're on a fool's quest if you think you can match her in his heart."

"You're wrong," I say to him, not quite feeling the full force of my words because of my own lingering doubts.

Levi shrugs. "Think what you will, but I would lay a heavy wager on Malcolm bedding the lovely Lady Sophia before this night is through. I mean, look at her! She's gorgeous and willing, just the way Malcolm likes his women. But don't worry, Anna; I will always be at your disposal to keep your bed nice and warm."

"You," I say with as much venom as I can, "will never touch me like that."

"We'll see, I guess," Levi says with a smirk and a shrug of his shoulders before striding off to mingle with some of the guests.

As I stand there, I feel wholly alone, even though I'm completely surrounded by people. I yearn to have my father back by my side and to regain access to his counsel. I begin to wonder what he'll think about his only daughter being soul mates with his best friend. I hope he'll be happy for me, but fathers can some-times be rather picky about who their daughters choose to give their hearts to.

I shake my head at my own thoughts. Here I am, already assuming Malcolm will let me inside his heart when I have no way of knowing if that will ever come to pass. His lingering love for Lilly, my ancestor, might prevent him from ever acknowledging his true feelings for me.

With this depressing thought, I turn to the staircase and begin my ascent to the top. Once there, I ask one of the servants to bring me my coat.

"Are you leaving already, my lady?" the herald asks me.

"Yes," I tell him, "and please don't announce it. I would like some time alone this evening. I don't think anyone will miss my presence."

I look back down at the crowd of partygoers and easily find Malcolm in the sea of revelers.

He's laughing heartily at something Lady Sophia has just whispered in his ear and doesn't even seem to notice that I'm about to leave. I turn my back on the scene, unable to make myself watch any more of it.

After the servant brings back my coat, he drapes it across my shoulders for me. I make my way outside the palace, unable to stand the sight of Malcolm enjoying the company of another woman for a second longer.

The artificial snow inside the dome is still falling. I stretch my hand out to catch some of the flakes against my palm, welcoming the cool tickle of their landing against my skin before they melt almost instantly.

The footman in charge of my carriage is soon standing in front of me, bowing deeply.

"Are you ready to go home, my lady?"

"Yes, but I want to walk there. You can put the carriage away until I need it tomorrow for the wedding procession."

The footman stands back to his full height, a worried frown on his face.

"I don't think the emperor would like you walking home by yourself, Lady Anna. I should at least go with you to act as your escort."

"No," I say in a voice which tells of my weariness from the night. "I want some time alone. Think of it as your wedding present to me."

The footman still looks uncertain but finally nods his consent to my desire.

I walk away from the palace and venture into the city streets.

The time is late and most of the residents of Cirrus are inside their homes, snuggled safely in their beds. The streets are vacant for the most part, and I relish the near silence surrounding me. The only sounds I hear are my own footfalls crunching the snow beneath my feet. As I walk with my head down, my thoughts become completely lost as I review the events of the night. I'm so preoccupied, I accidentally run into a woman walking in the opposite direction along the sidewalk. She ends up on her back, sprawled onto the snow-strewn street because I wasn't guarding my strength and ended up colliding against her at full force.

I rush to her and get down on my knees beside her.

"I'm so sorry," I lament. "Are you all right? Are you hurt anywhere?"

The woman looks a bit stunned at first, but then she begins to laugh. Her laughter is irresistible, and I soon find myself laughing along with her at the ridiculousness of the situation.

I stand to my feet and hold out a hand for her to take. She takes my offer of assistance, and I gently help her stand.

"Wow," she says, bending slightly at the waist to dust the snow off of her coat, "you're strong for such a little thing."

"Sometimes I don't know my own strength," I tell her, giving her the only explanation I can.

As I watch the woman continue to pat her coat free of snow, I begin to feel as though I know her. When she stands to her full height and looks at me, the chocolate brown of her eyes holds a tenderness some part of me seems to faintly recognize, like a long-lost memory.

"Do I know you?" I ask, studying her beautiful features and somewhat old-fashioned style of dress. Almost no one in Cirrus would wear a black wool coat or what looks like a homemade knit cap. The citizens of Cirrus are far too fashion conscious for such plain apparel.

The woman smiles at me, and I become even more confident that I know her. Yet I have no memories of her, and I never forget anything. I begin to wonder if perhaps I met her in another life.

"No, you don't really know me," she says. "But I know you. You're Lady Anna Greco, the future empress. Your wedding is tomorrow, right?"

I hesitate but then say, "Yes."

The woman tilts her head. "You don't sound too happy about it."

The more I look at the woman, the more I want to tell her everything about myself. It's strange that I would want to tell her so much, because I've always been one to keep things to myself. Yet, for some inexplicable reason, I feel as though I could tell her my deepest, darkest secrets and she wouldn't judge me by them.

"I don't love the emperor," I tell her.

The woman smiles at me knowingly and slowly nods her head. "I'm guessing there is someone else that you *do* love. Only trouble with a man could have made you so distracted that you ran into me on an empty street."

I feel my cheeks grow warm against the cold, feeling embarrassed that I let my thoughts completely blind me.

"I humbly apologize for that," I say to her. "I'm usually more careful."

The woman looks me up and down, but not in an appraising way. It's almost like she's seeing me for the first time and a look of pride enters her eyes.

"You're so beautiful, Anna," the woman says. "I can tell your spirit is a strong one. Any man would be lucky to have you love him."

I let out a small laugh. "Not when that man is already in love with someone else."

"I feel sure you can change his mind," she tells me with more confidence than I feel. "He would be a fool not to return the love of someone like you. Give him time. I'm sure he'll come around."

"I hope you're right. ..." I tell her, realizing I don't know what to call her. "What's your name?"

The woman holds out her hand, and I notice a bracelet hanging from around her wrist. It's composed of a multitude of little silver and gold charms.

I shake her hand as she says, "My name is Rayne Cole."

"Rayne? That's an unusual name."

Rayne smiles.

"Somewhat unique," she agrees.

"That's a beautiful bracelet you have," I tell her. "Where did you get it?"

Rayne lifts up her wrist and looks at the bracelet. "My children gave it to me on one of my birthdays. Over the years we've added charms to it to mark different events in our family life."

"I've never seen anything like it. Is it an antique of some sort?"

"I guess you could say that. I don't think they make them anymore."

We fall silent with one another, and I'm not sure what else to say.

"Well, I guess I should continue on my way home," I tell her. "It was nice to meet you. I would love it if you could come visit me sometime at the palace. I don't really have a lot of people to talk to, but for some reason, I feel like you and I could become friends."

Rayne's smile grows brighter. "I would like that, Anna."

"Good."

"Would you mind me giving you one small bit of advice before we part ways?"

"Of course."

"Fight for the man you love," she tells me fervently. "He's worth it."

With those parting words, Rayne leans into me and kisses me on the cheek. It's a breach in protocol between a royal and a commoner, but for some reason, I don't mind her casual familiarity.

She walks past me to continue down the street, and I watch her for a few moments more before turning to continue down my own path. For some reason, I decide to take one last look at her and turn back around, but she's already gone, almost like she vanished into thin air.

After I get home, Millie and Eliza help me undress and get ready for bed. Millie tries to ask me questions about the party, but I beg her to wait until the next day and plead that I'm just too tired. She doesn't seem to like my answer—most likely because she can sense something is wrong with me. All I want to do is go to sleep and not think about a certain someone for the rest of the night.

Unfortunately, all I end up doing is tossing and turning in my bed. Visions of Malcolm and Lady Sophia together in compromising positions haunt my thoughts. At one point, I grab my pillow and scream into it to muffle my pain. Unfortunately, it does nothing to relieve the ache in my chest, and I end up crying.

Then something happens.

A pain which greatly overshadows my own enters my heart. I sit up in my bed and wipe away the tears from my cheeks. The pain I feel is unlike anything I've ever felt before. It's a strange sensation—separate, yet a part of me.

I know what I need to do without even having to think about it.

I stand up from my bed and phase.

CHAPTER 11

The room I phase into is bitterly cold. I immediately cross my arms over my chest and place the palms of my hands on my exposed forearms in a vain attempt to retain what warmth my body has left before the coldness leeches it completely away. The thin, sleeveless white nightgown I'm wearing does nothing to help fight off the chill in the bedroom.

It's a room I've never been inside before, but I know exactly why I'm in it.

Sitting in a red velvet wingback chair, angled to face an unlit fireplace, is Malcolm. His head is bowed, causing the flow of his long locks to hide his face from my view. His elbows resting on his thighs, he conceals his features with his hands, like their flesh will hide him from the world. He's only wearing the black pants of the suit he wore earlier, leaving his chest and back bare.

I walk across the marble floor to him, dropping my hands back down to my sides. I stand in front of him and tentatively place one hand on his head, not sure how he'll react to my touch. Gently, I run the tips of my fingers through his silky strands, hoping to bring his tortured soul a small bit of peace.

Malcolm lets out a deep, trembling sigh, but I can't quite tell if it's one of relief or woe.

"Why are you here, Anna?" he whispers, sounding torn between wanting me near and not here at all.

I stroke the soft texture of his hair twice more before answering.

"I felt your pain," I tell him, trying to keep myself from crying because I can still feel his torment. "I had to come to you, just like you had to come to me the other night."

I continue to stroke the top of Malcolm's head until he drops his hands away from his face and slowly leans back in the chair.

I let my hand return to my side and meet his gaze with my own.

He looks haggard, like the pain of his soul has physically manifested itself in his expression. I want to reach out and touch him, but I don't. His posture looks guarded, and I get the feeling he doesn't want me to touch him in that moment. He continues to stare into my eyes but doesn't say a word. I remain still, patiently waiting for him to say something ... anything.

I involuntarily shiver against the cold in the room.

Malcolm's eyes slowly travel the length of me, and when his gaze travels back up, it stops at my chest.

"Are you ... cold?" he asks, an almost smile tugging on his lips as he continues to look at me, not even attempting to hide the fact that he's staring directly at my breasts.

I glance down at myself and immediately cross my arms over my chest, because the evidence of my body's reaction to the cold in the room is all too prominent.

"Yes," I tell him. "It's freezing in here. Aren't you cold?"

"I've always been a bit warm-blooded," he tells me, slowly

getting to his bare feet and walking over to the bed in the room. In one swift motion, he yanks the thin black blanket covering the bed off.

As he walks back over to me with the blanket in his hands, he says, "Fire, seventy-five degrees."

The fireplace instantly erupts with flickering orange flames, bringing with them much needed warmth.

Malcolm walks up behind me and drapes the blanket over my shoulders. After he pulls the edges together in front of me, I think he's going to take his hands away, but he does the complete opposite. He brings his arms completely around me and simply enfolds me in the ring of them. I close my eyes as my heart races with joy and gently lean my back against his bare chest, feeling safe within the confines of his embrace. I feel him rest his forehead against the top of my head and hear him breathe in deeply then let it out in a drawn-out sigh, like holding me brings him a small measure of peace.

I don't say anything because I know if I do, he'll move away. I keep quiet and simply enjoy the feel of him finally holding me again.

The moment lasts longer than I could have hoped for, but eventually, I feel him loosen his grasp on me and take a step back.

I want to ask him to take me into his arms again, but I know that's not what he needs right now.

He walks in front of me and sits back down in his chair. Not having the comfort of his warmth anymore, I go to sit in front of the fireplace for its heat. I turn so that I'm facing Malcolm at a slant. I find him staring at me with that bemused expression again.

"Have you ever been inside this room before?" he asks unexpectedly.

I shake my head. "No. I'm not even sure where I am."

"It's a room I rented today," he tells me. "We're still in Cirrus."

I know why he asked the question. If phasing was based on being able to travel between two points of space that you had actually been to before, he must be wondering how I was able to phase here without actually having ever been inside this room. The answer has to be obvious to him, but I get the feeling he's still trying to explain away our connection to one another.

I decide to take Jered's advice and not push the matter. But I also remember Rayne's words to me.

"*Fight for the man you love,*" she had said. "*He's worth it.*"

I couldn't agree with her more.

"I'm a little surprised to find you alone," I tell him, remembering how, just moments ago, I was certain Malcolm was in the amorous embrace of Lady Sophia.

Malcolm leans back even farther into his chair in a relaxed pose that does nothing but make him look even more devastatingly handsome. I find myself completely distracted by his bare chest and feel an almost uncontrollable urge to go curl myself on his lap to soak in his warmth. I swallow hard and look away from him for a moment, pretending to warm my hands next to the fire, just so I can compose my thoughts and gain some much needed clarity.

"If you're talking about Lady Sophia," Malcolm says knowingly, sounding somewhat amused, "I never had any intention of bedding her this evening. She simply served a purpose for me tonight."

I look back at Malcolm. "What purpose was that?"

"To introduce me to everyone of importance in Cirrus," he answers. "I might need their help one day, and it's vital to my plans that I get to know them."

"Help with what?" I ask. "You have more wealth than anyone here. You're possibly wealthier than the Amadors. What could the people of Cirrus do to help you?"

"Place you on the throne as sole ruler."

I sit there for a moment because I feel certain I misheard what Malcolm just said.

"Sole ruler?" I ask just to clarify.

Malcolm nods but says nothing, just watches my reaction to his plans.

"But women aren't allowed to rule here," I tell him. "Only a man can be on the throne of Cirrus."

"Which is exactly why I needed to befriend those people tonight," Malcolm says. "If they know there's something in it for them, they'll let you keep your place on the throne even after you kill Levi. Or do you intend to let him remain emperor?"

"No, I absolutely do *not* plan to let him rule Cirrus for very much longer," I say. The thought I had earlier that night creeps up out of the shadows of my mind. "Do I really have to kill him and the other princes? Isn't there a way to retrieve the seals without having to resort to murder?"

Malcolm shrugs. "I have no way of knowing. My Father didn't give us the specifics of what is supposed to happen or how it is supposed to happen. The only thing we were ever certain about was that you would fight Amon with Jess's sword. ..."

"Jess's sword?" I ask, interrupting him. "The same Jess who fell in love with a Watcher named Mason?"

"Yes," Malcolm says, looking surprised I know even that much. "Who told you about them?"

"Millie told me a little bit," I confess. "So the sword once belonged to Jess?"

"Yes. She retrieved it from the Garden of Eden. It was actually the sword of another angel named Jophiel, who used it to guard the Tree of Life there."

"How did you all know I would need it to defend myself against Amon?"

"It was seen in a prophetic vision a long time ago. We knew a girl from Caylin and Aiden's line would eventually be born to take back the seven seals from the princes. We've simply been waiting all this time for you to be born so we can finish the mission we were given."

"Jered told me that Caylin was Lilly's daughter. But who was Aiden?"

"He was a Watcher and Caylin's soul mate."

"And Lilly ... Jered said she married her soul mate, too. What was his name?"

"Brand."

"Was Brand a Watcher?"

"Yes."

I can't help but smile. "Did all of my ancestors fall in love with Watchers?"

"Some, not all. A few of them had the good sense to just fall in love with regular humans."

"You say that like there's something wrong with you Watchers."

"Some. ..." Malcolm says with a small smile, "not all."

"At least the women in my family are consistent," I mumble to myself, not expecting Malcolm to hear me since I said it so low, but apparently he has excellent hearing.

"Consistent about what?" he asks.

I look him in the eyes because I feel like this is one of those now or never moments for us.

"Consistent about falling in love with Watchers," I tell him, studying his reaction to my near confession.

His facial expression gives nothing away. He continues to stare at me but remains mute.

"Don't get your hopes up by what I'm about to tell you," he finally says, making me wonder if he's actually going to admit he has feelings for me, too. "Jered may have found a lead on where your father is being kept."

Of all the statements for him to make, the possibility of that one hadn't even crossed my mind.

"Where?" I ask, sitting up a little straighter. "Where is he?"

"He's being kept down-world somewhere. That's all we know for now. It'll take time, but we'll find Andre, Anna. You have my word on that."

"Maybe I should threaten him," I say harshly. "Maybe if Levi thinks his life is in danger, he'll tell me the location."

Malcolm shakes his head. "No, he won't."

"You say that like you know it for a fact."

"I do. Levi may be a complete ass, but he isn't stupid. He knows the only thing keeping him alive right now is Andre's safety. As long as he has that to hold over your head, he'll use it to get exactly what he wants from you."

"My father wouldn't want me to sacrifice myself or Cirrus for his safe return," I say. "But you should probably know that I plan to do whatever it takes to bring him back."

"You're right," Malcolm says, "Andre wouldn't want you to sacrifice yourself or this city for him. You do what you have to do, Anna, but just remember that your father has lived a very long life, and he never wanted to outlive you. It was the whole point of him becoming human."

"Did you ever want to become human?" I ask him.

"Once."

"Why?"

"Why, what?"

"Why did you want to be human?"

"For reasons similar to Andre's. I didn't want to live an immortal life after Lilly died. A part of me died the day she did," he says hoarsely. "The part she brought back to life when I first met her."

"Then why did you stay?"

"Because I made a promise to her that I would help you retrieve the seals from the princes and finish this once and for all. Maybe then we can all finally find a little peace."

I want to ask him what his plans are after we accomplish the mission I was born to undertake. I want to know if his love for Lilly is still so strong that he'll choose to be with her in death instead of with me in life. But I don't ask, because I plan to make sure he chooses me. I can't imagine my life being worth living without him in it.

I will do as Rayne advised and fight for him because willingly letting him go isn't an option.

I feel as though we've probably said enough to each other for one night and stand to leave. It's only then that I realize I can't.

"I'm not sure how I phased here," I tell Malcolm. "How do I phase back home?"

"Just think about your room and pull it to you mentally," Malcolm says. "It might help if you close your eyes and picture it in your mind."

I do as he instructs and picture my room but nothing happens.

I stand there for a few minutes more, attempting to return home, but just can't for some reason.

I finally open my eyes and find that Malcolm has stood from his chair and is now standing directly in front of me.

"It's not working," I tell him, looking up into his eyes. "What am I doing wrong?"

"I'm not sure," Malcolm says. "But there's something else we can try. I want you to follow my phase trail."

"Phase trail?"

"When we phase, we leave a small hole in space between the

point we traveled from to the point we travel to. I'll phase to your room first, and you try to follow my trail."

I nod. "Okay. I understand."

Malcolm phases, and I see the small hole in space appear like I did the first night we met and he returned home. I didn't know what it was at the time, but now I do.

I stare at the small portal to my room and stretch my hand out to touch it. I instantly find myself back inside my bedroom.

Malcolm is sitting on the side of my bed, waiting for me. His gaze is so intense as he stares at me that I immediately let go of my grip on the blanket and go to him.

He watches me with hooded eyes as I approach but says nothing. When I stand in front of him, he doesn't look up to meet my gaze, but he does wrap his arms around my waist and bring me in close to him. He rests his head against my breast and closes his eyes. I cradle his head with my hands and bring him even closer to me, never wanting him to let me go and hoping he will do more than just hold me.

Eventually Malcolm loosens his grasp around me and lifts his head until our eyes meet.

I see a storm of confusion in his sea blue eyes but am helpless in knowing how to erase it. We stare at one another wordlessly, but I have no doubt that he knows how I feel because I'm powerless in concealing the love my soul holds for only him.

"I need to leave," he murmurs but doesn't move an inch.

"Stay," I almost beg, hoping to change his mind. "I don't want you to go. Stay with me, Malcolm."

The confusion in his eyes changes to one of desire, and I know he wants to stay with me, too.

Unfortunately for me, he doesn't follow what his heart is telling him to do.

"I can't," he whispers. "I'm sorry."

Malcolm phases, and I see by his phase trail that he's returned to his room here in Cirrus.

I sit down on the bed and still feel the lingering warmth left there by his body.

I smile slightly, because I feel like we've taken a tiny step forward.

I know for certain now that Malcolm wants me as much as I want him.

And I won't let him hide from the truth of that fact forever.

CHAPTER 12

The next morning I wake up to face a living nightmare.

Even when I was going to marry *my* Auggie, I wasn't looking forward to the wedding day. I know it will be filled with pomp and circumstance—two things I hate most. It is supposed to be a celebration for the ages. For me, it is one of the worst days of my life.

The morning begins at the break of dawn with Millie coaxing me out of a dreamless sleep to make sure I eat some breakfast before the events of the day begin to unfold.

"I don't need you fainting away at the altar," Millie says as she fills my plate with food. "You have so much to do today, my sweet. I plan to do all I can to help you survive it."

"I'm not very hungry," I tell her, playing with the food on my plate, thinking about everything but eating.

"Try to eat just a little bit, Lady Anna," Millie urges. "If not for yourself, then for my peace of mind."

I force myself to eat half of what's on my plate, and this seems to satisfy Millie's need to see me nourished.

The rest of the morning is spent primping me into perfection for my wedding to the emperor. By the time everything is trimmed, powdered, and styled to perfection, I feel overly made-up. As I look at myself in the reflective wall in my room, I begin to cry.

"Anna, what's wrong?" Vala asks as she pads over to me and sits down on her haunches beside me.

The skirt of the dress is composed of so much fabric that she can't get too close because of its sheer circumference.

I wipe at the tears on my cheeks and force them to stop. Weakness is one emotion I cannot show today no matter how miserable I might feel.

"I just want this day to be over," I tell her.

Vala whines in sympathy over my plight.

"They're ready for you," Millie says as she reenters my room. "I wish I could come with you, but we commoners didn't get an invitation to the most important event of the year."

"There's no need for you to be there," I tell her, making my way to where she stands by the door. "It's not a real wedding anyway, only a pretense of one."

"Well, if circumstances change for the better, like I think they will, I expect to be invited to a real one soon."

I smile at Millie because a picture of Malcolm standing at an altar waiting for me floods my thoughts, making this day just a little more bearable.

"I promise you'll be there," I tell her.

Millie and Eliza help me get into the same crystal carriage I rode in the night before. I need both of their help and the help of the footman just to stuff myself into its interior and pile in the skirt and long, flowing train.

"This is a ridiculous dress," I moan as I finally sit down in a huff. "Next time I want something simple."

"I used to be quite the seamstress back in the day," Millie tells me with a sly grin.

"Then get to work, Millie," I tell her with a meaningful look.

Millie winks at me, and I know she understands what I'm really saying without having to ask for any more instructions.

It's only the thought of Millie making me a dress to wear at my actual wedding that makes the ride through town tolerable. As I look at the multitude of citizens lining the streets of Cirrus to wish me well on my wedding day, I vow to somehow become a ruler they can be proud of. I don't only want to make their lives better. I want to change the patriarchal way things have been run thus far in Cirrus. It's time for a woman to rule. It's time the world was made right again, and I feel confident I can do it.

I only want one thing for myself.

I want Malcolm by my side through it all. As long as he's with me, I feel as though we can make the world a better place and right the many wrongs that have been perpetrated during the last two hundred years.

Once my carriage reaches the palace, a group of ladies-in-waiting has to help me extricate myself from its confines. The ladies were chosen by the empress to stand with me at the altar during the wedding ceremony, but if you ask me what their names are, I can't tell you. In the grand scheme of things, it doesn't really matter. This day is a farce as far as I am concerned. The sooner it is over, the sooner I can get on with my real agenda.

I am given a gold, gem-encrusted scepter to hold instead of the traditional white rose bouquet most brides carry down the aisle. Since the wedding is doubling as a coronation ceremony to crown me empress, flowers aren't deemed necessary.

A full orchestra positioned on the back balcony of the sanc-tuary plays the wedding march as the doors to its interior open. I take a deep breath before making my way down the red carpeted center aisle leading to the altar. As I slowly walk to the altar, I see Levi standing tall beside the presiding priest with a lascivious smile on his face. It's far from pleasant and unnerves me slightly. He looks like a man about to take possession of new property, not a wife.

Just as I approach the steps leading up to Levi and the priest, I catch a glimpse of Malcolm out of the corner of my eye. I look over at him briefly because I don't want to bring unwanted attention to him, but one glance is all I need.

He looks distressed by the proceedings. His expression mirrors the way I feel about this wedding. But we both know it has to happen. There will be no reprieve from what is about to occur because I need to officially become empress. If Malcolm's plan for putting me on the throne of Cirrus as sole ruler is to come to pass, I need to *be* empress first. If that means I have to marry Levi, then so be it.

As I stand beside Levi and we begin to consecrate our vows of marriage to one another, I remember what Malcolm told me on the first night we met: A true marriage is one of the heart, not this mockery of one I am having to endure. I will never consider Levi my husband, even though that's what he will be by law. I need the power that comes along with being empress, and I pray it will be enough to help me find my father.

The wedding and coronation take almost an hour to complete. When all is said and done, I stand in front of all of Cirrus as the newly crowned Empress Annalisse Desiraye Greco Amador. The people in the cathedral cheer as the priest announces my new title, and I can hear the throng of Cirruns outside the palace adding their vocal approval.

"It seems the people of Cirrus love you," Levi whispers to me.

I don't respond to his comment because it's their love I'm counting on to not only help me change the future for all of Cirrus, but for the down-worlders and myself as well.

126

I let my gaze return to where Malcolm was standing before the wedding ceremony began, but notice he isn't there anymore.

Why did he leave? Where could he have gone?

The wedding reception is held in the ballroom of the palace, a place I now have to call my home. As Levi and I stand at the entrance of the room to greet our guests and thank them for attending our wedding, my mind wanders to Malcolm. Why did he leave the wedding before it was over? And why isn't he at the reception?

"I don't think it's very considerate to be thinking about another man while you're with your husband on our wedding day," Levi whispers to me as we wait for the last of our guests—the delegation from the cloud city of Nacreous—to greet us.

"You act like I care about your feelings," I say harshly. "If you dropped dead right this moment, it wouldn't bother me in the slightest. It would actually save me the effort of killing you myself."

"Ahh, but then you might not ever find your dear old dadums again," Levi remarks snidely. "I still can't believe the idiot asked to become human for you. What an imbecilic thing to do."

"He loves me," I say. "But I guess you wouldn't know anything about that type of devotion."

"True enough," Levi admits with a shrug. "Loving a human isn't exactly something I have on my to-do list in this life. Who would want to waste the time on someone who can die so easily? I mean, look at your mother. No sooner did she fall in love with the man who really fathered you before she died giving birth to the abomination that you are. They both should have known anything spawned from your father's loins would lead to nothing but heartache and misery. Of course, if your mother had simply kept her legs together, you wouldn't have been conceived in the first place, and she would still be alive."

"You really need to stop talking about my mother like that," I hiss, feeling my temper get the better of me. "Do you have a death wish or something?"

"Oh, on the contrary," Levi says. "I plan to live for a very long time—longer than your real father, in fact. You won't kill me. You wouldn't dare."

"Please, remind me why that is exactly."

"Because I'm the only one in this whole wide world who knows where Andre is," Levi informs me smugly. "I think that little bit of information is worth my life. Don't you, Empress Annalisse?"

Before I get a chance to respond, the herald announces, "Introducing the delegation from Nacreous: Empress Olivia Grace Ravensdale and Prince Consort Horatio Ignatius Ravensdale!"

Nacreous is the cloud city that sits above Antarctica. It's one of the poorer cloud cities because of the low population density, but it is renowned for its forward-thinking and innovation. Nacreous has the only matriarchal society among the seven ruling families of the world. From what I was told in my lessons with Auggie's mother, Empress Olivia is someone you would want on your side, not against it.

Empress Olivia is in her mid-fifties and my height with shoulder-length blonde hair that seems to have a natural wave running through it. Her skin is porcelain white, and her eyes are a deep, rich green. Even at her age she needs little makeup to accentuate her natural beauty. She holds herself tall and proud, and you can tell it's simply her natural stature. She isn't putting on airs because she doesn't need to.

Her husband is handsome, tall, and very trim. His short blond hair feathers naturally, and the lines around his mouth mark the passage of many smiles within his lifetime. He graces me with one of them as they come to stand in front of us.

"Empress Annalisse," Empress Olivia says, holding out her hand for me to shake.

It isn't customary for two royals to shake hands, but I immediately shake hers without even giving it a second thought. My automatic reaction to the handshake seems to please the empress, because she smiles while studying my face.

"You're quite gorgeous," she tells me without an ounce of envy. "I don't believe I've ever seen anyone to match your beauty, Empress Annalisse."

"Please, just call me Anna," I tell her, not caring for the formality of being called "Empress."

"Then you must call me Olivia," she responds in kind. "You also have my permission to call my husband by any name you see fit."

"Just don't call me Iggie," Olivia's husband says to me with a smile and a shake of his head. "It makes me feel like I'm a five-year-old."

I laugh. "Personally, I like Horatio."

"Now, *that* I can handle, Anna."

Olivia's attention diverts to Levi standing beside me.

"You look different, Augustus," she comments dryly, letting her gaze take in my new husband's visage. "I'm not sure I like it."

Levi smiles, tight-lipped. "Well, I really don't care what the Empress of Nothingdom thinks of me. In fact, I would rather you kept your opinions to yourself. I'm the ruler of the most powerful cloud city in the world. Your opinion of me holds about as much weight as a feather."

I notice Horatio stiffen after Levi's insult, but Olivia simply wraps her arms around one of her husband's to silently tell him now isn't the time or place for a confrontation.

Olivia looks back to me. "If you ever need my help," she says with an emphasis on the last word, "please, don't hesitate to come to me. Nacreous may not have much, but we do support our friends when they need us."

"Thank you," I tell her, feeling that I've made a new friend and ally in the empress.

Olivia gently tugs on her husband's arm and walks away from us.

"Uppity bitch," Levi spits out after they leave.

"You're going to cause a war if you don't rein yourself in."

"Maybe I *should* start a war," Levi snarls. "I could rule this world easily enough. These people are weak. It wouldn't take much to gain control over all of the cloud cities and finally put an end to everything."

Before I get a chance to ask him what he means, one of the servants comes up and instructs us that it's time to cut the cake.

The rest of the afternoon turns into a blur of formality. We go through the motions of everything a happy, newlywed couple is supposed to do at their reception. After cutting the cake, we dance the first dance together. If you ask me what song was played, I can't tell you. I can't tell you what the cake tasted like. I can't tell you what any of the presents given to us were. And I can't tell you what anyone who toasted to our good health and happiness actually said.

I can't tell you any of those things because I simply wasn't interested enough to pay attention to them.

I *can* tell you that I constantly searched for any signs of Malcolm. I don't even see Jered at the reception, which makes me wonder what the two of them are up to. It isn't until Levi stands up to make an announcement that my attention is diverted from my futile search.

"Ladies and gentleman!" Levi says as he stands from his throne beside me and addresses the crowd. "I would like to thank you all for coming today and helping Anna and me celebrate not only our marriage to one another, but also her crowning as your new empress!"

The crowd applauds enthusiastically.

"But," Levi says, "I'm afraid the empress isn't feeling well. I'm sure you can all understand what the stress of a day like today can have on someone. We will be retiring to our rooms to finish out the night." The way Levi says these words leaves no doubt that he's implying he and I will be sharing a bed soon. "Please stay for as long as you like. I sincerely doubt anyone will be seeing us again until late morning."

Levi turns to me and bows slightly as he holds out his hand to me.

I feel sure if I hit him across his jaw with my fist to wipe the smarmy grin off his face, it will cause an uproar. However, I have a feeling some in the crowd wouldn't fault me for such an action.

Instead, I place my hand in his and stand to my feet.

We walk out of the ballroom together and through the palace to our rooms. Stationed outside the doors are the two guards, Christopher and Clark, who have always been the ones to escort me to the palace for my lessons with Empress Catherine.

"Good evening, Empress," Christopher says to me as we approach the room while Clark opens the doors to the royal chambers.

As I pass by them, I hear Clark, who has never uttered a word to me in the many years he has been a palace guard, say, "Have fun."

Startled to actually hear him speak, I look up and meet his gaze. I see something in his eyes that warns me he is no longer the person he once was.

After we're inside the room, Clark closes the door behind me, and I hear the distinct hum of a lock being activated.

"I don't intend to stay here," I inform Levi. "I'll be phasing to my own home to spend the night."

"I assumed you might want to do that," Levi says, not seeming in the least bit put-out by my plans. "But maybe you could at least have one drink with me before you go."

Levi walks over to a crystal canister holding some light brown liquid and pours some of the libation into two crystal goblets sitting on the table.

I walk over and take one of the goblets he offers.

"To us," Levi says, holding up his glass to me. "Long may we reign."

He begins to sip his drink, but I do not. I'm not that stupid.

I set the goblet back down on the table.

Levi begins to chuckle. "What's wrong, Anna? Do you think I drugged the scotch?"

"I wouldn't put anything past you," I tell him. "You're not to be trusted."

Levi nods. "That is very true. Very true indeed. Too bad you didn't remember that I'm smart, too."

My vision begins to blur, and I lose my focus on Levi. I shake my head slightly to clear my muddled vision.

"Feeling a little drowsy, are we?" Levi asks in false sympathy, putting his glass down and taking a couple of steps toward me.

"But," I say, feeling like I might faint at any moment, "I didn't drink any of it."

Levi smiles, and it's far from pleasant.

"No, you didn't," he agrees. "I knew you wouldn't. I actually counted on it. That's why I coated the glass with the sedative, so it would simply absorb into your skin when you touched it."

I stumble back and head for the doors because that's the only thing I can think to do.

"There's nowhere to run," Levi mocks, "and nowhere to hide, my little dove."

I lean my back against the doors to the room and watch through my blurred vision as Levi approaches me. I try to phase, but obviously I still don't have the hang of it because I go nowhere.

"Why would you drug me?" I say, my speech sounding slurred.

"Because I want to know if you can conceive a child from me," he says in all seriousness, coming to stand directly in front of me and cupping my face between his hands. "I want to know what it feels like to have a descendant of my own, and you're the only one who can make that dream come true."

"I don't understand," I say, trying to hold onto consciousness. "Why me?"

"Because you are a descendant of Lilith, and only you can take my seed and conceive a child from something like me. Your father was able to do it with your mother. I should be able to do it with you."

Levi makes to move closer to me, but his plan is interrupted.

I see Malcolm phase in behind Levi, grab him by the shoulders, and throw him against the far wall of the room.

Malcolm turns to look at Levi, who is now sprawled out on the floor.

In a strident voice, I hear Malcolm say, "That will *never* happen."

CHAPTER 13

Levi stares up at Malcolm in surprise at first, but then he simply starts to laugh slowly as he sits on the floor and bends his knees up to prop his arms over them.

"You surprise me, Malcolm," Levi says, a cocky grin on his face. "Of all the people to come to sweet Anna's rescue, I didn't see it being you. Weren't you the one who banished her up here in the first place, just so you didn't have to look at her?"

"I didn't send her here so something like you could paw at her," Malcolm replies in a deadly voice.

"What do you care?" Levi asks. "As long as she has a child, what does it matter who fathers it? I'm as good a candidate as anyone else."

"She isn't yours to have."

"Oh?" Levi says, his eyes lighting up with mischief. "Are you claiming her for yourself, then? Because I distinctly remember you calling her an abomination to God and that you didn't want to have anything to do with her after she was born. Or has that rather large thing between your legs started to think *for* you after seeing what a beauty she's grown up to be? I can't say I blame you, really. She does look rather delectable. Good enough to eat, in fact."

Malcolm takes a threatening step toward Levi.

"You will *never* lay another hand on her if I have anything to say about it."

"Hmm, I seem to remember you saying those words once before to her mother's suitor. I guess we know how that turned out, since we have the proof of their union standing in the room with us. My, my ... what would Lilly think of you now, Malcolm? You weren't strong enough to keep Amalie from bedding the enemy. Now, you want to lie with her last direct descendant yourself. It's just shameful, really. How many epic failures can one person have in a lifetime?"

"Don't you dare sully Lilly's name by having it come out of your mouth," Malcolm snarls. "You're not good enough to even have it pass over your lips."

"Lilly ... Lilly." Levi pauses before taunting, "Lilly."

Malcolm descends on Levi and stretches his arms down to grab him up off the floor, but Levi phases to where I stand, forcing Malcolm to twirl around and face us. The anger he feels is etched clearly onto his face.

"Tsk, tsk," Levi taunts, "and here I thought you were in love with my little dove. Seems like that torch for Lilly is still lit and burning as brightly as ever."

"I will always love Lilly," Malcolm confesses as his eyes drift from Levi to me. "She will always be a part of me."

Levi grabs hold of my arm closest to him and pulls me roughly against his side. I'm still feeling completely drugged and helpless to stop him.

"Well, if that's the case, I don't see why I shouldn't be able to keep Anna for myself. She's obviously not of any use to you. Poor thing thinks she's in love with you, though. I feel sure after a few days with me I can remedy that little fantasy and bring her back to reality."

"How? By driving her insane?" Malcolm scoffs.

"By giving her something you can't—all of me. You Watchers might think you have the monopoly on being able to fall for human women, but you don't."

Malcolm crosses his arms in front of him. "Do you think you're in love with Anna? Is that why you tried to have Amon kill her the other night?"

Levi looks at me like he's considering Malcolm's question carefully. "That was a mistake. I never should have tried to kill her. She's much more valuable to me alive. I might not love her, but I could care for her better than you, especially if she gives me what I want," Levi says, looking into my eyes. "A child."

"Why does that seem so important to you?" I mumble, needing to know.

"Because it's the one thing your real father has that I don't, and I refuse to let him have anything over me."

Levi looks back at Malcolm.

"I'll even give you what you want without a fight," Levi tells him. "I'll give you the seal I have and not fight you from taking the other seals from my brothers. All you have to do is give me Anna, and you can complete your mission and finally die so you can be with Lilly again. I'll willingly give you everything you want, Malcolm. All I want in return is Anna and the child she can bear for me. Odds are she'll die like her mother in childbirth, but what will that matter to you? You'll be in Heaven with the real love of your life, and you'll finally have the peace you've been longing for."

Malcolm's arms unfold and fall to his sides as he looks at Levi thoughtfully.

"You would do all that just to have her?" Malcolm asks skeptically.

"Yes," Levi says, and I know he's telling the truth. I'm not certain Malcolm does, though, because he still looks dubious. "I'll do all of that to have her and the child for myself. What do you say? Do we have a deal?"

Malcolm is completely silent, and he seems to be seriously considering Levi's proposition.

"Malcolm. ..." I say, feeling a corner of my heart begin to tear over the real possibility that he will agree to Levi's terms. I can see the wheels of his mind tumbling back and forth between the easy way out Levi is offering and rescuing me.

How much can I really mean to him if he would consider trading me in a bargain with Levi to get what he wants—what he's always wanted?

Jered phases in and touches Malcolm on the shoulder. This seems to bring Malcolm out of his thoughts and back to reality.

"Everything is ready," Jered says to Malcolm, looking over at me with a worried glance. "You know you can't trust a word that comes out of his mouth."

Malcolm looks at Jered for a moment before finally nodding his head in agreement.

"I won't let you just take her," Levi says angrily, pulling me even more tightly against his side.

With his free hand, Levi raps his knuckles three times against the door behind us.

Instantly, Christopher and Clark are standing on either side of us without the flashing light associated with teleportation. I can only assume they phased in.

"I didn't think you would let her go without a fight," Malcolm answers.

Three men phase in beside Malcolm and Jered.

I take in a sharp breath because all three of them are glowing to my eyes, like Jered is. Malcolm is the only one among the five men who doesn't glow.

"Called in the troops, did we?" Levi says, not sounding as sure of himself as he did before.

Before Malcolm can answer, Levi phases away with me in tow.

Malcolm isn't far behind, though, because he's right beside us in a matter of seconds. Levi keeps phasing us over and over to new locations in Cirrus so fast I end up having to close my eyes because I start to feel ill.

"You're going to kill her!" Malcolm finally yells at Levi, making the prince of Hell stop phasing.

"I thought she could take it," Levi says, telling the truth.

"She's still part human, you idiot," Malcolm says to him, trying to be the voice of reason. "You know human bodies can't survive that much phasing."

Levi pulls me behind him and stands between me and Malcolm.

"I won't let you take her away from me. Not when I'm so close to having what I want," Levi says with grim determination.

"I won't be asking for your permission," Malcolm replies before phasing over to us and grabbing Levi by the throat, tossing him off to the side.

Without Levi to prop me up, I fall to my knees before completely sitting down.

I turn my head and see Malcolm and Levi fighting, but my vision is so blurry by this point that I can't make out much of what is happening. I feel my stomach begin to heave and completely lose what little food is still left inside me. Someone comes to me and lifts me into their arms. When I look at his face, I recognize him as one of the three men who phased into the room before Levi phased me away.

He's tall and has Asian features. The smile on his face is kind, and I know I can trust him.

The stranger doesn't waste any time and quickly phases me away from the fight.

We end up somewhere I've never been before but know of. It's one of the thousands of escape pods on the underside of Cirrus.

The interior is small and completely white. Escape pods are built to only carry four people at a time in case some catastrophic event befalls Cirrus and an evacuation is necessary. The man puts me in one of the command chairs at the front of the pod and activates the invisible protective shield, which helps hold me upright in the seat.

"I'm sorry you've been placed in the middle of all this, Anna," he tells me. "I hope we can resolve things quickly and eventually give you a normal life."

"Who are you?" I'm able to ask through the haze of my thoughts.

"My name is Daniel," he tells me before turning his attention to the control panel in front of me. He waves his hand over it to make the holographic controls light up. "As soon as Malcolm gets here, he'll launch this pod to the surface. Once it's moving, you won't have to worry about Levi anymore for a while."

"How are we going to lose him?"

"It's impossible to phase into a moving target," Daniel tells me. "He won't be able to follow you, and please remember not to phase once you're on the surface. There's technology Levi can use to track our phasing. He'll know exactly where you are in an instant if he catches you using it."

I nod because I simply don't have the energy to do anything else.

Malcolm phases in.

"Go!" he yells to Daniel, quickly sitting in the seat beside me and taking command of the controls.

Daniel takes one quick glance at me the second before he phases. In that one look I see a multitude of emotions but the most prominent one is worry.

I soon feel the pod's freefall from the magnetic lock holding it to the underside of Cirrus.

I silently watch Malcolm as his hands move quickly over the controls, guiding the pod where he wants it to go. He doesn't say anything to me and seems completely focused on the task at hand.

My heart aches inside my chest, and I feel the wetness of warm tears begin to trickle down my face.

How could he have even considered the offer Levi made? Is he so desperate to be with Lilly again that he will completely ignore the bond between us? I understand the fact that we have only just met and don't really know each other that well. Yet there isn't a doubt in my mind that we are each other's soul mates. The evidence of our connection is unmistakable to me.

Maybe I was wrong. Maybe I won't be able to share Malcolm's heart with Lilly. It seems as though she might have taken it all with her when she died.

The pain in my heart becomes unbearable, and my silent crying turns into an anguished sob.

Malcolm looks over at me in alarm.

"Are you hurt?" he asks in worry.

I turn my head away, unable to look at him anymore, but slowly I shake my head so he knows I'm not hurt ... at least not physically.

I force myself to stop crying because I don't want to divert Malcolm's attention from our getaway. I try to remind myself that Malcolm didn't agree to Levi's offer. He actually chose to rescue me instead. Yet if Jered hadn't shown up when he did, would

Malcolm's decision have been the same? Or would he have traded me off in a bargain that assured his quick reunion with Lilly in Heaven?

I have no way of knowing. The moment is gone, and now we are on the run.

A few minutes pass, and I hear Malcolm say angrily, "We have company."

Through the front glass of the pod, I see two drone warcrafts flying on either side of us.

"Please follow us to an approved landing area," a computer-generated female voice says to us inside the pod.

"I'm going to try to lose them," Malcolm tells me. "The ride from here on out might be a little bumpy."

I watch as Malcolm increases our speed and begins to maneuver us in an attempt to lose the drones. He tries his best, but the drones are just as quick in their adjustments to speed and altitude as Malcolm is.

"Damn it!" Malcolm says, becoming frustrated. "All right, hold on. We're going to have to make a crash landing in the ocean and use the autodestruct to destroy the drones before they can report where we are."

"I don't like the water," I say.

Malcolm looks over at me in surprise.

"Then I suppose you can't swim?" he asks, like he already knows the answer to his own question.

I shake my head. "No, I can't."

Malcolm does something to the controls and then stands up. He turns my protective shield off and lifts me out of my chair.

"You're so drugged," he says, "I doubt you could swim even if you knew how."

He holds me against his chest and reaches around to the back of my dress to open the closure there. I hear fabric tear as he rips the back of the skirt in two. He sits me back down and completely removes the wedding gown from me, leaving me in only my undergarments.

"Why did you just do that?" I ask.

"The dress is too big," he answers. "It would have just weighed you down like an anchor and sent you directly to the bottom of the ocean."

Malcolm picks me up in his arms and cradles me to him, much like he did the first night he came to my rescue.

"Open hatch," Malcolm says, and the pod door opens.

Cold wind rushes into the interior of the pod, but Malcolm keeps his hold on me, his feet firmly planted. I can see the watery surface of the ocean beneath us rapidly approaching.

"I've got you," he says, looking down at me. "I won't let you go, Anna."

I hope his words hold a double meaning, because it's not the water that I'm afraid of.

I'm more afraid of losing him to the ghost of Lilly.

Just as the pod is about to crash in the ocean, Malcolm yells, "Autodestruct, five seconds!"

Malcolm jumps out, holding me securely to him. As we hit the water, I instantly feel chilled to the bone from its coldness. It's a cold I've never felt before and hope to never feel again. I'm faintly aware of the pod exploding but am just too drugged and cold to care much about its destruction.

I've always hated the water. My father tried to teach me how to swim when I was young, but I didn't like getting in the pool. I didn't like the feeling of not being in complete control. There wasn't anything solid for me to hold on to, and I felt like I was at the mercy of a substance that didn't seem very reliable and could easily kill me.

Malcolm slips his left arm underneath my breasts and begins

to swim while pulling me with him through the water. The swim to shore seems to take forever, but eventually my body becomes completely numb to the cold, and I feel myself begin to drift off to sleep.

"Don't go to sleep, Anna," Malcolm orders.

"Tired," I say as my eyelids droop. The sweet release of sleep beckons me to accept her embrace and just let go. Let go of the pain. Let go of the nightmare my life has turned into. Let go of the heartache Malcolm has caused me because of his lingering feelings for someone who died long ago.

"Stay with me," Malcolm begs.

"Why?" I ask, seeing no reason good enough to stay.

Malcolm doesn't answer right away, but finally he says, "Because I need you. Don't leave me, Anna."

That ... is a good enough reason. ...

By sheer willpower alone, I keep my eyes open and force myself to concentrate on the moon hanging in the sky above us—our only source of light. I use every bit of energy I have left to keep myself awake as Malcolm swims us to shore.

Once we reach the sandy shore, Malcolm picks me up in his arms and cradles me to his warm chest. He runs to a stand of trees to help block out the wind battering the shoreline with its winter breath. When we reach the shelter of the forest, Malcolm gently sets me against the trunk of one of the trees and begins to hastily pull off his wet clothes.

I don't mind the private striptease Malcolm is giving me. In fact, I'm rather enjoying it, but I can't imagine why he's taking all his clothes off. I notice a series of black scars on his right calf and have to assume the injuries are what cause him to limp sometimes. Malcolm soon comes back and sits down beside me, only wearing a pair of tight white underwear. He pulls me onto his lap and cradles me in the safety of his arms. I'm shivering so violently by this time I begin to wonder if I'll end up breaking one of my own bones or hurt Malcolm.

"Anna," Malcolm whispers in my ear, his warm breath melting my heart, "concentrate on my voice. Stop thinking about how cold you are and just listen to me."

I nod my head because my teeth are chattering so hard I can't actually speak.

"I never would have let Levi touch you," he tells me vehemently. "And I sure as hell wouldn't have let him have a child with you. Do you understand that? I wouldn't have made that deal with him."

I want to believe Malcolm's words, but I was witness to his hesitation. I know he believes the words he was telling me, because if it had been a lie, I would have been able to see through it clearly. If I was able to speak, I would have asked him if, in that moment with Levi, he had considered the proposal seriously for even just a second. Was it his heart or his mind that had made the final decision?

I lean completely against Malcolm's warmth as my shivers subside. But even with his added heat, my core feels so cold I'm not sure I'll ever regain my own body's warmth. I'm so tired, and I feel alone, even though Malcolm is holding me and rocking me for comfort. Unable to keep my eyes open for a second longer, I fall asleep and faintly hear Malcolm yell for me to stay awake. But not even his desperate pleas are enough to stop me from freefalling into death.

CHAPTER 14

I feel a warm breath fill my lungs to bursting and faintly taste something sweet against my tongue but can't quite place the flavor. I take a deep, shuddering breath of my own and open my eyes to find an angel of mercy hovering over me. He's glowing, just like most of the other angels I've met, and his sweet blue eyes hold an ancient quality I've never seen in anyone before. His tousled blond hair hangs down over his forehead as he peers down at me.

"Hello, Anna," he says. "My name is Will."

I lift a hand to his face and cup the side of it, strangely feeling as though I'm in the presence of a dear friend. There's a connection between us that is so familiar, yet so strange. It's almost a mirror of the way I feel about Auggie. I instinctively know that he just saved my life. I just don't know how exactly.

Will closes his eyes at my tender caress, and I know he feels the same way I do.

"Thank you," I tell him.

Will opens his eyes and smiles down at me.

"You're welcome," he replies.

"Will ... what are you?" I ask.

"One of the people who hopes to help you make it through all of this," he tells me.

"Was I. ..." I have to swallow hard before I can finish my question. "Was I dead?"

"For a little while," Will tells me.

"Then how. ..." I don't even know how to ask what I want to know.

Will smiles.

"How did I bring you back to life?" he asks.

I nod my head.

"Protecting Caylin and Aiden's descendants is a job I was given a long time ago. To put it mildly, you girls have been high-maintenance."

"So, if we die, you bring us back to life?"

"Yes."

I feel my brow crinkle as I consider this fact, because one thing makes absolutely no sense if what he is saying is true.

"Then why did you let my mother die?" I have to ask.

Will's face droops with a mixture of guilt and sadness.

"I couldn't save Amalie," he tells me.

"Why?"

"Because you had been born," he replies gently, like he hopes this news won't upset me. "My protection automatically transfers to the next descendant. It's the way things have always worked."

"Then my birth caused her death in more ways than one," I say as I look up at him through a blur of tears, feeling the heaviness of my guilt over my mother's death crash into me all over again.

"No," he tells me in no uncertain terms. "You did *not* kill your mother. It was simply her time to leave this world. Amalie knew what she was doing. She loved you so much that she willingly gave up her life for you. You were everything to her. So don't ever think you killed your mother, because that's not what happened. The best parts of her are still alive within you."

"If I hadn't been born, she would still be alive," I try to argue.

"Or the line of your family would have ended with Amalie," Will argues back. "You have no way of knowing what might have happened. None of us do. So stop blaming yourself, Anna. Life is never certain. Every decision, every turn in the road, will lead you down a different path. All you can do is be satisfied with where you end up."

I try to take Will's words to heart, but I've carried the guilt of my mother's death with me since I was old enough to understand what happened. It won't just vanish with a few kind words.

As I continue to look up at Will, I still have this strange sense of déjà vu.

"Have we met before?" I ask him. "There's something about you that's so familiar to me. I feel like I know you."

Will's smile broadens. "Yes, we met in Heaven before you were sent to Earth. We were actually playmates while you were there."

"Playmates ... in Heaven?" I ask, finding the concept strange. "Like we used to play chase and hide-and-go seek with one another? I didn't realize I even existed before I was born."

"Some souls aren't allowed to stay in Heaven for very long. But yours was. We were friends in Heaven for what would be many years here on Earth. God allowed someone very special by the name of Utha Mae to keep you before you were sent here. He gave me the privilege of being your best friend while you were living with her and her husband. He didn't want you to be lonely, so he let me be your playmate."

"Don't take this the wrong way, but you seem kind of old to be a playmate."

Will chuckles. "In Heaven, you can assume any of your

previous forms that you want. I looked eight years old when you and I first became friends there."

"I don't remember that," I confess. "Yet something inside me seems to remember you."

I try to sit up, and Will helps me accomplish what should have been a simple task. I look around and see that we're inside an old house with furniture that looks like it's about to fall apart. I hear a rattle by the sliding glass doors that face toward the sea and watch as Malcolm opens them to step inside. A gust of cold wind follows him in, and I hug the blanket I'm lying underneath closer to my chin to block its chill. His arms are filled with short logs of wood. He slams the door shut behind him and turns to look at me.

I see him visibly take a steadying breath when he sees that I'm awake.

"How are you feeling?" Malcolm asks, dropping the logs onto the floor before walking over to me.

"Better," I tell him, realizing the coldness I felt before is gone now and my thoughts are a lot clearer.

Malcolm holds a hand out to Will. Will stands and shakes it.

"Thanks for coming. I was worried you wouldn't for a moment there," Malcolm says.

"There was no need to worry, Malcolm. I've been waiting for her to be born for as long as you have. Time might move differently in Heaven, but some things still seem to take forever to happen."

"Did Father send any instructions for us?"

Will shakes his head. "No, He didn't send a message. And before you ask, no one else sent a message either."

Malcolm nods that he understands but doesn't look too happy about what Will said. I have a feeling Malcolm was hoping for a message from Lilly. It just deepens the mystery surrounding her hold over him, even in death.

"I need to get back," Will says, looking down at me once again. He helps me to my feet.

Once I'm standing, I wrap the thin blanket around my body because I'm still only wearing my underwear.

"Am I ever going to see you again?" I ask, hoping this won't be the last time I see him.

Will smiles crookedly. "Let's both hope you don't need me to come down again for a long time. I'm only allowed to travel between Heaven and Earth when you need to be brought back to life. I love seeing you, but I would much rather just have you stay alive, Anna."

"Yes," Malcolm agrees wholeheartedly, looking me dead in the eyes. "Let's make that our top priority. I don't think I can take you having another near-death experience."

Malcolm turns his attention back to Will.

"Can you do me a favor before you leave?"

"What do you need?"

"Could you go to my home in New York and grab Anna's outfit, her sword, and my cane for us? They're on my bed. I had hoped we would be able to land closer to the city and rendezvous with Jered there, but that's not possible now. So leave him a note telling him where we are, and instruct him to bring the horses and other things we packed this afternoon here instead."

Will nods and phases, causing me to instantly panic.

"Daniel told me Levi can track our phasing," I say in alarm.

Malcolm nods. "Yes, he can track any phasing you or I might do, but he can't track Will's phasing."

"Why?"

"Because Will is a guardian angel. His phasing is different. He can travel through the veil between Heaven and Earth during the window of time he's given. As long as he travels to Heaven before coming back here, Levi won't be able to track him."

149

"Why didn't we just get Will to phase us to your home then?"

"Because he isn't allowed to phase other people."

A couple of minutes pass before Will returns with my sword, Malcolm's wolf-head cane, and a large package wrapped in brown cloth, tied with a string.

"Here," Will says, hurriedly handing the items to Malcolm. "Jered was already there, so I told him where to find you."

"Thanks."

Will turns to me and wraps his arms around me for a brief hug. "I've got to go. I've stayed too long as it is. Hang in there, Anna. Have faith that everything will work out for the best in the end."

Then he phases, leaving Malcolm and me alone.

The quiet in the house is disturbing. The only sound is the howling of the cold winter wind outside as it gusts past the ramshackle structure.

Malcolm hands me the brown cloth-wrapped package.

"You'll find some clothes and shoes in there that should fit," he says. "There's also a baldric to keep your sword in. You wear it on your back to make carrying it easier."

I take the package from him, grateful to have some dry clothes to put on. Malcolm hands me my sword before turning his back to me to lean his cane against the wall by the fireplace. He then goes to pick up the wood he brought in earlier from off the floor. I watch as he walks to the fireplace in the small living room we're in and begins to stack the wood into it.

I get the feeling his actions aren't only to build a fire to chase away the cold, but to give me a minute to put my new clothes on.

I untie the string around the package and remove the fabric protecting what's inside. Within the folds of cloth, I find a white leather jacket and pants, white shirt, matching knee-high boots, and something that looks like a sheath for my sword, which I assume is the baldric.

I drop the blanket and begin to put the clothes on. Once I have the pants and shirt on, I lift up the jacket and ask, "Is this a zipper?"

Malcolm, still crouched by the fireplace, turns on the balls of his feet to face me.

He begins to smile. "Yes, it's a zipper. I know it's a bit old-fashioned, but it's what was used back when the outfit was made."

"How does it work?" I ask, wondering why anyone would find the metal teeth of a zipper safe to wear, considering how prickly they feel.

Malcolm rises from the floor in one fluid motion and walks over to me.

He takes the jacket from my hands and holds it out for me to put on. I turn my back to him and slip my arms into the sleeves. Malcolm wraps his arms around me and holds the bottom front of the jacket together.

"You have to slide this side of the zipper, which is called the pin, into this little box on the other side," he says, his mouth right next to my ear, washing my senses with his warm breath. His attention is captured by his little demonstration, but mine is completely seized by him. "Then just pull up on the tab to zip the teeth together," he tells me, going through the motions of closing the zipper and raising it up to just underneath my breasts.

I turn my head slightly to look at him. He hesitates but finally meets my gaze.

"Did you mean what you said?" I ask, wanting to know the truth but also fearing what I might learn at the same time.

"I always mean what I say," Malcolm answers. "But what are you talking about in particular?"

"That you wouldn't have taken the easy way out that Levi offered you. And ... that you needed me. ..."

Malcolm studies my face for a moment before answering.

"I had no intention of taking his offer. But I'm not going to lie and say I didn't consider it for a moment there."

He is telling the truth, even if it is hard to hear, and quite honestly, I would rather have the truth from him than a lie to spare my feelings.

"And the other thing?" I ask.

Malcolm remains silent and just looks at me.

"Like I said," he finally replies in a whisper, "I always mean what I say."

Malcolm steps away from me and returns his attention to the fireplace.

"I wish I had some matches," he grumbles as he stares at the dead pieces of wood.

Then suddenly, and quite unexpectedly, he begins to laugh.

"What's so funny?" I ask, unable to suppress a smile of my own because the joy in Malcolm's laughter is contagious.

He shakes his head and turns back to look at me.

"An old inside joke," he tells me with a smile.

"What's the joke?"

Malcolm shakes his head resolutely. "You're far too young and innocent to know it yet."

It's only then that I remember something.

"I turned twenty-one today," I tell him. "I think that makes me old enough to be able to understand most things."

Malcolm's eyes narrow on me. "I completely forgot today was your birthday. I'm sorry it wasn't a happier one for you."

"It may not have started out very well," I admit. "But ... I have high hopes that it will end well."

The smile on Malcolm's face slowly dissolves as he stands in front of me stock-still, as if he's waiting for me to complete my thought.

"How do you want it to end, Anna?" he finally murmurs.

I swallow hard, because my heart begins to race inside my chest. I have a feeling he knows exactly what I want. But he wants me to declare it out loud. I'm not sure I feel quite brazen enough to say the words directly to him. A lady isn't supposed to tell a man about such carnal desires. Plus, I'm not quite sure he understands how deeply my desires run for him. I don't just want a kiss from him. I want all of him: heart, body, and soul. I desperately yearn for him to take me into his arms and make love to me until the sun kisses the horizon the next morning, and even after that, I'm not sure I'll want him to stop.

I feel my lips part, and the braver part of my soul pushes her way to the surface to voice what my heart and body desire the most and to tell him explicitly what I want from him.

Deafening howls rip through the air around us, forcing me to cover my ears because their high pitch feels like needles piercing my eardrums. I realize it can't be the howl of just one creature but a multitude of them.

As quickly as the sound came, it dissipates.

"What was that?" I ask Malcolm, cautiously lowering my hands but being on guard for them to sound again.

Malcolm's face darkens.

"Hellhounds," he replies. "They've found us."

CHAPTER 15

"What's a hellhound?" I ask, never having heard the term before. "Some sort of animal here on the surface? Like a wolf?"

"They're ten times the size of an ordinary wolf," Malcolm says, absently rubbing his right leg. "But they're not creatures of this world. They were made in Hell."

"Are we safe in here?" I ask, looking at the walls of the beach house and not finding a lot of comfort in their apparent thinness.

"No," Malcolm says, confirming my suspicion.

"Then what should we do?"

"I say we stand and fight," he answers. "Levi probably sent a lot of packs out to track us down, which means he doesn't exactly know where we are yet. If he did, he would already be here."

"What's the best way to kill them?"

"You have to separate their heads from their bodies. And whatever you do, don't let them bite you."

"Why?" I ask apprehensively.

"Just trust me," Malcolm says, walking over to the wolf-headed

154

cane Will brought, which he propped next to the fireplace. "You don't want to get bitten by one."

He lifts the cane in his hand, and I watch as he grabs the upper portion of it between the wolf's head and the strange wing-shaped silver protrusions. With one swift yank, I hear the metallic ring of a blade being released from its sheath. I have to admit I'm impressed with how Malcolm has his sword camouflaged. He was even able to fool the guards in Cirrus into allowing him to bring a weapon up there.

I grab my sword off the couch, and the blade instantly bursts into red-orange flames, like it has a mind of its own and knows it's time for a fight.

"It's been a while since I've seen that sword in action," Malcolm remarks. "Andre told me you were the best he'd ever seen with a blade. That's high praise, considering how much swordplay we've seen in our lives."

"My father trained me well," I say, not wanting to sound like I am boasting. I just want Malcolm to know I can handle myself in a fight without him feeling as though he needs to protect me, which would only serve to divide his attention.

"Just don't let them bite you," Malcolm warns again, like nothing else matters. "Their venom causes a pain worse than anything I wager you've ever felt before. I wouldn't wish it on my worst enemy ... much less you."

My heart is warmed by his apparent concern for my safety. Before I can ask anything about our strategy in defeating the creatures outside, something crashes through the sliding glass doors and lands on the floor in between us.

I've only seen pictures and videos of wolves, but this one seems unnaturally large to me with its head as high as my chest. Its white fur is fluffy and seems to be swaying in an imaginary wind, because it doesn't match the tempo of the glacial gusts coming in from the outside. Its pristine coat is surrounded by reddish-orange flames, but the fire seems to be only for show, because it doesn't give off any heat or seem to burn anything.

The hellhound looks at Malcolm and snarls fiercely before whipping its head around to look at me. It blinks twice as it considers me with its large black eyes and gives a silent whine like it's confused by me for some reason. There's intelligence behind the hellhound's eyes, but also a primordial viciousness that seems to overrule whatever sense of intelligence it might possess.

Malcolm takes advantage of the animal's momentary lapse of action and jumps onto its back, wrapping one arm around its neck to lift it up and slice its throat with one swift stroke of his blade. I would have expected blood to splatter everywhere, but it doesn't. The hellhound's body crumples to the floor beneath Malcolm, and a black substance trickles out of its body from the open wound. The flames of its coat die down, and all that's left is the sad remains of a creature that seemed to suffer from a torment of its own.

Malcolm hops off of its back and tosses the hellhound's head into a corner of the room.

I look at the shattered remains of the glass doors.

"How many more do you think are out there?" I ask Malcolm.

"From the sound of the howls earlier, I would say at least three more."

"Why aren't they coming in?"

"I'm sure they sense the death of this one," Malcolm says, looking at the corpse of the hellhound he just killed. "He was probably the runt of the litter and expendable to them. I think the others just used it to judge what they were up against."

"He was the runt?" I ask, wondering just how large hellhounds could get.

A lopsided grin graces Malcolm's face. "The others will be

bigger and smarter. In the end, they're just animals. They might put up more of a fight, but we can kill them just as easily as this one."

I heft the hilt of my sword in my hands. "Then I think we should go on the offensive before they have time to strategize a plan."

Malcolm nods in agreement, and we walk to the broken glass doors together.

As we reach the entrance, Malcolm holds up a hand to silently signal me to stop. He stands completely still, only tilting his head slightly, like he's trying to listen to something. I briefly wonder what it is he hears until I hear it, too. I look up toward the ceiling as tiny creaks and shuffles become evident, revealing the presence of something heavy walking on the roof of the structure right above our heads. If we had walked out onto the porch, the hellhound on the roof would have probably pounced on one or both of us. Malcolm grabs hold of my free hand and turns me around. We quietly make our way to the front of the house and the door there. Malcolm lets go of my hand and turns the doorknob while keeping his grip on the slim sword with his other hand.

"*One*," he mouths to me but doesn't vocalize.

I hold the blade of my sword up with both hands on the hilt, spreading my legs apart slightly to brace myself for an attack.

"*Two*," he mouths silently, his grip on the door handle tightening.

He doesn't have to say "*three*" because he simply opens the door.

A gust of cold wind rushes in, but nothing jumps out of the darkness.

Malcolm cautiously looks outside, directing his gaze to either side of the entrance.

He motions for me to follow him outside.

We make our way to the front exterior of the house. The only light to see by is given off by the moon, which is a notch higher in the sky than it was earlier, marking the passage of time. Malcolm tilts his head to the left of the house, and we make our way to that side. Once we reach the corner of the building, we stand behind it together, and Malcolm slowly peeks around the edge to see what's there. He holds up one finger to me. I assume it means he only sees one hellhound on that side of the house.

If his assumption of there being three hellhounds surrounding the house is correct, that means we know where two of them are. It makes sense to think that the third one is on the other side of the house.

Malcolm looks away from the hellhound and lightly taps the wall at our backs with his fist, making a slight noise that hopefully only attracts the nearest hellhound. It takes a minute, but the hellhound's head soon appears around the corner. Before it even has a chance to see us, Malcolm swings his sword down against its neck. The force of the blow is so fierce it completely decapitates the hellhound before it can release even a whisper of a whine.

Apparently it doesn't need to. Its death seems to be automatically sensed by the other two. We soon hear the one on the roof run toward the front of the house, and the one on the other side of the house comes barreling around the opposite corner.

Malcolm and I stand away from the protection of the wall and face the two hellhounds as they approach.

"Do you feel confident you can take one on your own?" Malcolm asks.

"Yes, I can take one."

"Good," he says, keeping his eye on the one on the roof. "You take the one on the right, and I'll take that one."

"Works for me," I tell him.

Just before I begin to make my way to meet the hellhound I've been assigned, Malcolm says, "Anna. ..."

I take a few precious seconds to meet his gaze and find concern for me.

"Be careful," he finishes.

I nod. "I will."

I return my attention to my hellhound. Its marble black eyes glow from the reflection of the flames surrounding its body, making him look even more sinister than the first hellhound Malcolm killed. I get the feeling it's mocking my ability to slay it as it approaches me, like it thinks I'll be easy to kill.

Malcolm was right. The first hellhound must have been the runt of the litter because the hellhound I'm facing is able to meet my gaze at eye level. After it gets a good look at me, it blinks like it's slightly confused by me, much like the first hellhound did.

"You don't have to do this," I tell it, seeing an opening into its dark spirit. "You don't have to be this way."

The hellhound tilts its head at me, like I'm a curiosity and it can't quite figure out why I seem to be such a novelty to it. Instead of taking my advice, however, the hellhound bares its teeth at me, lowers its head, and runs straight toward me.

I stand my ground and wait for it to get close to me. I can feel its breath wash over my face. As it reaches out with its open mouth, filled with razor sharp teeth that seem determined to snap my head off, I spin on my right heel and swing the blade of my sword at a downward angle to slice through its neck cleanly in one stroke.

The hellhound's headless corpse continues to run for a few more feet before falling to the ground in a motionless heap of white fur.

I look over at Malcolm and see that the hellhound on the roof must have jumped down while I was confronting my own. It snarls and snaps its teeth at Malcolm.

"Come on, you big fur ball," Malcolm taunts, hefting his thin-bladed sword in his hand. "What are you waiting for?"

Nothing, apparently. The hellhound charges Malcolm with its head held down like it intends to ram him. Malcolm holds his sword out horizontally so that the tip of the blade is pointed directly at the hellhound's forehead. The beast does most of the work for Malcolm as it impales its own head on the sword. Malcolm yanks the blade upward with such force it completely slices its way through the upper portion of the hellhound's skull and splits it in half. The beast collapses to the ground but is still breathing. Malcolm walks over to it and releases the creature from its pain with one swift motion of his sword through its neck.

Malcolm turns to me, quickly taking inventory of my physical welfare.

"It didn't bite you, did it?" he asks worriedly.

I shake my head. "No, it didn't bite me. I'm fine."

I see Malcolm's bare shoulders sag in relief.

"That wasn't so—" I begin to say before I feel a heavy weight slam into my back, propelling me into the air before I come back down to earth, hitting the ground hard.

Before I know it, a hellhound is standing over me, preparing to clamp its jaws down on my left shoulder. Out of the corner of my eye, I see Malcolm ram his right leg into the creature's gaping maw just before it bites me. The hellhound clamps its razor sharp teeth down onto Malcolm's calf just as the force of his kick catapults the creature into the air. Malcolm falls to the ground onto his back, like the bite knocked him completely unconscious. I stand to my feet quickly and pick up my sword. Before the hellhound can recover from being stunned by Malcolm's kick, I slice its head off.

I turn my back to the fallen corpse of the hellhound and rush to Malcolm's side.

He's lying on the ground, completely motionless. I kneel down beside his leg and rip the bottom half of his right pant leg in two to view the damage of the hellhound's bite. Not only are the fresh wounds oozing a horrible-smelling black substance, but the old wounds I saw earlier have popped open and are seeping the same malodorous fluid.

"There's not much you can do to help him," I hear a strange male voice say to me.

I look up and see a man standing at the edge of the woods near the house. The new arrival's features are obscured by the hooded cloak he's wearing, which billows around him in the cold winter wind.

There's something oddly familiar about the man, but I can't quite place where I know him from. His voice holds a memorable quality. I feel as though I've heard it before but have no real memory of ever meeting him prior to this moment.

I stand to my feet and hold my blazing sword out in front of me.

"Who are you?" I demand, thinking anyone who just shows up after a hellhound attack probably isn't someone I can trust.

"No one to you," he says, and I instantly know he's lying.

"Did you lead the hellhounds in the attack against us? Do you work for Levi?"

The man begins to laugh like what I've said is totally absurd.

"Me? Work for Levi?" he says in disgust. "Now that's a rich idea. No, I most definitely *do not* work for Levi."

"Then who are you?" I challenge. "Why are you here?"

The man is silent, and I'm not sure he's going to answer me.

"I wanted to see you in person," he finally says, almost too low for me to hear against the howl of the wind. "I wanted to see how much you looked like your mother."

"You knew my mother?" I ask, remembering that my mother lived on the surface when she was alive. Could this man actually be a friend of hers? Is that why he seemed so familiar to me? But how on earth did he find us out in the middle of nowhere?

"Yes," he tells me. "I knew her quite well."

"Can you help us?" I ask, lowering my sword just a notch, because I don't fully trust the man standing in front of me, but I don't want to offend him either with a raised sword if he can help Malcolm.

"No," the man says succinctly. "I can't help you."

"Then what do you want?"

"Nothing. Like I said ... I just wanted to see how much you resembled Amalie."

I don't feel any reason to fear the man and lower my sword.

"If you can't help me, then please leave. I need to take care of my friend."

I'm not sure what to do with my sword, so I hurl it through the door opening of the beach house before reaching down and pulling Malcolm into my arms. I can't imagine what it must look like to the stranger for a person of my stature to effortlessly carry someone as large as Malcolm in her arms.

To my dismay, Malcolm is unnaturally cold to the touch and shivering. I turn to walk back into the house when the man says something that stops me in my tracks.

"You might want to seal the wounds with the fire from your sword," he advises. "That's how they sealed them the first time. If I were you, I would do it while he's still unconscious. Otherwise, you might have to deal with his screams of pain if you wait until he awakens."

"Is there anything I can do to heal him completely?"

"No," the man says so assuredly that, even if I couldn't tell a truth from a lie, I would have no doubt it was the truth. "There's nothing you can do. Only the person who created the hellhounds can take the curse away."

"Curse?" I ask in alarm. "What kind of curse?"

"A pain more torturous than any normal person can live with for very long."

"Where can I find the person who made the hellhounds?" I ask. "I'll make him cure Malcolm."

"He can only be found when he wants to be, Anna. Even if you located him, he wouldn't help Malcolm."

"Why wouldn't this man help Malcolm? Are they enemies?"

"For almost as long as time has existed. Rest assured your plea would receive a resounding 'no.' "

"Since this is the second time he's been bitten," I say, "will that make the pain he's been living with worse?"

"To an extent," the stranger admits. "But I'm sure Malcolm is accustomed to living with pain by now. I daresay he's numb to most any pain or pleasure after living with it for this long."

"You're just full of good news," I quip.

The man chuckles. "Would you rather I lied to you?"

"No," I admit with a sigh. "I need to know the truth. And I need to get him inside."

"Then I will leave you to do what you can for him."

The man turns his back to me.

"Wait!" I call out.

The man turns halfway around to face me again.

"What's your name?"

The man doesn't move a muscle, and I can feel the heat of his stare from underneath the hood of his cloak.

"My name is Lucifer."

I know instinctively this isn't just someone unlucky enough to be named Lucifer at birth. I'm standing in the presence of the devil himself. What's stranger still is that I feel connected to him for some inexplicable reason.

"Who are you?" I ask, feeling sure he knows what I'm really asking with my question because the connection between us is undeniable, at least to me.

Lucifer tilts his head down like he's looking at the ground, but I have a feeling he's trying to decide whether or not he wants to answer my question.

Finally he looks back up at me and says, "I'm the man your mother gave her heart to and who she abandoned just so she could give birth to you."

I suddenly can't seem to take in a breath but manage to ask, "Are you my father?"

"Like I said before," Lucifer says, "I'm no one to you, Anna. No one at all."

CHAPTER 16

Before I can even process what Lucifer just said to me, he phases. I can see by the phase trail he's left that wherever he went is completely void of light. I get the feeling that even if I had the time, I wouldn't want to follow him to his location.

I look down at Malcolm and notice that his breathing has become even shallower. Without having the luxury of time to ponder the revelation that I just met the man who fathered me, even though he refused to admit it, I carry Malcolm into the house. I lay him down in front of the fireplace and rush back to pull my sword out of the floorboards near the front door.

When I get back, I thrust the blade of the sword into the middle of the pile of wood and will it to ignite. I'm not sure it's going to work, but just a few seconds later, the blade bursts into its red-orange flames, lighting the wood quickly and chasing away the chill permeating the room.

As the fire crackles and sputters to life, I look down at Malcolm's injured leg and remember Lucifer's words to me.

With my sword still flaming, I touch the tip of it to each of the open wounds and watch as they seal shut from the cauterization. The scent of burning flesh permeates the air as I continue my ministrations, but I know this has to be done before Malcolm awakens and force myself to finish the task at hand no matter how gruesome I might find it.

After I'm done, I will the sword to extinguish itself. To my surprise, it does just what I want.

I walk over to the couch where I left the blanket I woke up underneath earlier and spread it over Malcolm.

I quickly dispose of the corpse of the first hellhound Malcolm killed. I'm then able to find some more blankets in an adjacent bedroom to put up a makeshift curtain in front of the shattered sliding glass doors. I hang them over an old curtain rod running across the top of the opening. The blankets prove to be heavy enough to not be blown much by the winter wind and stay in place for the most part.

By this point, Malcolm is shivering almost as badly as I had earlier. So I crawl underneath the blanket, hoping to share some of my warmth with him. Strangely enough, ever since I put on my new leather outfit, the cold hasn't bothered me. It's almost like the clothes I'm wearing keep my body at a constant, comfortable temperature.

Malcolm stirs and wraps his arms around me, apparently feeling my presence even in his unconscious state. I lay my head on top of his chest and listen to the slow, steady rhythm of his beating heart. I close my eyes and will him to get better. I've only just found him. I can't lose him now. I have no way of knowing if he can actually be killed, since he's an angel, but just the thought of having him torn from my life is completely unacceptable.

"Just live," I beg him, "Just live, and I promise I'll do everything within my power to bring happiness back into your life. Stay alive for me, Malcolm. Please."

He sighs, sounding almost content as his arms continue to hold me close. I hear him say something, but his voice is so weak I can't make out the word he keeps repeating like a litany. I lean up so my right ear is barely an inch away from his mouth as he whispers once again, "Lilly."

His arms squeeze me tighter, just as I feel the tear in the corner of my heart—which started when Levi made his offer and I saw Malcolm consider it—rip just a little bit farther, manifesting itself into a sting of warm tears, burning my eyes.

I lay my head back on his chest, suddenly finding it hard to breathe. I close my eyes and try to shut out the sound of Malcolm saying Lilly's name over and over again, like his memories of her are the only things keeping him alive.

I don't try to stop myself from crying because there's no reason to. Who would hear me? Who would care?

I squeeze my eyes shut and continue to cry until sleep provides my only escape from the pain in my heart.

I suddenly find myself on a darkened street, standing underneath a streetlamp, and I instantly know that I'm not seeing things through my own eyes, but Malcolm's. I don't know how, but I have a feeling I've entered his dreamworld by some miracle.

He watches a pretty girl with smooth, pale skin and long dark hair, wearing a black dress, cross his path only a few yards away. The fragrant smell of her blood from a fresh wound on her foot arouses his senses, causing a jolt to his system that he can't explain and has never experienced before. The smell of her, the very essence of her being, draws him in, and her effect on him is as unexpected as it is overwhelming. Instead of her newly spilt blood awakening the darkness within his heart, igniting the craving that has always resided there, he instantly becomes intrigued by her. In that moment, she becomes a true enigma to him that he must figure out.

She turns her head and looks over at him from across the street, having sensed his presence.

In that one brief glance, when he fully sees her for the first time, I feel the beat of Malcolm's heart literally stop inside his chest. He's seen a lot of beautiful women during his time on Earth, but none of them can even remotely compare to the beauty of the girl looking at him now. Her physical beauty is undeniable, but it's the inner glow she radiates around her that draws him in like a moth to a flame.

The girl begins to walk in the opposite direction, seeming bent on staying as far away as she can from him. But Malcolm phases over to her and gently grabs her by the elbow. When she turns to face him, and he looks into her soft, brown eyes, Malcolm's heart thunders back to life, beating with a new sense of purpose, a new reason to live. She's unlike anyone he's ever met in Heaven or on Earth, and he doubts he will ever meet anyone like her again.

"Hello, Lilly," he says to her, confused by what he feels for someone he doesn't even know, someone he was sent to kill.

In those few seconds before she speaks back to him, he instantly realizes that he would die for the woman standing in front of him. He's at a complete loss to explain why he feels the way he does, but in that moment, the reason really doesn't matter. All he wants to do is protect someone so rare, so utterly matchless in all of time, from all and any harm. He yearns for her to know him better, to see the real him and not the monster he's become.

The scene fades, and a new one appears.

Malcolm is lying in a small bed beside Lilly, watching her sleep. He's phased to her room while she sleeps a few times now. He doesn't mean her any disrespect by coming to her while she's in such a vulnerable state, and he rationalizes invading her privacy by thinking he does it to help protect her, but deep down, he knows the real reason is because he hates being separated from her. They've become friends of sorts by now, which is a notion Malcolm never thought possible, especially with someone as pure of heart as Lilly and so beautiful it causes his own, tortured soul to ache inside his chest each and every time she smiles at him. Why she continues to let him be a part of her life is completely beyond him. If she knew of the terrible things he's done in his past, he feels sure he would lose her forever.

He feels unworthy of her trust in him because of the evil deeds littering his past like unwelcome nightmares. But somehow, through her willingness to be his friend, she's made him feel like he can rise above his primitive nature, become a better person, and possibly find that part of him he thought was lost forever. Perhaps ... he isn't beyond saving.

Lilly has given him the first glimmer of hope about himself that he's had since being cursed. And maybe, just maybe, he can find a way to be forgiven for his multitude of sins—so many sins that he feels sure he's simply forgotten about some of the lesser ones he's committed since being exiled from Heaven and abandoned by his father.

He reaches out a hand and gently caresses her exposed cheek, being careful not to wake her.

"I will always protect you," he whispers to her slumbering form, feeling his heart swell with an emotion he thought was long dead, irretrievable. "I will be whatever you need me to be: friend, lover ... both. From this moment on, my life is yours to do with what you will. I will never forsake you. I will always remain loyal and true to you. I will always ... love you, Lilly."

The scene changes, but Malcolm is still caressing the side of Lilly's face. The only difference is that she's standing and awake now. They're inside an unfurnished room in a house, and Lilly seems to be blushing about something.

Malcolm built her the house they're standing in as a gift to show her how much she truly means to him. Building things is his talent, and in the back of his mind, Malcolm hoped to be able to bring her here and show her proof of his complete and utter devotion and love. He had planned to bring her here before she made a permanent commitment to Brand, but he's too late. She's already engaged to Brand, a promise he knows, deep down in his heart, she will never break.

Of anyone in this world, she is the one person who has even gotten close to breaching the barrier he uses to protect his heart. He may use sexual innuendos and humor to show how much he desires her physically, but what he truly wants, what he desires the most, is a place inside her heart. He wants to say these things to her but knows he shouldn't. It would only ruin the happiness Lilly is feeling in that moment and making her unhappy is something he will never knowingly do. The only thing he can do now is try to support her decision and continue to keep his deepest desires to himself.

"I thought it would be nice if you had somewhere all your own to go to," he tells her instead, continuing to caress the side of her face with his hand. "You deserve this and so much more, dearest. I could give you the world if you would just let me."

"Malcolm, I. ..."

"No, don't say it," he tells her, not needing a reminder of her love for Brand, because that's all too evident every time they're around one another. "I know. Just let me fantasize for a moment that this is our house and that you love me more than you do him."

He pulls her into his arms and holds her for a long time, much longer than he intends to. He doesn't want her to see the pain or tears in his eyes as he tries to come to terms with the fact that she will never be his to love and cherish. They will never live in this house like he hoped and raise a family together. He will never be allowed to have true happiness on this Earth because she will always belong to another.

The blinding light of the sun dissolves the tender moment, and I hear the crash of waves lapping against the shoreline.

Malcolm's sitting in a lounge chair, watching Lilly walk along the edge of the white, sandy beach picking up the occasional seashell as incoming waves bring them ashore. He's thinking about a striptease dance he did for her and how she almost let him kiss her not long afterwards. He had felt her desire for him in that private moment they shared and gained a new sense of hope that maybe she and Brand weren't actually soul mates after all. Perhaps, with just a little bit of persuasion, he can find a way to make her face her feelings for him. He knows she loves him ... in some way. But is it just the love of one friend for another, or has it grown into the same type of all-consuming love he feels for her?

No woman has ever thwarted his advances like Lilly has. In all of history, he has been able to have whomever he wanted whenever he wanted. Is that part of her appeal to him? Is he simply trying to conquer her heart because her love for Brand seems beyond his ability to break through?

Lilly looks over at him and smiles, holding up an unbroken sand dollar she just found.

No, he decides in that moment he doesn't want Lilly just because she's someone he can't seem to have. He wants her because he loves her and can't pass up what might be his last opportunity to have her choose him instead of Brand. This will be the last day they'll be able to share before she consecrates her marriage vows, a forever commitment to Brand. It's now or never, and Malcolm plans to make sure she knows how much he loves her. He knows he can be just as good for her as Brand. He also knows things might not be that simple. If she and Brand are destined to be together, there will be nothing he can do to change that.

The scene shifts to what seems like sometime later in the day. Lilly is lying down on one of the lounge chairs underneath the umbrella, sleeping. Malcolm just watches her for a long time, uncertain if he should tempt fate and possibly ruin their friendship, or jump in with both feet and make her face her feelings for him. Never being one to just stand idly by, he decides on the latter.

He stands from his chair and walks over to her. After he kneels on the sand beside her, he gently traces the outline of her face with the tips of his fingers, marveling at her beauty—inside and out. He gently caresses every contour of her face, finally sliding his fingers lightly across the bridge of her nose, over the plump, tender flesh of her lips, then down the gentle slope of her neck, stopping at a point just above her breast, not daring to disrespect her by going further but yearning to touch all of her and bring her the pleasure he knows he can if she would let him. His hand trembles slightly from his desire, but he holds himself back.

He feels her staring at him and knows this is the moment that will decide his fate. When he looks up at her, he silently questions whether or not she'll let him kiss her.

He feels like this might be his one and only chance to find out if she can love him more than Brand. He has to find out if there's any hope at a future with the woman he's given his heart to, or if he will always have to stand in the background and watch her be happy with another man.

He lowers his lips to hers tentatively at first, but when she doesn't push him away or ask him to stop, his heart flares with hope that maybe she's chosen him. Maybe he wasn't deluding himself into thinking he could never win her heart.

He plunges both of his hands into her hair as he worships the feel of her lips against his, causing him to let out an involuntary moan of pleasure. He soon feels the warm trickle of tears escape the corners of her eyes and slide over each of his hands as he continues to cradle her. He pulls back and tenderly kisses the wet trail of tears away.

"Lilly, why are you crying?" he asks. It is one of the happiest moments in his life, yet the woman he loves, the woman he would do anything for, is crying.

"This isn't right, Malcolm," Lilly says to him, shaking her head.

"Of course it is," he replies, planting small kisses all over her face. "You love me."

"But I love Brand more."

Malcolm looks down at her and sees the certainty of her love for Brand inside her soul. The pain of this simple truth completely engulfs Malcolm as he realizes she is truly lost to him. She was never meant to be his, and he will have to live with that fact for the rest of his life.

"If we still had four years, do you think you could come to love me more than him?"

Lilly doesn't even hesitate in her answer, "No."

Malcolm sighs in defeat, knowing his dream of making Lilly his was never meant to be. He was deluding himself, thinking someone like her could be meant for him. He wasn't good enough for her. He would never be good enough for someone like her. Maybe the real curse from his father was having Lilly thrust into his life but never being able to build a future with the woman who stole his heart.

He leans his forehead against hers, seeing her refusal of him as proof of this assumption.

"May I have one last kiss, dearest Lilly, before I make my heart let you go?"

Lilly nods to my surprise, and apparently Malcolm's, too.

Not wanting to waste his last chance to truly kiss her like a man kisses the woman he loves with every part of his being, Malcolm leans down and presses his lips to hers, feeling the hot sting of his own sorrow burn his eyes.

The scene changes to one of Malcolm and Will walking Lilly down the aisle of a church toward an altar where a handsome man, who I assume is Brand, awaits her. Malcolm looks over at Lilly and feels his heart completely break at the happy smile on her face.

He knows she is happier in that moment than she has ever been in her life. He welcomes her joy and makes a silent promise to her that he will never let her know how much this moment is costing him. The pain deep within his soul is almost unbearable, yet he smiles at her when she looks over at him, because he never wants to be someone who makes her cry. He never wants her to pity him, because he can't seem to make his heart let her go. He may have told her that he would that day on the beach, but forcing himself to let her go is an impossible task. She will always hold his heart, and he knows he is doomed to live with the knowledge that she has always, and will always, belong to another.

The only way he can truly show his love for her is to be her friend and simply love her from afar. He intends to remain a part of her and Brand's family for as long as they will allow, because not having her in his life would not be living at all. Living with the pain of his loss will be bearable as long as they can remain friends. He secretly vows to her in the house of his father that he will always protect her and her family.

Years pass and Malcolm stays true to his vow to Lilly. He becomes an uncle to her and Brand's children and dotes on them like a second father. In fact, that's exactly what the kids seem to think of him as. Malcolm's love and loyalty to Lilly stays strong and true through everything—never wavering, never slackening in strength.

The next memory finds Malcolm standing on the front porch of a house with a woman I haven't seen yet, but I know who she is: Jess.

Malcolm grins at her. "So I heard about the date last night."

Jess's eyes narrow on him. "Who told you about that?"

"Isaiah."

She simply shakes her head in resignation. "I didn't realize he was the gossiping type."

Malcolm shrugs. "Like I've told you before, we've all been worried about Mason for years. We like seeing him happy for probably the first time in his life. Don't begrudge us sharing in your happiness. It's been a long time coming."

"It's just ... kinda weird—all of you rooting for us. Freaks me out a little bit. I feel like everything we do is being judged by all of you."

Malcolm shakes his head. "Not judged, just observed from afar."

"What about you?" Jess asks.

Malcolm is confused by the question. "What about me?"

"I don't understand how you can be around Lilly and Brand so much. Even I can feel the love they share for one another when I'm around them, and I barely know them. How can you stand to be around them when you're in love with Lilly?"

Malcolm isn't prepared for such a question from Jess and isn't completely sure he wants to answer it. Finally he says, "I love her enough to only want to see her happy."

"But don't you deserve to find happiness with someone who can love you back?"

"My happiness stems from Lilly and her family's happiness. Besides, I'm not sure there is a person for me."

"Maybe she just hasn't been born yet," Jess suggests wisely.

"Perhaps," Malcolm reluctantly agrees but feels certain true love is something he's never meant to find.

Malcolm briefly thinks back to a time when his father offered him forgiveness from his sins. Apparently it was sometime right after he helped Lilly defeat Lucifer. Lucifer had set into motion a plan to destroy the universe, which ended up resulting in something called the Tear. Malcolm refused His forgiveness then, because he simply didn't feel like he had done enough to deserve it.

It wasn't until after Jess and some people who were vessels for six other archangels sealed the Tear that he finally accepted forgiveness from his father.

"Why have you let yourself be tortured for longer than you needed to be?" his father asks him.

They are standing near the top of a pyramid. It is nighttime and only the light of the moon lights the scene.

God doesn't look like what I expected. He is tall with skin so dark I can barely see him in the shadow of night. His eyes are penetrating as he looks at Malcolm, waiting for an answer.

"I had to feel like I earned it," Malcolm replies. "I think I have now."

God rests His hand on Malcolm's shoulders, and I instantly feel the weight of guilt Malcolm has been carrying around for centuries finally lift from his soul as he fully accepts God's grace.

When God drops His hand from Malcolm's shoulder, Malcolm turns to Him because he needs an answer to a question he has been pondering for the past few years.

"Why?"

God looks at Malcolm, and you can tell from the knowing expression on His face He understands the real question he is asking.

"Because you needed Lilly to show you that you could love

again, My son," God answers. "She made you realize that there was more to life than what you were allowing for yourself. Your guilt was eating your soul away until only a few fragments were left by the time you first met her. By allowing her inside and proving to yourself that you were a person worthy of befriending, she helped you rebuild your soul and become whole again."

"I want to be made human after she dies," Malcolm says with no hesitation in the request. "I don't want to live here any longer than I have to after she's gone."

God nods. "I will grant you your wish if you ask it of Me. But I hope you will reconsider the request before that time comes."

"What would be the point?"

"I have only wanted what was best for you, Malcolm. And I think you would miss out on your own happiness one day if you chose to end your life prematurely."

"I don't see how I could possibly find happiness without Lilly being with me to share in it."

God sighs. "Lilly was never yours to have," He says as a gentle reminder. "I think you know that."

"Yes," Malcolm admits. "I've known that for some time now. I've accepted it. But I feel happier with her as just a friend than I have ever felt with anyone else. You know what her death will do to me. If I had the luxury of becoming human now, I would. But since Brand is human, I feel like I need to remain the way I am to watch over her and the kids. No," Malcolm says resolutely, "the day Lilly passes from this world into Heaven is the day I want you to make me human, so I can eventually die, too."

Night turns into day again.

Malcolm is standing on top of a half-built structure, looking down at a man leaning against an exposed post, staring at a mountain in the distance. Malcolm phases to the man.

The man turns his head to look at Malcolm, but he doesn't

seem surprised by his sudden appearance. Malcolm has visited Aiden quite a bit in the last few months. He even helped Aiden design the house he's building. It's a home Malcolm knows Aiden plans to share with Caylin one day, a home where they can raise their children and build a life together.

"How did it go?" Aiden asks.

Malcolm grins.

"She loved it," Malcolm says. "But I'm sure she would have loved it even more if I had strapped you to the hood of the car instead of a big red bow."

Aiden smiles shyly and chuckles. He turns his head to look back at the mountain.

"I'm not ready," Aiden admits. I can feel the pride Malcolm has in Aiden in that moment. "She deserves to have all of me, and I'm just now beginning to regain who I was before the curse."

"Well, if it's any consolation," Malcolm says, crossing his arms over his chest, "I wouldn't let you near her anyway, not yet at least."

"I've never felt this kind of love before," Aiden confesses. "There isn't anything I wouldn't do for Caylin. She could ask me for the world, and I would find a way to give it to her. Have you ever felt this way about anyone?"

"All the time."

Aiden looks at Malcolm.

"Lilly?" Aiden asks knowingly.

"I've given her everything I can," Malcolm tells him, "everything she'll let me."

"You're stronger than I've ever given you credit for," Aiden tells him. "I've always thought of you as selfish and conceited. And you are. ..."

Malcolm looks over at Aiden and sees the other man's smile.

"But," Aiden continues, "when it comes to Lilly and her

family, I think you're the most generous and humble person I know."

"Two words I never thought anyone would use to describe me," Malcolm admits but is secretly proud to hear.

"When the time is right," Aiden says in all seriousness, "I will be that for Caylin, too. I want you to know that I'll protect her with my life and never do anything to hurt her."

"I feel that I've made it abundantly clear what will happen if you do hurt her," Malcolm says ominously.

"You'll never have to worry about that," Aiden assures him with such certainty Malcolm can find no reason not to believe him. "Hurting her would kill me faster than you could."

The scene changes again, and Malcolm is lying in a bed with his back propped up against some pillows. I know this takes place after the first hellhound attack Malcolm suffered. He's in excruciating physical pain but somehow finds a way to hide it from Lilly. He doesn't want her to worry any more about him than she already does.

"Here, drink this," Lilly tells him, handing him a glass filled with tea.

Malcolm has to force himself to drink it, but he does because he knows it will make Lilly feel better.

"Thank you, dearest," he tells her as he hands the glass back to her.

"Do you want some more?" Lilly asks, looking like she needs to do something, anything, to help Malcolm.

"No, not right now," he says, trying to sound stronger than he is but not quite making it.

Caylin walks over to the side of the bed.

"How do you feel?" she asks.

"A little tired," Malcolm tells her. "I'll be fine, though. Don't worry about me."

"Any … pain?" a blond-haired man asks, and from Malcolm's memories I know the man is Mason.

"There's some," Malcolm admits. "But not as much as there was at first. Whatever you did seems to have alleviated the vast majority of it."

Both Caylin and Mason narrow their eyes on Malcolm, and he knows they can sense he isn't telling the whole truth. It's then I realize my sixth sense in being able to tell when someone is lying to me is inherited.

Malcolm tells them about a fight he had with one of the seven princes, Baal, and how the hellhound found an opening during the fight to bite him on the leg.

"Are you hungry?" Lilly asks afterwards. "You need to keep up your strength."

Malcolm looks into Lilly's worried brown eyes and hates that he's the one who has made her so sad. She's been acting strangely ever since she and Caylin got back from their trip to Heaven. He doesn't know what's wrong, but he can tell she's hiding something from him.

"If it would make you feel better," Malcolm tells her, "I will eat whatever you bring me."

"Okay," Lilly says, standing up. "I'll be right back."

Malcolm watches her phase and secretly hopes Lilly doesn't try to cook something for him herself. He knows that she's so worried about him she might lose her common sense. Lilly is talented in many things, but cooking is apparently not one of them.

Caylin sits down in the spot her mother just vacated. She leans in to give Malcolm a hug. Malcolm hears her gasp when she touches him and instantly knows she used a bracelet that once belonged to Jess on him. He knows that she's felt the pain he's in, but he's grateful in the knowledge that she can't distinguish the physical pain he feels from the hellhound bite from the emotional pain he's lived with since the day Lilly and Brand were married.

Malcolm gently presses his lips to one of Caylin's ears and whispers, "Don't tell anyone."

Caylin holds onto him even tighter, as if silently telling him she's fully aware that the pain he feels in that moment will never go away.

With each passing year, Malcolm watches Lilly and her family grow. And with each passing year, he watches as more and more wrinkles line her face and sees her body weaken due to the passage of time. He's never considered time his enemy, but now he considers it his nemesis because it's slowly taking the person he loves away from him. There is no battle he can fight to save her, and there is no miracle cure to return her to her youth. All he can do is watch and pray that his father will keep his promise that after Lilly's death He'll make Malcolm human so he, too, can pass from this Earth in time.

In the next memory, Malcolm is sitting in a porch swing with a frail, much older Lilly wrapped securely in a wool blanket sitting on his lap. Her head is leaned against his shoulder as they look out across a blue lake to a distant mountainside. I know they're at the home Malcolm built Lilly all those years ago. It's the place she's chosen to die.

"Malcolm," Lilly says in a weak voice.

Malcolm looks down at the woman he loves, holding back the pain he feels as he looks at her, knowing he will lose her soon.

"Yes, dearest?"

"I have to ask you to do something for me."

Malcolm sees the tears in Lilly's eyes and knows what's coming.

He's known it for a long time now but hoped through the years that they might find a way around it.

"You know I would do anything for you," he tells her, brushing a stray gray hair off her cheek.

"I need you to stay alive," she tells him. "I need you to protect my family until the girl from the vision is born. She'll need your help."

In his heart, Malcolm knew this would be the price he would have to pay for loving someone he was never supposed to. In a way, he felt like God was punishing him all over again for such a sin. No one knew how long it would be before the girl who was supposed to take the seven seals back from the princes of Hell would be born. But just the fact that she lived in a city built in the clouds told Malcolm it would be more years than he wanted to think about.

"I don't want to live that long without you, dearest," Malcolm tells her, secretly hoping she won't make him promise to stay on Earth after she's gone.

A single tear rolls down one of Lilly's wrinkled cheeks. Malcolm leans in and kisses the path of her tear away, wiping away all evidence of its existence.

"You must," Lilly says in a sob.

Malcolm holds her closer to him as she cries. His heart feels like it will collapse in on itself, but he knows what he has to do.

"Then I promise you I will," he says to her, even though he would rather die in that moment than live without her in his life. "I will protect them all and help the girl when she's born."

The scene switches to one inside the house.

Lilly is lying in a bed, and Brand is sitting beside her, holding her hand. The room is filled with Lilly's children, their children, and their children's children.

Malcolm stands in the background and simply watches, because he knows there is nothing he can do to stop what's about to happen. For one of the few times in his life, he feels completely helpless. Death isn't an adversary he can fight against. It's simply the natural progression of a human life, and there's nothing he can do about it.

Lilly stares up at Brand with the same love and devotion I saw on her face on her wedding day.

"Thank you," she tells him. "Thank you for giving me such a beautiful life."

Brand reaches out with his free hand, caressing one side of her face.

"This isn't the end for us," he assures her.

Lilly nods her head, letting him know she understands that they'll eventually be reunited in Heaven.

"And I'll be waiting there for you when it's your time to come to me."

"I have a feeling it won't be a long wait," Brand says, his voice breaking. "I don't think my heart can beat for very long without you near it."

She smiles lovingly at him just before she closes her eyes, like she's about to go to sleep. I can hear one last shuddering breath come from her parted lips, marking her passage from this world into the next.

Malcolm feels someone staring at him and looks away from Lilly to meet Caylin's gaze.

Of anyone in the room, she knows the pain he feels. She knows that he will have to live with the loss of Lilly for many years to come.

Malcolm phases away from the room, knowing he won't be able to hide the pain he feels over the loss of Lilly for very much longer, especially not from Caylin.

He goes to the beach where they spent that day before her marriage to Brand. It's nighttime, and a multitude of stars fills the sky.

Malcolm falls to his knees, holding his head in his hands. His pain is beyond the relief tears would bring. It's an agony that rips him apart at the seams, and he doesn't feel like he'll ever be whole again, at least not while he remains on Earth. He continues to kneel on the sugar- white sand, filled with such unimaginable pain I simply can't stand it anymore.

I feel myself separate from Malcolm. I stand beside him and place my hand on his bowed head, hoping to bring him out of the torture his memories are causing him and back to reality, a reality I can make better if only he would let me.

As soon as he feels my touch, his head snaps up. He stares at me like he doesn't know who I am, but then the memory of me seems to flood back into his mind.

"What are you doing here?" he demands, standing to his feet in one swift motion, towering over me. "You shouldn't be here!"

I shake my head. "I'm not even sure where 'here' is."

"You had no right to see my memories of her!" he roars as the ground beneath my feet begins to tremble and the stars fall from the sky in quick succession.

"I'm s-s-sorry," I stammer, feeling frightened of Malcolm for the first time since we met. "I didn't mean to. I just fell asleep and found myself here in your memories."

Malcolm grabs my arms and squeezes hard as he shoves his face right in front of mine.

"You will never replace her!" he says, his features twisted into a mask of rage. "I don't care what you feel for me. I don't care what you might think is supposed to happen between us. I don't care what mind games my father is trying to play. Lilly is the woman I gave my heart to, and you're simply a cheap imitation of who she was. You will never mean as much to me as she does. Now, get out of my head!"

Malcolm shoves me back so hard I begin to fall, but I never reach the ground.

I wake up.

"Get away from me."

I lift my head from Malcolm's chest and look at his face.

He still looks drained from the recent hellhound attack, but the total and utter disgust in his eyes as he looks at me isn't tempered by his weakened state.

"Get away from me *now*," he orders with more vehemence.

I want to say I'm sorry, but I'm not exactly sure what I should be sorry for. How was I able to slip into his dreams and share his memories? I don't understand what just happened, but Malcolm doesn't look like he's in any mood to explain things to me.

I sit up and then stand. Malcolm grabs the edge of the blanket and lifts it to his chin. He turns onto his left side to face away from me and doesn't say another word.

I stand there not knowing what to do, but Malcolm obviously knows exactly what he wants me to do.

"Leave," he says.

I don't want to leave, but I feel as though I owe him the courtesy of doing as he says. It was never my intention to invade his private thoughts, but I'm not sure he understands that. I think his emotions are still too raw from reliving the time he spent with Lilly to think straight. I turn my back to him and walk into the foyer. I sit down on the bottom step of the small staircase there and lean my head against the wall.

Malcolm's last words to me inside his dreamworld echo in the corners of my mind over and over again.

"Lilly is the woman I gave my heart to, and you're simply a cheap imitation of who she was. You will never mean as much to me as she does."

What would Malcolm think of his Lilly if he knew she'd visited me instead of him?

The moment I saw Lilly in Malcolm's memories I knew who she was. She was the woman I knocked down the night of my wedding party as I made my way home through the streets of Cirrus. She called herself Rayne Cole then. She was the one who told me I should fight for Malcolm because he was worth fighting for.

I simply didn't know at the time that my fight would be against his memories of her—memories which seemed to be so fresh to him they could have happened yesterday instead of a thousand years ago.

I close my eyes to just rest them for a moment, because I feel so tired from everything that's happened, everything I've learned in such a short span of time.

I faintly remember that it's still my birthday.

"Happy birthday, Anna," I say out loud before gifting myself with the solace of sleep.

CHAPTER 17

I'm awoken the next morning by the smell of something being cooked close by. I feel my stomach grumble its discontent at being left completely empty and ravenously hungry. I cautiously stand up and stretch my legs. My body feels like someone beat it during the night, but everything seems to still be working properly. I cautiously peek around the corner and find Malcolm kneeling on one knee with one arm resting against his raised leg in front of the fireplace. I lean back and take a deep, calming breath. I have no idea what to say to him this morning. After seeing his memories of Lilly the night before, I feel like I know Malcolm better, but it wasn't in the way I wanted to learn more about him. I feel like I invaded his privacy, his deepest and most close-kept secrets, and from the way he reacted last night, I feel sure that's the way he feels, too.

There's nothing I can do to change what happened. I didn't do it on purpose. I just hope he realizes that fact in the light of day.

I take another deep breath and walk around the corner to face whatever mood Malcolm might be in this morning.

I walk until I'm standing beside him.

"That smells good," I tell him as I see the four fish he has roasting over the fire on metal skewers.

Malcolm is silent for a while but then says, "I thought you might be hungry."

"Where did you get the fish?"

This makes Malcolm look up at me with a raised eyebrow.

"I know you've lived in Cirrus all your life, but surely Andre educated you."

"Of course he educated me," I say in defense of my papa.

"Then what lives in an ocean, Anna?" Malcolm asks a bit condescendingly.

I feel my cheeks burn. "Fish."

Malcolm looks back at the fire. "And the empress gets a gold star for answering correctly."

He doesn't say anything else, and he doesn't look like he intends to say anything else any time soon.

"I'm sorry," I blurt out, feeling an uncontrollable urge to make things right between us, and an apology seems like a good place to start.

Malcolm bows his head and closes his eyes.

"You couldn't have understood what you were doing," he says in a low voice. "I know that."

"What did I do?" I ask, needing to know so I can prevent it from ever happening again. "How did I go into your dreams?"

"All Watchers are able to construct their dreamworlds to be whatever they want them to be. Your ability to join our dreams was inherited. There's no way you could have prevented it from happening."

I want to ask more about what I saw and experienced inside his dreamworld, but I don't want to push the matter. He's talking to me, and I'm just grateful for that small miracle.

"You need to know something," Malcolm says, looking back up at me. "What I said to you there at the end … on the beach. …"

I hold my breath and wait for him to finish.

"I meant every word," he tells me. "I thought it only right that you know what I said was real and not just part of a dream."

I feel my heart twist inside my chest and suddenly hate Malcolm for making me feel this way. I want to hurt him like he's just hurt me, and I know just how to do it.

"I've met Lilly before," I tell him, selfishly hoping my next words hurt him. "I met her on my way home the night of the wedding celebration in Cirrus."

Malcolm stands to his feet in one fluid motion and turns to me.

"That's impossible," he says confidently, looking at me like he thinks I'm a liar.

"She told me her name was Rayne Cole when we met," I tell him, and I can see by the surprised expression on his face that the name instantly registers with him.

"What did she say to you?" Malcolm asks in a whisper.

"She asked about the wedding. I told her I didn't love the emperor because I had feelings for someone else. She also gave me some advice. …"

"What advice?"

"She told me I should fight for the person I did care about because he was worth fighting for."

Malcolm shakes his head. "It couldn't have been Lilly."

"Why? Because she chose to come see me instead of you?" I ask. "Has she not come to you in all the years you've been waiting for me to be born?"

Malcolm is completely silent, giving me my answer.

I can see the hurt I've caused enter his eyes. His perfect Lilly isn't quite so perfect anymore. I should feel happy because I did exactly what I set out to do with my revelation, but instead, I feel

Malcolm's pain as he realizes the woman he gave his heart to abandoned him in more ways than one.

I take a step forward, intent on trying to comfort him, but Malcolm turns away from me and walks over to the couch where his shirt and jacket from the night before have been laid out to dry. He slips on the white undershirt and then the jacket.

"I'll be back," he says and walks past the makeshift curtain I put up the night before in front of the broken glass doors.

I watch him go and feel a sting of guilt from causing him even more pain than what he's already suffering through.

"Malcolm will be all right," I hear a man say behind me.

I look back at the fire and see a man with dark skin and a bald head standing there. I know who He is because I saw Him in Malcolm's memories the night before.

"God?" I ask, simply needing clarification that He's actually there and not just a wishful figment of my imagination.

God smiles at me. "Hello, Anna."

"Why are you here?" I ask Him.

"I thought you might need a friend right about now."

I sigh, realizing a friend is exactly what I need. But that's not all I need from God. I need some answers, too.

"Did you make me for Malcolm?" I ask, needing to know if our connection to one another is real or if I'm simply deluding myself.

"If you're asking me if the two of you are soul mates," God says, "then the answer to that question is yes. But I wouldn't say I made *you* for Malcolm."

"What's the difference?"

"Has it not occurred to you by now that I might have made Malcolm for *you*?"

"Made him for me?" I ask, completely confused. "Didn't you make Malcolm before you made me?"

"Your soul was made in the Guf a very long time ago, Anna. In fact, you were one of the first souls ever created. I've known for quite some time I would need you to fulfill an important mission one day, one only you can accomplish."

"To take back the seven seals?" I ask, not knowing of anything else I was sent to Earth to do.

"I have hope that you can also accomplish something else during your mission to retrieve the seals. I've been waiting longer than anyone for you to be born, Anna. I simply hope you can do something many have tried to do, including Me, but failed."

I can tell God isn't going to go into any more details about this special mission He apparently thinks only I can undertake. So I decide to get as much information on other subjects as I can from Him while He's here.

"Do you know where my papa is?" I ask. If anyone should know where my father is, it would be God.

God nods. "Yes, I know where he is, and I can tell you he's perfectly safe for now."

"Where is he?"

"I'm sorry. I can't tell you that. I don't like to interfere with the natural progression of events. You'll find him soon enough on your own."

"If you can't tell me that," I say, "can you tell me how to make Malcolm face his feelings for me?"

"I believe you'll be able to find a way to do that on your own, too, Anna."

"And you're sure You made Malcolm for me? Because I feel sure I wouldn't have asked for someone so hardheaded."

God chuckles. "Malcolm is exactly who you need. I think you know that."

"Are you sure *he* does?"

God smiles. "He knows. He's just fighting against the idea because of his feelings for Lilly."

"Will he ever be able to let her go?"

God tilts His head to the side as He considers the question.

"Would you want him to let her go so easily after finding out how he truly feels about her? Would it make you feel better if he was able to completely forget his feelings for someone he's loved for so long? Is that the type of man you would want to be with?"

I think about God's questions and realize how crucial Malcolm's feelings for Lilly are to who he is. Once Malcolm gives his love to someone, it isn't just a transient event. It's forever.

"I don't want to make him forget her," I admit, not only to God but to myself. "I just want him to stop hiding behind his feelings for her and using them to push me away."

"I have no doubt you will be able to make him stop hiding, Anna. He just needs some time to come to terms with what he feels when he's with you."

"Why hasn't Lilly visited Malcolm like she did me the other night?"

"Lilly knew Malcolm would have a hard time letting her go. She felt it would be unfair to him for her to come back after her death. We all hoped he would move on, on his own."

"He hasn't," I tell him. "Not if what I witnessed last night is any indication."

"Have faith in your love, Anna. Have faith that it was always meant to be. Not even Malcolm's memories of Lilly will be able to change that fact. Malcolm will come to understand that in his own time. He simply has to reach a point where he's able to allow Lilly to be a part of his past and make you his future."

"I don't suppose you know how long that will take?" I ask hopefully.

God smiles. "If I know you at all, I feel sure it won't be much longer. You have always been rather tenacious, especially when it comes to something you really want."

"You sound like You've known me for a long time," I say, finding it strange the way God talks about my past in Heaven.

"Like I said, you were one of the first souls ever created. I've known you for longer than this Earth has been in existence."

"Why did You wait so long to send me here then?"

"Because it took some time to get things ready for you. It's just like a good chess game. You have to have all your pieces in place before you bring out your queen. All of My pieces are now in play. It's simply a matter of whether or not the game can actually be won."

"Can't all games be won?"

"Not necessarily. Sometimes there are no winners."

I hear Malcolm's heavy footfalls on the back porch, indicating he's about to reenter the room.

"Keep your faith in your love for Malcolm," God tells me. "If you need Me, simply pray, and I will come."

God vanishes just as Malcolm moves the makeshift curtains hanging over the broken glass doors.

"I thought I heard you talking to someone in here," Malcolm says as he lets the curtains fall back into place behind him, surveying the near-empty room.

"I was," I say, not seeing any reason to lie. "God came to see me."

Malcolm looks surprised at first but then just rolls his eyes and shakes his head.

"Of course He did. Seems like everyone in Heaven wants to come down and have a little chat with you."

"I'm sorry I told you about Lilly coming to see me," I tell him, feeling a need to confess why I did it. "I wanted to hurt you, and it seemed the easiest way. I hope you can forgive me for being so selfish."

"You didn't hurt me," he says with a heavy sigh. "She did, by coming to see you instead of me. And I'm sorry if what I said in the dream hurt you, but it's the truth, and I don't want to give you any false hope about the two of us."

"I don't accept that."

Malcolm looks confused. "I don't think you have a choice," he says bluntly.

"I don't accept that you can only love one person," I tell him. "Plus, I have it on good authority that you were made for me, Malcolm Devereaux. I think the sooner you accept that fact, the happier we'll both be."

"Made for you?" Malcolm asks, continuing to look baffled. "You *do* realize I'm far older than you are, right?"

"My soul was one of the first ever created," I tell him. "So, in point of fact, I'm probably older than you think. Possibly even older than you. So you can try to hide behind your love for Lilly and push me away, but you need to know that—"

A heavy knock resounds against the front door and echoes throughout the house, effectively interrupting what was supposed to be my confession of love. I had intended to lay all my cards out on the table and not hide anything from Malcolm, but apparently a higher power doesn't think it is the right time.

Malcolm walks out of the room to the front of the house and opens the door.

"About time you got here," Malcolm grouses to whoever knocked.

"Sorry," I hear a familiar voice say. "It took me a while to find a safe way out of New York without drawing suspicion."

I walk around the corner of the room toward the front of the house and see Jered step over the threshold wearing a heavy, black, hooded cloak.

He smiles at me when our eyes meet, and I feel thankful to see a friendly face.

Jered's eyes take in my outfit in one sweeping glance.

"It looks good on you," he compliments. "Like you were born to wear it."

Before I can even respond, Malcolm asks gruffly, "Did you bring the horses and the other things I asked for?"

Jered lowers the hood of his black cloak.

"Yes, everything is outside."

"There's fish cooking on the fire," Malcolm tells him brusquely. "You and Anna should eat before we leave."

Malcolm doesn't say another word before he walks out the door, slamming it rather harshly behind him.

Jered returns his gaze to me and looks troubled.

"What happened?" he asks.

"Maybe I should tell you everything while we eat," I say. "I get the feeling Malcolm's in a hurry to leave."

I go on to tell Jered everything about what happened the night before. I also tell him something I haven't had time to even tell Malcolm.

"Lucifer came here last night after the hellhound attack."

Jered stops eating and leans the skewer his half-eaten fish is still on against the side of the fireplace.

"What did he say to you?"

"Not much. From what little he *did* say, though, I know he's my biological father, even if he didn't exactly admit to it."

Jered's eyes slide to the floor before meeting mine again.

"I'm sorry you had to find out like that."

"Is that why Malcolm sent me away when I was born?" I ask. "Because I'm the child of the devil himself?"

"Malcolm and Lucifer have hated each other for eons, Anna. That part of it has nothing to do with you. When your mother fell in love with Lucifer, it broke something inside Malcolm. He felt like he completely failed in his mission to keep the line of descendants safe. I think he's only now realizing that it was all part of God's plan. It was an important piece of the puzzle none of us understood until after you took Amon's seal from him."

"When I told Levi I killed Amon," I say, "he didn't believe me. He said even my real father couldn't kill an archangel. Do you know how I was able to do it? Have all the descendants been able to kill archangels?"

"No, they haven't. You're the only person, besides God Himself, who has ever been able to destroy an archangel. I've been thinking about that since Amon's death, though," Jered admits. "The only logical explanation I can come up with is the fact that you are the only child of Lucifer and you are a descendant of Michael."

"Michael?" I ask, thinking over what I know of the Bible and what my father taught me. "Archangel Michael?"

"He was Lilly's father," Jered says. "You are one of his descendants, too. A connection between what Michael passed on to Lilly and Caylin and what Lucifer passed on to you must have been made when you were conceived. I don't think I'm over exaggerating when I say you are the most powerful angel and/or human to ever be born, Anna. You're stronger than any angel I know of and most definitely stronger than any human who has ever existed."

"What does that make me?" I ask, suddenly feeling like I'm having an identity crisis. "I'm not completely human, and I'm not completely an angel."

Jered shrugs his shoulders. "You're something unique. There's nothing wrong with being different."

"God said that my mission to retrieve the seals is also meant to help me accomplish something no one else has been able to do yet. Do you know what He was talking about?"

Jered pauses to think about what I just said before answering. "No. I can't say that I do. Did He give you any other hints?"

"No. That's all He said."

Jered sighs. "Our father has never been very forthcoming when it comes to giving us helpful information. I suppose you've figured that much out on your own by now."

"Yes, I did. But I don't think He means for it to be as aggravating as it is."

Jered laughs.

"No, I don't think so either, but it always tends to feel that way."

Jered's laughter dies, and his expression turns serious.

"I know what Malcolm said in the dream must have hurt you," he tells me. "But I think you're smart enough to understand he said those things because he's trying to push you away. I think he's holding onto his memories of Lilly so hard, especially now, because he's rebelling against the idea that he can care for someone else just as much as, or even more, than her. Don't give up on him, Anna. He needs you more than he realizes or is willing to admit to himself."

"I have every intention of fighting for him," I tell Jered. "God made him for me, at least that's what He said, and I know it wasn't a lie. Malcolm is mine, and I'm his."

Jered smiles at me and nods his head. "Good. Just keep that in mind when he tries to push you away next time. I have no doubt he'll keep trying. I just hope he comes to his senses before you get tired of forcing him to face his feelings."

We hear the front door open and know that Malcolm has returned. The sound of hard- soled shoes walking across the floor-boards gets louder as he approaches. I turn my head to see Malcolm walk around the corner and into the room.

He's wearing a sleeveless, hooded, long black duster coat. On each arm he has black leather bracers with silver bindings. Underneath the coat, he's bare-chested but wearing black leather pants with silver striped accents across the thighs and a silver buckled belt cinched around his waist. The boots are matching black leather with thick, heavy soles.

With the hood of the cloak pulled over his head, Malcolm looks the part of an overlord.

"We should get going," Malcolm says to us. "We have a long way to travel today."

"Where are we going?" I ask.

"I need to visit a friend near New Orleans and pick up a package I left with them," Malcolm says. "We can't use a public teleporter. Levi would have to be an idiot not to have people watching all of the teleporters in this part of the country after our escape."

"Are we going to ride horses all the way to New Orleans?" I ask, mentally calculating where we are versus where I know New Orleans is located.

"No, that would take too much time," Malcolm tells me. "But there are always people willing to do things for a price."

"I really don't like doing business with that man," Jered says, standing to his feet and offering me a hand up.

"What man?" I ask, accepting his assistance in standing.

"He's a black marketer we do business with on occasion," Jered tells me. "His name is Bartholomew, and he's about as trustworthy as a snake."

"He can get us to New Orleans today instead of a week from now," Malcolm argues. "And we need to move the package I stashed before Levi finds it."

"What's in this package that's so important?" I ask.

"You don't need to concern yourself with it," Malcolm says dismissively. "As soon as I finish helping you retrieve the seals, you and I will be parting ways, and I have no intention of ever seeing you again, Anna. The package will be of no consequence to you after that."

Malcolm turns his back to me and heads toward the door without waiting to make sure we're following him outside.

I hear Jered sigh beside me, and I turn to look at him.

"That man is too stubborn for his own good sometimes," he mutters.

I look back the way Malcolm disappeared and say, "Don't worry, Jered. Everything will work out the way it's meant to."

"You sound confident."

I look back at Jered. "I am confident."

"Why?"

"Because I know in my heart that we're meant to be together. He just needs to stop fighting what he feels for me."

"What if he doesn't?"

"Then I'll let him go."

Jered tilts his head, like he's confused by what I just said. "Why would you do that?"

"Because I love him, and I want him to be happy. If his memories of Lilly make him happier than I can, then I don't deserve him. But I won't let go unless there's no hope, and I don't think I've reached that point yet."

"Now I know the bloody fool doesn't deserve you," Jered grumbles. "You're far too good for him, Anna."

"Malcolm does deserve me," I say. "He just has to accept the fact that he's earned the right to be happy. I think that's hard for him to believe. He's been so hard on himself for so many years that the mere thought of a happy ending with someone who loves him the way I do has become a foreign concept, an intangible wish he never thought possible."

"You're right," Jered admits with a sigh. "I think Malcolm gave up on finding someone who could even compare to Lilly a long time ago."

"I don't want to replace her in his life. She's too important to who he is. I understand that now. I also think his heart is big enough to love us both equally, if not me just a smidge more."

Jered smiles. "I think you could make him love you more than just a smidge."

"But that's just it, Jered. I don't want to *make* him love me." I look back at where Malcolm disappeared. "I want him to give me his heart all on his own."

CHAPTER 18

I just stand and stare dumbfounded at the horse I've been assigned. It's huge—gargantuan, in fact. I feel totally intimidated by it because I know underneath its black and white coat beats the heart of a living creature with a mind of its own. The only other real animals I've ever seen were the hellhounds, and they seemed far less formidable than the horse pawing at the earth with one of its giant, hairy front legs and snorting at me. At least I knew where I stood with the hellhounds: kill them or die. Apparently I'm expected to entrust the creature in front of me with my life to provide me safe passage to wherever it is we're going today.

"Do these things come in a smaller size?" I ask hopefully, looking to Malcolm for an answer as he stands beside his own jet black behemoth, tightening the cinch of its saddle.

Malcolm looks over at me, and I see one corner of his mouth lift in a reluctant half-smile, like what I just said amused him in spite of himself.

"Just get on," Malcolm says, walking over to me. "She might look formidable, but she's actually very docile. She's been trained to just follow behind my horse. You shouldn't actually have to do anything but stay in the saddle."

I look back at the horse and realize I can't even reach the pommel of the saddle to lift myself into the seat.

"Can you at least help me get on?" I ask Malcolm.

Malcolm walks behind me, placing his hands on either side of my waist, easily lifting me with both of his hands by the waist.

"Put your left foot into the stirrup," he instructs.

I do as he says and feel his right hand slide from my side to underneath my bottom as he supports me there to help give me a little added push as I swing my leg around to the other side. The stirrups end up being too long, and Malcolm takes a little time to shorten the straps so I can rest my feet against them. He gently places my left foot into its stirrup and then walks around to place my right one in the stirrup on that side. I feel his hand linger on my calf a little longer than it needs to, like maybe he doesn't want to stop touching me. But the moment is fleeting, and he walks away without saying a word. I involuntarily sigh my disappointment as I watch him leave my side.

My discontent must be obvious. When I look over at Jered standing by his own horse, he winks at me, silently giving me some encouragement.

As we leave the little cottage by the beach, I suddenly have mixed feelings about abandoning it. I want to get started on the mission God sent me to Earth to accomplish, yet so much happened inside the little home in such a short period of time. I met Will, my best friend while I was in Heaven and my guardian angel here on Earth. I discovered who my biological father is. And I met God. How many people get to claim they met the Lord and the devil himself within a few hours of each other?

I also learned so much about Malcolm when I was inside his dreamworld—things I'm glad to know and not glad to know. As my father used to tell me, knowledge is power. I just hope something that I saw in his dreams will help me find a way to make him finally open up to me.

During the ride, we keep to the forest for the most part. It makes the ride a bit slower, but I suppose the cover provided by the trees keeps us safe from prying eyes and surveillance drones. Malcolm and Jered ride ahead of me, quietly speaking to one another for the most part, leaving me to follow behind them. I don't mind the solitude. It gives me time to think and consider things like how in the world I'm going to break down the wall Malcolm has built around his heart.

Not to sound completely immodest, but I know I'm beautiful. Physically, I have all the attributes a man would find attractive. Yet it doesn't seem to be enough for Malcolm. He has probably been living on Earth so long that physical beauty doesn't impress him anymore. I'm smart, but so is he. I wrack my brain for almost an hour, trying to think of some way to make him face the connection we share, but a solution doesn't readily present itself.

While I'm lost in my own thoughts, I don't notice Malcolm bring his horse to a halt, jump off, and storm toward me, looking completely furious, until it's too late.

He wraps an arm around my waist and unceremoniously yanks me out of my saddle with little effort, practically slamming my back against the nearest tree trunk.

"Why didn't you tell me you saw Lucifer last night?" he demands, his face so close to mine his warm breath mingles with my own.

"Considering everything else that happened last night," I say, trying to catch my breath from the unexpected attack, "it kind of slipped my mind."

"You should have told me first, not Jered," Malcolm says,

hitting his fist above my head in aggravation, causing the trunk of the tree to tremble behind me.

"Yes, I should have," I agree. "I just forgot, Malcolm. I didn't mean any disrespect by it."

Malcolm pushes back from me and turns to walk a couple of steps away.

"What exactly did he say to you?" Malcolm asks, turning around to face me again. "Why was he even there last night?"

"He said he came to see how much I looked like my mother," I say. "He's the one who told me to use my sword to seal your wounds, and he also said the curse you're under can be cured but that the person who can lift it probably wouldn't do it even if you asked."

Malcolm shakes his head as he looks at me in disappointment. "And here I thought you were smart."

I bristle at the remark, but it doesn't take me long to understand why he made it.

"It's his curse, isn't it? Lucifer is the one who can take your pain away."

"And yet another gold star for the empress," Malcolm says scathingly. "You're just racking them up today, Anna."

"Malcolm," Jered says almost like a reprimand, coming to stand with us, "there's no need to be rude to her just because you're in a bad mood. All of this is new to Anna. You can't expect her to understand every single little thing in a day. We've lived with it for centuries. Cut her some slack."

When I look back at Malcolm, I can see Jered's words have sunk into his thick skull, somewhat at least.

"Then maybe you should educate her," Malcolm grumbles. "It's not like we have anything else better to do on the ride to Bartholomew's place."

Malcolm walks back over to his horse and settles himself in his saddle, waiting on us.

"Come on," Jered says, holding his hand out to me. "I'll help you back onto your horse and tell you all you need to know about your family history while we ride."

For the rest of the day, Jered and I ride side by side as he explains everything important about my family. I sit in amazement at the stories he weaves about them all. All I can think while I'm listening is that I hope I can live up to the high standards they have set for me. I don't want to be the one member of my family who fails in her mission from God. I don't want to disappoint all those who laid the ground-work before me and not accomplish the important task God thinks only I can achieve, even if I'm not sure what all that encompasses.

Near nightfall, I feel like I understand things a lot better. I have a clearer image of what needs to be done.

"So when will we be going to the other Watchers so I can take the seals from the princes?" I ask.

"As soon as possible," Malcolm grumbles, still riding ahead of us but apparently listening in on our conversation. He hasn't said a word since the earlier altercation, but to be honest, I was so enthralled with the tales Jered told I didn't pay him too much mind until now.

"We'll get to them," Jered promises me, ignoring Malcolm completely. "The princes are safely hidden where each of the other Watchers put them."

"So, how did Amon escape?" I ask. "He was hidden by my papa, right?"

"Yes," Jered says. "We assume Levi probably blackmailed Andre into giving up his location somehow. Odds are it was part of the deal to release you from prison. But Andre wouldn't have had any doubts that you would kill Amon. It was the one thing we knew would happen at some point. You were never in any real danger from him. It was just a part of your destiny."

"How many Watchers are still here on Earth?" I ask.

"Just the ones put in charge of keeping the princes safe. All of the others either found their soul mates and lived their lives out as humans or died."

"Papa never found his soul mate?" I ask.

Jered smiles. "After you were born, Andre said he couldn't imagine ever feeling more love for anyone else. On your first birthday, he asked God to make him human because he just couldn't bear the thought of outliving you. Over the years, we've had to watch all of the people we've loved die, but the thought of enduring your death just wasn't something Andre could see himself doing. I think that's when I finally understood how sure Andre was that you were the one we had been waiting for. That's when I started to believe he was right."

"God said Papa is safe," I tell them, realizing this was something else I forgot to mention. "But He wouldn't tell me where he was. He said He doesn't like to interfere with the natural progression of events."

"Typical," Malcolm mumbles in irritation, keeping his back to us as we continue to ride through the forest.

I look over at Jered.

"So what do you normally do about that," I say, nodding my head in Malcolm's direction, "when it happens?"

It takes Jered a minute to understand what I'm really asking, but then he smiles as realization dawns.

"Sometimes it's just better to let grumpy bears lie until they can learn to be *civil*," Jered tells me, not bothering to lower his voice and actually raising it. "We've learned over the years that it likes to growl, but surprisingly enough it rarely bites."

"If you're trying to hide the fact that you're talking about me by using a metaphor," Malcolm grouses, "you're doing a piss-poor job of it."

"I don't believe I was trying to hide that fact at all," Jered says, completely unapologetic. "In fact, I hope it makes you realize what a total ass you're being to Anna."

Malcolm doesn't reply, just keeps riding on ahead like Jered didn't even speak.

I look over at Jered and see him scrunch up his face like a grouchy old man. I instantly know he's doing his best imitation of Malcolm and can't help but giggle.

Jered looks over at me and smiles.

"That's better." He leans slightly toward me in his saddle and whispers, "And don't worry about the grumpy old bear. He'll come around eventually."

I nod my head, letting Jered know I heard what he said and silently hope that he's right. I also steel myself for the real possibility that I'll have to do what I said to Jered and let Malcolm go someday. I pray it doesn't come to that point, but if it does, if I can't make him loosen his grip on Lilly's memory just a bit, I'll leave him alone. I won't have a choice, because my heart can't take much more of this.

I try to keep in mind how he was the night I phased to his room when I was drawn to him because I felt the pain of his soul. He had been so tender and almost loving then. I hold onto that memory because there has to be some part of him that cares for me, possibly even loves me.

Near nightfall, we come upon a ramshackle cabin in the middle of the woods. If you didn't know its exact location, I seriously doubt you would just stumble across it by accident. An elderly man is sitting in a rocking chair, whittling on a small piece of wood. The felt top hat on his head is tattered-looking, and the wool coat he wears must have been black at one time but is now worn to a faded gray. I know he has to have noticed our approach, but he never looks up, just keeps working on his project.

Malcolm brings his horse to a complete stop in front of the house and dismounts. He saunters over to the set of steps leading up to the small porch and rests the sole of his right boot on the bottom step.

"Evening, Harvey," Malcolm says to the man.

Harvey holds up the piece of wood he is working on and surveys his craftsmanship from different angles. Even from where I sit, I can tell he's carved the piece of wood into the shape of a rabbit.

"Evening, Overlord Devereaux," Harvey says, finally tearing his eyes away from his handiwork to look at Malcolm. "Can I help ya?"

"My companions and I need to see Bartholomew," Malcolm says.

Harvey turns his gaze directly to me. "Well, I'll be damned. You do actually have her."

Harvey stands but immediately kneels on the creaky floorboards of the cabin's porch and bows his head in my direction.

"Empress Annalisse," Harvey says reverently. "Welcome to the down-world."

I swing my right leg over the horn of my saddle and hop off my horse.

I walk up the few steps to the porch and stand in front of the man.

"Please stand, Harvey. There's no need to kneel in front of me."

I can tell age is making it hard for Harvey to get to his feet easily. So I place my hands on his forearms and gently help him rise.

"Thank you, Empress Annalisse," Harvey says, keeping his head bowed and not meeting my gaze.

I slip the tip of my index finger underneath his wrinkled chin and tilt his face up until he's looking me in the eyes.

"There's no need to keep your head bowed in front of me," I tell him. "And please, just call me Anna. I'm not much on formal titles when people talk to me."

A touch of amusement brightens Harvey's old brown eyes. A smile stretches his cracked lips, which causes the wrinkles on his face to become even more pronounced.

"How can I help you, Anna?" he asks.

"Could you please take us to Bartholomew? We need his help," I say, basically asking for the same thing Malcolm had, just with a tad more honey in my words.

Harvey holds out a crooked arm for me to take. I slip my arm through his and allow him to escort me into the cabin. I'm faintly aware of Malcolm and Jered following in behind us.

The interior of the cabin looks normal enough with a small bed, table, and cast iron stove inside. On the opposite wall from the front door is another solitary door. Harvey walks me over to this door and opens it to reveal what looks like a square iron cage hanging in an open shaft.

Harvey opens the door of the cage and seems to expect me to get inside.

"What is it?" I ask him.

"It's an elevator," Harvey tells me. "Not as fancy as the ones you have in Cirrus, I'd wager, but it'll getcha down safely to where Barlow is."

I want to look back and confirm this with Malcolm, but I feel like such an action would make Harvey think I don't trust his word. So I simply nod and smile while I step into the elevator.

Malcolm and Jered aren't far behind me. Once all three of us are in the elevator, Harvey closes its door.

"Safe journeys, Anna," Harvey says to me before closing the cabin's interior door.

A light illuminates the ceiling of the elevator as it begins to make its descent down into the earth.

"Where exactly are we going?" I ask.

"Bartholomew practically has his own city built underground," Jered tells me. "It keeps his operation out of sight from the prying eyes of the royal family."

"Isn't he going to be upset that you're bringing the empress of Cirrus into his inner lair?" I ask Malcolm, forcing him to talk to me even if it's just to answer a simple question.

"He won't be upset," Malcolm says, keeping his back to me. "In fact, he's been waiting for you. They all have."

"Waiting for me? Why?"

Malcolm finally turns around as the elevator continues to make its slow descent underground. The hood of his cloak is masking half his face, but that does nothing except make him look even more handsome to my eyes.

"All the down-worlders have been waiting for you to ascend to the throne," Malcolm answers. "Everyone knew that Augustus wasn't anything like his mother or his father. And with someone who was actually born down here ruling by his side, they all have hope that the two of you can change things for the better."

"That was our plan," I tell Malcolm. "I intend to do what Auggie and I wanted to do before Levi killed him. I have every intention of bringing the down-world into the present."

"I plan to give you your chance, Anna," Malcolm says, causing me to catch my breath slightly when he says my name. "And I hope you can accomplish what no one else has been able to."

"I plan to accomplish a great many things during my time," I tell him, hoping he knows winning his heart is at the top of my list.

Malcolm stares at me for a moment then says, "I'm sure you'll try. But you can't always get everything you want."

"I was always taught that if you worked hard enough, you can achieve anything," I reply.

Malcolm tilts his head at me. "And how many times have you failed to get what you want?"

"Never."

"Hmm," Malcolm says, considering my answer. "Well, there's always a first time for everything, Anna."

Malcolm turns around again, seeming to completely dismiss me from his mind.

I feel an elbow gently prod me in my right side. I look over at Jered and see him wink at me. He then proceeds to roll his eyes in Malcolm's direction, looking completely exasperated by the other man's attitude toward me, and shakes his head in dismay.

It makes me smile but doesn't exactly lift my spirits much.

The elevator finally comes to a stop, and I hear the sound of live music being played.

Malcolm opens the door of the elevator and walks out, holding the door open for me and Jered to exit. I feel as though I just stumbled upon a carnival of some sort. There are women dressed in colorful dresses, some of which are in two parts and showing more flesh across the midriff than the people of Cirrus would consider decent. The men are wearing loose-fitting cotton shirts and dark pants. The cavernous space I find myself in looks like a large room carved within a mountain. Lights are strung up from the center of the room's ceiling outward, like a canopy of illumination.

Everyone in the room seems to be captivated by a man and a woman dancing in the center of the room. As a group of musicians plays some lively music off to the side, the couple dances around each other but never seem to touch. They keep their eyes locked on one another as each takes their turn dancing. It's almost like a competition between the two dancers. The woman is wearing a red and black two-piece dress with the top tied together in the front by a knot between her breasts and a long flowing skirt that flares out when she twirls. She tosses her long, curly black hair to the beat of the music during her turn, then stops and holds out her hand to the man, challenging him to try to out-do her.

The man is handsome with short black hair and startling gray-green eyes. His plump lips spread into a smile like he was simply awaiting his chance to take his turn. His dance is composed of a lot of rhythmic stomping of his feet, not as elegant as the woman's dance but nonetheless captivating in its movement. At one point, the man bends his knees and squats down but still manages to keep his balance and kick his booted feet in time with the music. When he stands back up, the music stops, and everyone in the crowd cheers enthusiastically. The woman throws her hands up in the air in defeat but doesn't seem in the least bit angry that she lost.

The man goes up to the woman and says something to her. She leans up and kisses him on the cheek before walking away.

People in the crowd go up to congratulate the man. He graciously accepts their praise but looks modest while doing so. As he's holding court with the crowd in front of him, he notices us standing by the elevator. He makes his excuses to those around him and walks over to us.

"Overlord Devereaux," the man says, holding out his hand to Malcolm. "To what do we owe the pleasure of your company this evening?"

"We need some transportation, Bartholomew," Malcolm says, shaking the other man's offered hand.

Bartholomew's eyes soon rest on me.

"Empress," he says, bowing his head in my direction, "we heard that you were here in the down-world. I must say I didn't think I would have the pleasure of your company so soon."

"Yes, about that," Malcolm says. "Harvey mentioned a little something when we arrived. What exactly have you heard about the empress?"

Bartholomew tears his eyes away from me and looks back to Malcolm.

"We heard that the fair empress here was kidnapped against her will by you on her wedding night, and that you're holding her for a hefty ransom."

Malcolm sighs and folds his arms across his chest. "I guess I shouldn't be surprised that's what he's saying. Is there anything else I need to know?"

"That the emperor has promised a lordship or ladyship to any person who provides information leading to the safe return of Empress Annalisse."

I hear Jered groan in dismay. "Well, that's certainly not going to make things any easier for us."

"And do you intend to turn us in for a title?" Malcolm asks Bartholomew point blank.

Bartholomew smiles. "No, I do not. None of my people will. We have no desire to go to the up-world. We like it down here just fine."

Malcolm looks over to me and raises an eyebrow. I instantly understand what he wants to know.

"He's telling the truth," I say, learning in that instant that Malcolm and Jered must not have my ability to ferret out a lie.

"So," Bartholomew says, "are you going to make the formal introductions, or am I going to have to introduce myself?"

Malcolm turns to me.

"Empress Annalisse Desiraye Greco Amador," Malcolm says, "I would like to introduce you to Bartholomew Stokes."

Bartholomew holds out his hand to me, palm up. I hesitantly place my hand in his. He bends at the waist and lightly presses his lips to the top of my hand.

"It's a great pleasure to meet you, Empress Annalisse," Bartholomew says as he stands back to his full height.

"Please, just call me Anna, Bartholomew."

"Then I must insist that you, in turn, call me Barlow," he replies with a friendly smile.

"Why does she get to call you Barlow and I get stuck with Bartholomew?" Malcolm asks, sounding irritated by the disparity.

Barlow raises an eyebrow at Malcolm. "Because only my friends are allowed to call me Barlow. You and I are business associates. There's a difference. And as a friend," Barlow says, turning to look at me again, "I have to ask you, Anna, are you with these two men of your own free will?"

I look at Malcolm and Jered briefly before replying, "Yes. Malcolm didn't kidnap me. He saved me. The emperor is not himself and wishes to harm me. I am abundantly safer with Malcolm."

"I had to ask," Barlow tells me with a shrug. "I want you to know that if you ever need my help, I am here to serve you no matter the task."

"Thank you," I tell him, not completely sure why a man in Barlow's line of work would make such an offer.

"Why don't we just get down to business now that you know I didn't kidnap the empress," Malcolm says. "We need three tele-ports to New Orleans for tonight."

"Easily arranged," Barlow tells him. "Where to exactly?"

Malcolm looks to Jered. "You need to procure us some rides.

But we can't chance you going back to my house to get any of my horses."

"I should just go to the Elysian Fields Market to get what we need. No one will ask any questions there," Jered says.

"Okay, you go there, and Anna and I will go get the package I left at Celeste's place."

Barlow begins to chuckle. "You're taking the empress of Cirrus to Celeste DuBois's house?"

"Celeste is a friend," Malcolm says, like where we're going isn't as bad as Barlow seems to think it is. "I left something there that I need to get back before the emperor finds it."

Barlow looks at me and shakes his head. "Please remember when you arrive there that it wasn't my idea to send you to such a place."

"Why?" I ask apprehensively. "Who is Celeste DuBois, and what's wrong with her home?"

"It's a house of—"

"Enough, Bartholomew," Malcolm says, cutting off Barlow's words. "She doesn't need to know everything. She might not even notice."

Barlow looks at Malcolm like he's lost his mind. "She's not an idiot. She'll know as soon as she gets there."

"Then it doesn't matter, does it?"

Barlow shakes his head in dismay at Malcolm. "Do I at least have your word that you'll look after her while you're visiting Celeste? I would hate for Anna to be mistaken for something that she isn't."

"She won't even be allowed inside the house," Malcolm says before his attention gets distracted by something laying in a chair nearby.

Malcolm walks over to the chair and picks up a folded, dark green, wool blanket. When he walks back over, he hands it to me.

"Here. You'll need this for later," he tells me without further explanation.

"I assume you're in a rush?" Barlow says to Malcolm.

"Yes," Malcolm answers curtly. "We need to get going as soon as possible."

"I suppose this will be going on your account?"

"You know I'm good for it."

Barlow nods. He looks over at me and holds out his arm.

"Please, Anna, let me escort you to where we need to go," Barlow says.

I take his offered arm and follow him to one of the many tunnels that are drilled into the mountain, branching off from the main room we're in. I'm fully aware that people are watching me. Whether they're in awe of me or frightened, I can't exactly tell. Quite honestly, I would rather they be neither. I never intended to be a ruler who is worshiped. I only ever wanted to lead the people of both Cirrus and the down-world into an enlightened age—one in which we could all coexist and prosper.

We walk up to what looks like a cart of some sort sitting on top of two metal tracks. The tracks disappear deeper into the dark tunnel.

The cart is divided into a front and back section, both with a padded bench for passengers to sit on.

Barlow steps up first and offers me his hand to follow him into the front of the cart. Malcolm and Jered get into the back section and sit down.

A tall metal rod is attached to the floorboard of the cart between Barlow and me.

"I hope you're not afraid to go fast," Barlow says to me.

"This little cart is supposed to go fast?" I ask dubiously.

Barlow smiles and flips a switch that turns on a light at the front of the cart, illuminating the dark tunnel ahead.

"If you get scared," Barlow tells me with a twinkle in his eyes, "you can always hold onto me, Anna. I'll keep you safe."

I know flirting when I see it, and Barlow is definitely flirting with me.

"Keep your hands to yourself, *Bartholomew*," I hear Malcolm growl behind me.

Barlow gives Malcolm an irritated sideways glance.

"Are you sure you wouldn't rather just stay here with us for a while?" Barlow asks me. "I wager we would be better company than at least one of your current companions."

I smile at him but shake my head. "No, I have things that I need to do. But thank you for your kind offer."

"It's an open offer," Barlow tells me. "Anytime you need us, we'll be more than willing to help."

"Why?" I ask. "Why are you so willing to help someone you don't even know? Someone you just met?"

"I knew your father," Barlow says. "Andre has always been a good friend to my people. We would do anything for a member of his family, especially his daughter. We have high hopes for you, Empress. We have hope that you can change the world."

I smile wanly because I know what he wants from me—what they all seem to want from me. It will take time and a lot of hard work to accomplish, but I know in my heart that it's what I was born to do.

"I promise you I'll do everything within my power to change things for the better. You have my word on that."

Barlow nods his head, like he believes my promise to him. "Then hold on, Anna; you're in for the ride of your life."

Barlow pushes the rod forward, and the cart begins to move down the track.

I soon learn that Barlow wasn't overexaggerating. The little cart zooms through the tunnel at a speed I didn't think it could achieve. It makes me giggle, which causes Barlow to laugh heartily. It feels like we're kids traveling together on a mysterious adventure through the center of a mountain.

I close my eyes to enjoy the exhilaration of the ride when Barlow yells, "Anna, open your eyes! You have to see this!"

I open my eyes and find us traveling over a large body of water. Something seems to be alive in the water, which makes it glow a bright, bright blue, illuminating the wide open space above the underground lake.

"It's beautiful!" I tell him.

"Just like you," he says back.

I look at him and roll my eyes in total exasperation at his overt flirting.

Barlow just laughs, completely shameless.

When we finally come to the end of the ride, Barlow pulls the rod backward, which seems to act as a brake, and slowly brings the cart to a stop.

Barlow hops out of the cart and reaches a hand back in to provide me his assistance in exiting the cart. While I'm standing there beside him, he holds my hand for a bit longer than is necessary, but then suddenly drops it.

I look up at him and notice his gaze is set to some point over my shoulder. I turn around to find Malcolm glowering at Barlow, like he might be on the verge of attacking the other man.

"I was just helping her out," Barlow says, like he has to defend his actions.

"Oh?" Malcolm questions, not seeming at all convinced. "Is that what all the flirting was doing? Helping her out?"

Barlow smiles and shrugs his shoulders. "I'm a man, and she's a gorgeous woman. Can you blame me?"

"No, but I can hurt you. ..." Malcolm says, taking a step forward.

Jered puts a hand on one of Malcolm's shoulders to hold him back.

"Why don't we just do what we came here for? We'll be gone soon enough," Jered says, acting as the voice of reason.

Malcolm doesn't look ready to stand down.

"Malcolm," Jered says, trying to draw his attention, "remember we need to move the package quickly. It's only a matter of time before it gets discovered."

This seems to be the only thing that makes Malcolm regain his senses.

"Lead the way," Malcolm tells Barlow, not even trying to temper his words as anything but an order.

Barlow turns toward the tunnel we stopped at. "Follow me."

This tunnel is lit with old-fashioned lightbulbs, much like the large cavern we just left was. At the end of the tunnel is a glass room with something I actually recognize inside it.

"You have a teleport pad here?" I ask. "But I thought they only worked in the approved areas."

"You're standing right beneath one of the rare areas where teleporters are allowed," Barlow tells me. "We've tapped into the power grid above us to fuel the pad we have here."

"That's brilliant," I tell him, not giving him false praise.

Barlow opens the door to the glass room, and we all step inside. A control panel stands off to the side on a glass pedestal.

As Barlow walks over to it, he says, "Jered, why don't you get on first?"

Jered walks over to me and takes both my hands into his.

"I'll see you tomorrow," he promises, leaning down to give me a kiss on the cheek. "Remember," he whispers to me, "the grumpy bear rarely bites."

I can't help but smile and nod at his words.

Jered stands on the white teleporter pad and soon disappears as he travels to his location.

"Okay, you two next," Barlow says, running his hand across the controls.

"Are you able to transport us exactly to where we need to go?" I ask, knowing that in Cirrus you can only travel between stationed teleporter pads.

"Yes, we modified it so all we have to do is input the exact coordinates to reach any place in the world." Barlow lifts his gaze from the control panel and looks at me. "Remember, Anna ... if you ever need anything from me, all you have to do is ask. Anything at all. ..."

"Just push the damn button or whatever you have to do to get us out of here," Malcolm grumbles.

"Until next time, Anna," Barlow says just as we teleport to our location.

I instantly find myself standing on the front porch of what looks like an old-fashioned mansion made of red brick. We're standing in front of a red door. The roof of the front porch is held up by thick, white-painted wood pillars.

"Your friend has a big house," I comment, wondering who this Celeste is and what she must do for a living to own such a home in the down-world.

Malcolm pounds his fist against the door.

"She needs it for her business," he tells me, not bothering to look at me, just staring straight at the door, waiting for it to be answered.

"What exactly is your problem, Malcolm?" I ask, finally getting tired of his attitude toward me. Enough was enough.

"I have no problem," he mutters.

"You made it abundantly clear this morning that you don't want to have anything to do with me after I take the seals from the princes, yet you acted like you were about to beat Barlow up for some innocent flirting. You realize that makes absolutely no sense, don't you?"

"What did you want me to do?" Malcolm says, finally turning to look at me. "Just let Barlow make passes at you without trying to protect you?"

"Why do you care?"

Malcolm falls silent for a second before saying, "Because you're my responsibility. You're under my protection, and as long as you are, it's my duty to look out for you, even from unscrupulous would-be suitors like Bartholomew Stokes."

"Is that the only reason you care?" I ask. "Because you feel an obligation to protect me? Isn't there any other reason?"

Malcolm just stares at me, his expression indecipherable.

Before he has a chance to give me an answer, the door is slammed open.

Standing in the doorway is a pretty woman with free-flowing blonde hair that reaches halfway down her back. She's wearing a rather old-fashioned dress, but it's a style I recognize because the people of the cloud city of Nimbo adopted nineteenth-century European clothing. Except, instead of being modest, the dress this woman is wearing has the front of the skirt hitched up to show off her long legs, and the bodice is so low you can clearly see the tops of her rather large breasts.

When she sees Malcolm, her eyes light up, and I instantly know this woman is in love with him. She practically throws herself at Malcolm, who catches her easily, like this isn't the first time this particular scenario has played out.

"What took you so long?" she moans as she looks lovingly up at Malcolm and proceeds to press her lips to his mouth in a demanding kiss.

CHAPTER 19

As I stand there and watch the woman virtually devour Malcolm's lips with her own, my first instinct is to draw my sword from the baldric on my back and force her ravenous mouth to back away from his. Fortunately just before I reach behind me to grab the hilt of my sword, Malcolm raises his hands up to the woman's arms, gently removes them from around his neck, and pushes her away. I hear a faint sucking sound as her lips are forced to release their hold on his.

"Celeste," Malcolm says, "we need to talk."

The woman seems completely unperturbed by Malcolm pushing her away. As I watch, she reaches down with her right hand and grabs hold of Malcolm in a place that no decent woman would touch a man who isn't her husband—and most certainly not while someone else is looking on.

A confused look crosses Celeste's face as she fondles him there.

"What's wrong with Little Malcolm?" she asks. "He should be

in proud fighting form and ready to play with me after a kiss like the one I just gave you."

I grab the hilt of my sword.

But Malcolm takes a step back from Celeste before I pull my sword from its sheath. His action forces her to drop her hand away from what she so lovingly called 'Little Malcolm.'

"We're not alone, Celeste," Malcolm says, turning to look straight at me.

Celeste follows Malcolm's gaze and seems to notice my presence for the first time.

"Well, I'll be damned," Celeste says, placing her hands on her hips. "We'd heard a rumor that you kidnapped the empress, but I didn't think it was true. I didn't think you would be that stupid, Malcolm!"

"I wasn't kidnapped," I politely inform her, knowing now exactly what she is and what type of "business" Barlow tried to warn me Celeste DuBois is involved in. "I left with Malcolm of my own free will."

Celeste looks me up and down in an appraising way that a woman does only when she deems you her competition.

Despite myself, I smile when I see a hint of worry enter her eyes.

"It doesn't really matter whether you came with Malcolm willingly or not," she says to me. "The emperor has placed a pretty price on your head that a lot of people down here would sell their soul to cash in on."

"Which is why she'll be staying in the barn tonight," Malcolm tells Celeste. "I don't want any of your girls to know she's staying here. As soon as Jered arrives in the morning, we'll be on our way and you won't have to deal with any of this. The last thing I want to do is cause you problems, or disrupt your business for any longer than I have already."

"Then go ahead and take her out back to the barn before one of the girls sees her," Celeste says to Malcolm. "I'll take her some food myself later. I'm assuming you're hungry?"

It's not until then that I realize I haven't eaten anything since the fish that morning.

"Yes, some food would be nice," I tell her. "Thank you."

Celeste sets her eyes back on Malcolm, like a rapacious beast setting its sights on its next prey. She walks up to him, slipping her arms underneath his long coat and around his waist until their chests are pressed against one another.

"After you get the empress settled in," she croons to him, "come back inside so we can ... have a quiet moment with one another."

Malcolm kisses Celeste on the forehead. "Thank you for your help, Celeste. I won't be long."

This seems to pacify Celeste, and she steps back to let Malcolm go.

Malcolm turns on his heels and steps off the porch. He doesn't ask me to follow him. He just assumes I will. I do follow him, of course. It's either that or stand on the porch with Celeste DuBois.

Malcolm walks to the back of the house where a large red barn stands. His strides are long and fast. I have a hard time keeping up with him without having to jog part of the way. Once we reach the barn, Malcolm opens up a normal-sized door built into the much larger one at the front of it.

Once we step inside, Malcolm grabs something off the wall beside the door. I hear a whirring noise and see a faint light come from the object he's holding as he turns a small crank on its side, and I see that it's a mechanically powered lantern.

After Malcolm turns the crank as far as it will go, he hands it to me.

"The light should last for a couple of hours before you have to crank it again," Malcolm tells me. "Your outfit will keep you warm enough. It was designed to keep your body at a comfortable temperature, but I'm sure you've already noticed that."

"Are you planning to sleep with her?" I ask point-blank, wanting an answer.

"If you need anything," Malcolm says, completely ignoring my question and keeping his eyes averted from mine, "go to the back door of the house and tell one of Celeste's girls. They'll come and get me. But try to keep your face hidden. I would rather none of them know you are here."

Malcolm turns his back to me to leave, but I clamp my hand down on his left shoulder and use my strength to spin him around, forcing his back up against the wall of the barn. The hood of his cloak keeps his features in shadows, but I can see his eyes meet mine clearly enough.

"Are you planning to sleep with Celeste DuBois when you go back into that house?" I ask him, making sure there isn't any way he can misunderstand or ignore the question again.

Malcolm's eyebrows lower. "I don't really think that's any of your concern."

"You know perfectly well why it should be my concern," I tell him, on the verge of losing my temper. "How can you even think about being with her when I'm right here? Don't you know what that would do to me? Don't you care that it would hurt me?"

"Maybe it will finally make you realize we can never have a future together," Malcolm says—the words sounding like a lame excuse because they are.

"If that's what you think, then you would only be fooling yourself into thinking that's the truth," I tell him, not about to let him feel like he has the upper hand in the situation.

We stare at one another for a moment, and I feel like if he leaves me to go back into that house, I might lose him forever.

I gently cup Malcolm's face with my free hand. He closes his eyes, and I hear him sigh, like my touch brings him comfort, even though he doesn't want to admit it to me or himself. I wish I could make him see reason. I wish I could make him give into what he's feeling in that moment and come to me. I pray that he does it soon, because I feel like the window of our future together is closing fast, and just the thought of losing him so soon after finally finding him tears me to pieces.

"Stay with me," I urge him, not wanting to beg but wanting him to know that even after the way he acted that day I still want him. "I could bring happiness back into your life if you wouldn't fight me at every turn, Malcolm."

I slide my hand from his face down to his bare chest. Malcolm keeps his eyes closed, breathing steadily, not telling me to stop but not giving me any encouragement to continue either.

"I belong here," I tell him, resting my hand over his heart. "You know that. You have to. I just wish you would stop denying what you feel when we're together. I would give you all of me if you would just take it. You deserve so much, yet you refuse to believe that you do. Stop being so stubborn, Malcolm, and let me in."

Still Malcolm says nothing, just stands there with his eyes closed.

He doesn't try to move my hand away, and I feel like that's at least a small victory.

Minutes pass by, and I feel like Malcolm is having a silent war with himself about what he should do. I desperately want to take his pain away, both physical and emotional. I want to be the one person in the world he can come to when he needs a shoulder to lean on, and I want to become the love he so richly deserves but doesn't think he does.

"You should try to get some rest," he finally says to me,

opening his eyes but refusing to meet my gaze. "I'll see you in the morning."

Malcolm pushes himself off the wall and brushes past me as he leaves.

I feel the sting of tears threaten to overwhelm me, but force them back. I refuse to give into despair, but I feel like I've reached one of my lowest points.

For some reason, I remember Auggie's words to me when I asked him if he thought I would ever find someone to love me.

"He's out there somewhere, longing to meet you as much as you are him. And when you finally find one another, God help anyone who tries to come between the two of you."

I wonder what Auggie would say to me if he knew the person coming between me and the love of my life is actually the man who holds my heart but seems hell-bent on refusing to accept it.

I don't feel like there's much else I can do that evening besides storm inside Celeste DuBois's house and make a scene. I have more self-respect than to do something like that. I can't force Malcolm to love me any more than I can make myself stop loving him. Besides, if he doesn't give me his love of his own free will, then what's the point?

Feeling tired all of a sudden, I look around the barn and find a pile of hay on the floor not too far away. It looks sufficiently comfortable enough to sleep on.

I walk over to it, set the lantern down beside it, and throw the green wool blanket on top of it. As I'm unbuckling the belt of the baldric from around my waist, doing my utmost not to think about what might happen to Malcolm while he's in the clutches of one Celeste DuBois, I hear the door to the barn slowly creak open.

I turn my head to look in that direction, expecting to see Celeste coming in with my promised food, but the person I end up seeing makes me completely stop what I'm doing and turn to face him.

A boy around the age of six with chocolate-colored skin and spiral, textured hair, practically sprouting from his scalp, peeks in through the crack of the door. I watch as his adorable little face lights up with joy when he sees me, and I hear him take an excited breath like he's just found the best present in the world waiting for him. Foregoing shyness, he slams the door open and runs straight to me as fast as his little legs will allow. He lunges his small frame at me, hugging me around the hips and resting one side of his face against my belly.

"I knew you would come," he says with a mixture of relief and excitement in a voice that is possibly the cutest I've ever heard in my life. "I just knew it!"

I have no idea what to say to this heartfelt declaration.

All I can do is place my hands on his shoulders and gently pry him off me so I can get a better look at him. I bend down on one knee so that we're at eye level with one another.

Considering he's someone I've never met before in my life, I don't understand the love I see in his startling blue-green eyes for me.

"Who are you?" I ask him.

"My name is Lucas," he says, smiling at me and inexplicably making me feel happy all of a sudden. The mess of Malcolm is completely pushed to the back of my mind as I look at Lucas.

"How do you know me, Lucas?"

"You're going to be my mommy one day," he tells me matter-of-factly, still smiling his little smile and sounding so confident I almost believe him.

His answer is definitely not one I am expecting to hear, and I have to admit it takes me a minute to let his words sink in.

"Don't you already have a mother?" I ask gently.

Lucas shakes his head.

"She died a long time ago," he tells me, his smile faltering as he delivers this sad news. Not to be deterred by the loss of his mother, he smiles again, and it not only brightens his face but the dreary barn as well. I notice that he's missing one of his top front teeth, giving him a beatific gap-toothed grin. "But I knew you would come so you could be my mommy. I've been waiting a long time for you, Anna."

"But. ..." I'm at a loss for words but have to ask, "What makes you think I'm supposed to be your mother?"

"Because I had a vision of you when I was three years old."

I smile at this statement because of the way Lucas said it, not particularly because of what he said, like at the age of six he's so much older and wiser than he was at three. It's a childlike quality that makes him irresistibly adorable, as if he isn't already.

I feel sure Lucas simply saw a picture of me somewhere and imagined that I would someday become his mother. But what in the world is he doing here? Why is he at Celeste DuBois's house?

I'm about to ask him these questions when I hear a woman clear her throat at the door, drawing our attention.

"Now, Lucas," Celeste says admonishingly, "you were asked not to leave the house. Why are you out here bothering this woman?"

"Because," Lucas says, looking away from Celeste to me, his face beaming with pride, "I wanted my new mommy to meet me."

When I look back at Celeste, the expression on her face isn't hard to read. She's fuming mad. What Lucas just said has made her livid, but I'm not sure why.

"Go back into the house before you're missed," Celeste tells him, keeping her voice calm in an attempt to not betray her true feelings.

Lucas reluctantly begins to walk toward the door, stuffing his hands inside his coat pockets. Before he goes too far, he looks back at me and smiles.

"You'll see I'm right," he tells me before he walks out the door and into the night, presumably to go back into the whorehouse Celeste DuBois owns.

"Why are you letting a child that age stay in your home?" I ask Celeste as she steps into the barn carrying a wood tray with a plate of food on it covered by a white napkin. "It doesn't seem like the best environment for an impressionable young boy to be living in."

"Why don't you keep your holier-than-thou opinions to yourself," Celeste tells me with a snarky attitude. "I'll do what and ... *whoever* I please in my own home, thank you very much, Your Majesty."

Celeste walks over and hands me the tray rather forcefully.

She smiles a crooked, knowing smile at me as I take it from her.

"In fact," she says, "Malcolm is waiting for me in my room right now. I just wanted to keep my promise to bring you something of your own to eat while I have a private and—dare I say it?— meaty feast of my own."

My mind goes completely blank for a comeback to such an explicitly suggestive statement. All I can think about now is Malcolm lying in bed with Celeste with her paws all over him.

Seeing that her remark has had the desired effect on me, Celeste smiles and turns to leave.

"Enjoy your meal," she tells me over her shoulder as she steps out the door and turns around before closing it. "I know I will."

She slams the door shut, and I'm left alone in the quiet of the barn.

I set the tray she gave me beside the lantern, having completely lost my appetite. I spread out the green wool blanket on the pile of fresh hay and finish unbuckling the belt of my baldric to set my sword aside.

After I lie down on the blanket, I feel an ache in my chest so heavy I'm certain my heart will stop beating because of the weight of it.

I close my eyes and pray for sleep so I can find succor in the land of dreams.

Unfortunately, my prayer goes unanswered for a long, long, long time.

CHAPTER 20

The next thing I know, the barn door is unceremoniously slung open with a crash, drawing me out of my hard-fought-for sleep.

"Let's go," I hear Malcolm say gruffly, startling my sleep-addled mind and causing me to jump slightly as I fully awaken. "They're waiting for us."

I sit up and look over at Malcolm as he stands in the doorway. The murky morning light from the outside world filters its way into the barn. I just stare at him for a minute, wondering what his night was like. I seriously doubt he feels as miserable as I do.

I can't seem to pluck up my nerve to inquire how he spent his night, but I do nod to him, letting him know that I heard his surly request.

I stand up from the pile of hay and grab the blanket to fold and take with me.

When I step out of the barn, I see Jered standing by three horses. Unfortunately, they're all as big as the last ones we rode.

"Couldn't find a small one?" I ask Jered when I walk toward him.

"Sorry, they were all out of little white ponies," Jered tells me with an affable grin.

"How come you don't like big horses, Anna?"

The question comes from beneath the horse, and I recognize the voice instantly.

I look down to see Lucas's inquisitive face staring up at me from his squatting position beneath the horse.

"Lucas!" I hear Malcolm bellow, storming over to us and quickly sweeping Lucas into the safety of his arms. "How many times have I told you it's not safe to crawl underneath a horse like that? It could kill you instantly with just one kick."

Lucas looks at Malcolm—eyes wide open—and says in a properly contrite voice, "I'm sorry, Dad. I forgot. I just wanted to surprise Anna."

I stand there for a moment and feel totally bewildered.

"Dad?" I ask Malcolm.

"Adopted son," Malcolm tells me. "Lucas's parents were killed in a freak accident right after he was born. He didn't have any other family. So I brought him home with me."

And then everything makes perfect sense.

"He's the package we came to get," I say, not really needing to have the answer confirmed. A whorehouse is the perfect hiding place for a child. Who would think to look for him inside one? "Where are we taking him?"

"Hopefully somewhere he'll be safe," Malcolm replies. "We can't exactly take him with us to the places we need to go."

"But I want to go with you," Lucas protests. "I don't like being away from you for so long."

Malcolm smiles wanly at Lucas. "I know. I don't either. But it's not just for your safety. It's for ours, too. There are bad people who would use your life against us to hurt us."

"Okay," Lucas says with a pout, "I understand. Just don't take too long to do what you gotta do."

"Aye, aye, captain," Malcolm says, and I see a genuine smile grace his face as he looks at his son. I think it's the first glimpse of happiness I've seen Malcolm express, and I decide then and there that I want to see him happy more often.

"Malcolm!"

We all turn when we hear Celeste's strident and somewhat angry call of Malcolm's name.

Malcolm walks over to Jered and hands Lucas to him. He strides over to Celeste, meeting her halfway across the misty lawn of her backyard. They stop and talk in low but heated voices. Celeste reaches up and slaps Malcolm across the face so hard we all hear the crack. She then storms off back toward her house without a single glance backwards. Malcolm watches her go for a few seconds then turns around, not looking at all bothered by the altercation.

"What was that all about?" I ask.

"She's mad," Lucas answers unexpectedly. "She got mad last night because Dad wanted to stay in my room with me. I'm not sure why."

I'm happy to know Lucas doesn't exactly understand why Celeste is upset. And even happier to discover that Malcolm might have spent the night in a house full of whores, but he obviously didn't partake of any of the ladies' wares, not even those of one very vivacious Ms. Celeste DuBois.

"We should probably get going," Malcolm says, lifting Lucas back into his arms and walking over to the black horse that's obviously his ride.

Malcolm sits Lucas in the saddle and instructs him to hold on before he walks over to me.

Malcolm takes the blanket from my hands and tosses it to

234

Jered to take care of. He then walks up behind me and places his hands on my waist. I feel the hood of his coat brush against the side of my face as he leans down and whispers, "Are you ready, Anna?"

I nod my head because I suddenly find speaking impossible with his closeness.

Malcolm lifts me easily with his hands and helps me into my saddle.

I look back down at him and say, "Thank you."

Malcolm gives me an almost reluctant lopsided grin and nods his head before walking away to mount his own steed, holding Lucas in front of him. I watch as he lightly presses the sides of his horse with his heels, signaling it to move forward.

Jered brings his horse up beside my own just as it begins to follow Malcolm's horse of its own accord.

"You don't look like you got much sleep last night," Jered comments with a note of worry.

"I didn't," I confess. "I had things on my mind that I couldn't stop thinking about."

"Am I right in assuming if you had known a certain someone spent the night in Lucas's room, you might have gotten more rest?"

I grin and look over at Jered. "I think you're starting to know me a little too well, Jered."

Jered laughs. "The day I know a woman too well is the day I ask that woman to marry me."

It's a comment that brings to mind an interesting question.

"Have you not met your soul mate yet?" I ask him.

Jered shakes his head. "No, I haven't been lucky enough to meet her. When the time is right for me to, I'm sure my father will find a way to introduce us."

"I hope you aren't as stubborn with her as someone else, who shall remain nameless," I mutter.

Jered chuckles. "I pledge to you that I will do my best to treat her far better."

I look back at Malcolm, and see Lucas peek around the side of his dad to look back at me. The smile on Lucas's face is infectious, and I can't help but smile back. Malcolm gently makes his son sit upright in front of him again.

"By the way, when did you and Lucas meet?" Jered asks me. "I'm a little surprised Malcolm introduced you to him last night."

"He didn't," I confess. "Lucas came to see me in the barn."

"Really?" Jered asks in surprise. "He's usually very shy around people he doesn't know. Did he say why he came to see you?"

"He told me he had a vision about me when he was three years old," I say with a small laugh, thinking such a concept is the fanciful notion of a child who obviously just wants a mother.

Jered doesn't laugh. Instead, he looks thoughtful.

"It makes perfect sense that you would be the one he saw," Jered finally says, like pieces of a puzzle are finally forming a picture he can recognize.

"The one he saw?" I ask. "Are you saying you think Lucas actually saw me in some sort of prophetic vision?"

"Do you remember what I told you about the vessels?"

"The ones who carried the archangels' souls and helped Jess and Mason close the Tear?"

"Yes. Do you remember me telling you about the different powers they possessed because of their archangels?"

"Yes."

"Well, Lucas is a descendent of Gabe. His archangel gave him the power to see visions about the future."

"So the power each vessel possessed because of their archangel was passed down?"

"Yes and no," Jered says, looking perplexed. "Not every descendent received the power. Sometimes it would skip through

236

ten generations before showing up again. We still don't understand how the powers were passed down. It was almost as if a part
of the archangel each vessel carried did something to their genetic
code after they were awoken. But it wasn't a dominant gene that
was altered; it was a passive one that only seemed to activate in
particular descendants. Lucas is the last of Gabe's line, now that
his biological father is dead."

"Then he really can see into the future?"

Jered nods. "Yes, but the vision he had of you is the only one
he's told us about. As he grows, his power may strengthen."

I sit there for a moment, absorbing this new information.

"He said," I say hesitantly, because I fear if I voice my next
words they won't come true, "that I was going to be his new
mommy."

"Yes, he told us that when he was three and had the vision.
Well, he said he saw the woman who would become his mother. I
guess his vision of you has stayed with him since then."

"I haven't been around many children," I tell Jered. "And I
don't know if it's just because he's a cute kid or what exactly, but I
already love him to pieces. Is that natural?"

"With Lucas? Yes, I would say that's perfectly natural, Anna.
He has that sort of effect on people ... always has."

We fall silent and simply enjoy the ride. Malcolm decides that
we need to keep to the trails within the forest again that day. I
don't mind the slow progress. It gives me a chance to ponder
things.

"Jered," I say in a low voice, hoping Malcolm is far enough in
front of us that he won't hear my next question, "what type of relationship did Malcolm have with Celeste?"

"Business mostly," Jered replies, also keeping his voice low,
"though I think Celeste took Malcolm's frequent visits to her as
meaning he felt something deeper. But he never cared for her

beyond friendship. Malcolm's just always had a healthy appetite when it comes to … uh … physical activity with the fairer gender."

I have to smile at Jered's euphemism.

"So you're saying he likes to have sex," I clarify for him.

Jered grins and seems to almost blush. "Well, if you want to put it bluntly, yes."

I grin back at him. "Good to know."

In spite of, or because of, my audaciousness, Jered laughs.

Malcolm turns his head to look back at us.

"Everything all right back there?" he asks.

I smile back at him. "Everything is absolutely fine. We're just getting to know each other a little better is all."

Malcolm raises an eyebrow at this but doesn't make a reply. He simply turns back around in his saddle.

"You're too good for him, Anna," Jered says with a shake of his head, still grinning. "But you're exactly what he needs."

"I hope he realizes that soon," I tell Jered. "If he doesn't, neither of us will ever find happiness."

"Have faith," Jered tells me, mirroring the words God said to me only the day before.

I nod. "I do," I tell him. "But Malcolm has to have it too, or it's never going to work out between us."

Jered doesn't make a reply because he knows I'm right.

The horses come to a stop suddenly and begin to back up of their own accord.

"What's going on?" I ask.

But there's no need for anyone to make a reply.

Twenty Cirrus guards teleport in around us, holding laser swords pointed in our direction.

"In the name of the emperor," one guard shouts to Malcolm, "we demand that you let Empress Annalisse go or suffer the consequences!"

I watch as Malcolm looks around at all the guards, sizing them up. Apparently he finds them wanting, because he begins to laugh.

"So, do these humans not know what you are, or are we really going to pretend you aren't a rebellion angel?" Malcolm asks the guard who spoke. "Seems a bit ridiculous, don't you think?"

"Give us the girl," the guard says, losing the pretense of actually being one, "and we'll let you go, Malcolm."

"I lost the ability to tell a lie from the truth a long time ago," Malcolm replies, "but even I can hear the lie in what you just said clearly enough."

"We'll let the boy live if the empress comes with us willingly," the guard says, trying another tactic.

I hop down off my horse and draw my sword from the baldric on my back, causing it to ignite into its red-orange flames instantly.

"Unfortunately for you," I tell them all, "I *can* tell the difference between a lie and the truth." I look at the guard who seems to be the mouthpiece for the group. "And that was a lie."

"We have you outnumbered," the guard says, trying to sound threatening. "Just come with us, Empress, and I promise we'll let the others go unharmed."

"If I thought there was even a remote chance you would keep that promise," I tell him, "I would go with you willingly. But we both know you have no intention of ever letting them go."

"You'll die if you try to fight us," the guard threatens with so much conviction I almost believe him.

"I would rather die fighting than let you slaughter my friends."

"Don't worry, Empress Anna, you won't be dying today," I hear a friendly voice say behind the guard I'm talking to.

I look over the guard's shoulder and see someone I haven't seen for quite some time: Gladson Gray, Auggie's former lover and leader of the rebel faction in Cirrus.

Before I know it, all hell breaks loose. A group of men and

women seem to erupt out of the forest, attacking the surprised Cirrun guards.

Jered phases off his horse to join the fray, drawing the sword from his scabbard and showing a practiced skill with it against his opponents.

Malcolm jumps off his horse and pulls out his sword from its sheath at his side. He quickly picks Lucas up and sets him down on the ground behind him.

A guard attempts to take Malcolm by surprise while he's tending to Lucas, but I phase the short distance to him and use my sword to block his swing at Malcolm's back. The guard attempts to fight me but quickly realizes he's outmatched in strength and swordsmanship. In three swings, I have his head separated from his shoulders.

I quickly turn around to make sure Malcolm and Lucas are all right. Lucas is staring up at me in shock. I realize he just saw me kill the guard and hope that he understands I didn't have any choice.

Malcolm quickly takes off his long coat and places it on Lucas, covering his son's face with the hood.

"Put your hands over your ears and shut your eyes," Malcolm instructs him.

I can see the worry on Malcolm's face over Lucas being in the middle of a fight.

"Phase him away from here," I urge Malcolm. "We can handle this."

Malcolm looks over at me, and I can tell by the stony expression on his face that phasing isn't an option.

"No," he says decisively. "I'm not leaving you. We stand and fight together."

A part of me loves that Malcolm doesn't want to leave me, and another part of me just wants him and Lucas somewhere safe. Yet

I know from the stern look on Malcolm's face that he won't leave, no matter how strenuously I make my plea.

So I turn around to face what's coming next with Malcolm by my side.

Malcolm and I keep Lucas sandwiched between our backs. Any guard who is foolish enough to attack us is dealt with quickly by either me or him.

The fight between the guards, us, and Gladson's people is fast and furious, but finally all the guards are killed and the threat to our lives is contained, for now.

Once the bedlam is settled, I quickly turn and kneel toward Lucas, pulling the hood from his face to make sure he's all right.

Lucas's face is tear-stained, and his little body is shaking uncontrollably. When our eyes meet, he takes a step toward me and wraps his little arms around my neck, burying his face against my chest as if he's trying to hide his eyes from the death surrounding him. I rise to my feet, and as I cradle him in my arms, Malcolm's coat falls away from Lucas to the ground. I walk over the bodies of the fallen until I'm out of the circle of death. I sit down by the trunk of a large oak and just hold Lucas close to me and let him cry. I suddenly remember the lullaby Millie used to hum to me and begin to sing the tune to Lucas, hoping it calms his fears like it always did mine.

After a while, Lucas lifts his head and looks up at me.

"I was scared," he tells me, like he's making a confession.

I try to smile at him reassuringly. "You had nothing to be frightened of, Lucas. Your dad and I would never let anything happen to you. I want you to remember that."

Lucas nods. "I know, Anna. I shouldn't have let myself get so scared because I already know what will happen."

"What do you mean?" I ask. "What have you seen?"

"I've seen us living in a castle built in the clouds."

"You have?" I ask, feeling my heart swell with hope for the future.

Lucas nods. "Yep, and we're all happy ... even the babies."

"Babies?" I ask, completely taken off guard by the simple use of this word. "Whose babies?"

"The ones you and Dad will have one day," Lucas says, like I should know this already. "Liam and Lilianna. I can't wait to have a brother and a sister. I promise I'll be the best big brother ever."

I sit there, stunned into silence.

"Have your visions ever been wrong?" I ask, holding my breath as I wait to hear the answer.

"I'm not sure yet," Lucas says, shrugging his little shoulders. "I've only had visions that have you in them. But you turned out to be real."

It isn't exactly the reassurance I am looking for, but at this point I decide to take what I can get.

"Everything all right?"

I look up and see Malcolm standing beside us. His eyes hold a worry for Lucas as he looks down at his son.

Lucas stands up from my lap and walks over to his dad. Malcolm bends down and picks his son up into his arms. Lucas wraps his arms around his dad's neck, and I watch as Malcolm rests his chin against one of Lucas's small shoulders, closing his eyes like the embrace is bringing him as much comfort as it is Lucas.

"Sorry I got scared, Dad," Lucas says to Malcolm.

"You don't have to be sorry about that," Malcolm tells him. "There's no shame in being scared of bad people."

Lucas pulls back slightly so he can look into Malcolm's eyes.

"When we go to live in the castle with Anna, will you teach me how to fight with a sword?"

Malcolm's face scrunches up in bewilderment.

"Live in a castle with Anna?" Malcolm asks.

Lucas nods. "Yeah, the one in the clouds that I've seen. Will you teach me?"

Malcolm still looks confused and at a loss for words.

I stand up.

"Maybe you're asking the wrong person," I say to Lucas. "I'll teach you how to use a sword when we go. I promise."

They both look at me—Malcolm in confusion and Lucas with a bright, expectant smile on his face.

"Thanks, Anna." Lucas's smile falters some. "When can I just go ahead and start calling you 'Mommy'?"

"Mommy?" Malcolm asks rather loudly. "She is not your mother, Lucas."

Lucas looks back at Malcolm. "But she will be, Dad."

Malcolm is silent for a moment, like he's trying to make sense of what Lucas just said.

Then he asks, "Anna's the woman you saw in the vision you had?"

Lucas nods his head.

"Why didn't you ever mention that before?" Malcolm asks. "You've seen pictures and holograms of her on the news, but you never said she was the one."

"I thought she might be made up," Lucas says. "I didn't think anyone so pretty could be real. But now I know she's real, and she'll be my mommy one day. I just don't see why I can't call her that now."

"Because she's not your mother," Malcolm says a little too stridently.

"But she will be," Lucas insists again, like it's a forgone conclusion.

Malcolm begins to open his mouth to say something else but seems to think better of it and closes it again.

Malcolm looks over at me but apparently he doesn't know what to say to me either. Finally he settles on, "Come on. Gladson wants to have a word with you."

Malcolm walks away with Lucas in his arms to where Gladson and Jered are standing, talking to one another.

Gladson Gray was one of the most sought-after lords in Cirrus. His exotic Middle Eastern looks make him stand out in a crowd. His light brown hair has a natural body to it that is envied by many women, and his deep-set brown eyes let you see the pureness of his soul. It is easy to understand why Auggie fell in love with him the first time they met. Many a lady had set their sights on Gladson, at least until he turned rebel. He became one of the most vocal proponents on how the citizens of the cloud cities were misusing their power by keeping the down-worlders as indentured servants, as he put it.

When we approach, Gladson turns to me and brings me into his arms.

"I'm so glad you're safe," Gladson says to me. "We've been looking for you since you disappeared. Anna, can you tell me what's wrong with Auggie? He's ... changed, and not for the better. He won't even see me anymore."

"It's a long story, Gladson. One I'll tell you about in just a minute. Right now, I need to know how you found us and how you knew we were going to be attacked."

Gladson pulls away to explain. "Like I was telling Overlord Devereaux and Emissary Alburn, I have spies everywhere. We learned your whereabouts when a message was delivered to the emperor this morning, telling him you would be traveling this way today. Someone was trying to cash in on the bounty he's placed on your safe return to Cirrus."

"Do you know who it was?" I ask.

"Did we *seriously* miss out on all the fun?" a new but familiar voice says behind us.

We all look over and see Barlow Stokes and about ten of his men walking toward us, surveying the carnage all around.

Malcolm hands Lucas to Jered and phases over to Barlow, grabbing the other man by the throat and lifting him into the air.

"Are you the one who betrayed us? Did you come to get your reward?" Malcolm demands, roughly throwing Barlow to the ground.

Barlow chokes out his answer. "I wasn't the one who betrayed you."

Malcolm looks to me, and I nod that Barlow is telling the truth.

"Then why are you here?" Malcolm demands. "You act like you knew we would be ambushed."

Barlow stands to his feet, rubbing his now sore neck.

"Obviously, I did know," he tells us, coughing a little. "We just got word that a deal was made between Celeste and the emperor. What the hell did you do to piss her off enough to betray you to him?"

Malcolm sighs and runs a hand through his hair in agitation.

"That's none of your business," Malcolm tells him irritably. "I knew she was mad, but I never thought she would put Lucas's life in danger like this."

Barlow looks over at me. "We came as soon as we heard, Anna. I'm sorry we weren't here in time to help."

"Well," I say, an idea forming in my mind, "maybe you can still help me, Barlow." I turn to Gladson. "Gladson Gray, I would like to introduce you to Barlow Stokes, the best black marketer here in the down-world. I think the two of you might be able to help each other ... and me. Maybe by working together we can all change the world for the better."

We take a few precious minutes to tell them both what's really going on with the emperor. Gladson takes the news hard but keeps himself together because he knows Auggie would want us to avenge his death, not waste time mourning it.

We also discuss what each man has to offer toward my plan to rebuild how our society functions, and they both seem eager to do their part. Once the two men I've just recruited know their roles in the new world order I see, we decide it's best to split up and get busy doing what needs to be done.

"So how long will it take you to complete this mysterious mission you're on?" Gladson asks me before he gets ready to leave.

"I'm not sure," I tell him. "But I have to do it. It's what I was born for, and it's the best way I can honor Auggie's memory."

"Can I help in any way?"

"I'll let you know if I need your help," I assure him. "Right now, I just need you to keep your ears and eyes open for any move the emperor plans against me. It's the best thing you can do to help me … for now at least."

"Then you have it," Gladson says, bending at the waist to pledge his fealty to me.

"I'm still a little confused about something," Barlow says. "If the emperor sent his men here, why hasn't he sent anymore men by now? He has to know exactly where you are."

"Oh, well, that's partially my doing," Gladson says with a sly grin. "I had my people disable the teleportation system in Cirrus after we teleported here so we didn't have to deal with any more guards than we had to. We also disabled aerial surveillance in the area, at least for a little while. Things should be coming back online within twenty-four hours though."

I look to Malcolm. "But there was a rebellion angel leading the human guards, right? If he has more angels masquerading as guards, they could just phase in at any time."

Malcolm nods. "Yes, but Levi probably doesn't have many

under his command. Most of the rebellion angels still follow Lucifer. I think it's best if we all leave before Levi figures out his ambush didn't succeed and decides to come down himself."

"I don't suppose you have personal teleporters?" Barlow asks Gladson. "Otherwise, my men and I will have a long walk ahead of us."

Gladson smiles. "We do, but they're offline until the system in Cirrus comes back up. Sorry."

Barlow sighs. "Then I guess it's a long walk for all of us back home. The nearest teleporter is in New Orleans."

"My men and I will walk with you," Gladson says. "But it would be best for us to not use a public teleporter. We'll just wait things out in the city until the system is back online in Cirrus so we can go back discreetly."

Barlow turns to me.

"I really am sorry we weren't here in time to come to your rescue, Anna. I promise to do better next time. Scout's honor," Barlow says, holding the three middle fingers of his right hand up into the air.

"I have no idea what that means," I tell him, thinking the pledge odd.

Barlow shrugs. "Old Earth saying," he explains. "Means you have my promise."

"Then I gladly accept your scout's honor."

"Ready when you are to leave," Gladson says to Barlow. Gladson turns to me and gives me a brief hug. "I'll keep an eye on things in Cirrus until you're able to return."

"You have my word that we *will* bring Auggie's killer to justice, Gladson. Please don't try to do anything yourself. He's too strong. I'm the only one who can deal with him."

"I can't say I completely understand everything you just told me about angels and demons," Gladson says. "But I do know I can't wait for the day you make that bastard pay for what he took away from the both of us. Take care of yourself down here, my friend."

Gladson kisses me on the cheek before turning to follow Barlow out of the forest.

"I don't think it's safe for us to go to Rory and Lora's place now," Malcolm says to Jered.

"Are they the ones who are supposed to take care of Lucas while we're dealing with the princes?" I ask.

"Yes," Malcolm says.

"Why don't I go to their house alone first to make sure they're not being watched?" Jered suggests. "You can take Anna and Lucas to the house in Lakewood, and I'll bring Rory and Lora there if it's safe."

Malcolm nods. "Okay. Just be careful, Jered. Celeste knows where we are going. If she made a deal with Levi, I have a feeling Rory and Lora have either been taken in by now for questioning, or there's an ambush planned in case we made it that far."

Jered nods. "I'll be careful. I should get there by the end of the day, and then it'll take us another two days to make it to Lakewood." Jered turns to me. "I bought you some necessities I thought you might like while I was at the market. They're in the satchel on my horse."

I follow Jered to his horse while Malcolm settles Lucas into the saddle of his mount.

Jered pulls the large satchel from his saddle and hands it to me.

"This might give the two of you some much-needed private time together," Jered whispers to me. "Use it wisely, Anna. Make the idiot realize what he's pushing away."

I nod. "I'll try."

Jered raises his eyebrows at me. "I still think you're too good for him, just so you know. But I guess I'm not the one in charge of pairing soul mates."

I smile. "No, I'm not too good for him. I'm just right."

"Too good," Jered mumbles before getting on his horse. "I'll see you in a few days," he promises before riding away.

I turn back to my horse and hook the satchel onto the horn of the saddle.

Malcolm walks over to me.

"Are you ready?" he asks.

I look up at him and know he's asking me if I'm ready to get on the horse, but my heart is ready to finally make the man standing in front of me mine.

"Yes," I tell him, "I'm ready."

I'm ready to fight for what I want.

And if I don't win his heart once and for all ...

... I'll set him free.

CHAPTER 21

As we ride, I notice Lucas constantly peeking around Malcolm, trying to look at me. It's cute to me, but apparently annoying to Malcolm. Finally I hear him let out an exasperated sigh and pull on his horse's reins to bring it to a halt. My horse walks up beside his and stops.

Lucas's face beams with joy when he sees me, making my heart truly happy for the first time in a long time.

"I think Lucas has a thousand and one questions he wants to ask you," Malcolm says to me, ruffling the hair on Lucas's head, making him giggle.

"What's it like up in Cirrus?" Lucas asks excitedly. "Do you have a dog? I've always wanted a dog, but my dad won't let me have one."

"I don't like dogs," Malcolm grumbles.

I feel sure Malcolm's aversion to dogs has something to do with his experiences with the hellhounds.

"Yes, I do have a dog," I tell Lucas. "Her name is Vala, and she's a sentient robotic dog. Real animals aren't allowed in Cirrus."

"Wow," Lucas says, eyes wide with wonder.

We begin walking the horses at the same pace when he asks, "Does she like to play fetch? Or is she too smart to do real dog stuff?"

"Vala loves to play fetch," I assure Lucas. "And I'm sure she will fall in love with you the moment she sees you."

"You think so?"

"I know so. I did."

Lucas giggles and smiles so brightly I feel as though anything is possible in his world. It's a realm filled with a child's magic and not burdened with the weight we adults feel sometimes.

For most of the day, Lucas questions me about life in Cirrus. He seems especially curious about the castle he saw in his vision. I suppose his interest is born from the belief that it will be his home one day. Malcolm even chimes in every once in a while, asking me questions about my life, and I'm given hope that maybe he's getting to know me a little better through Lucas's natural curiosity about me.

It's near dusk before we reach the place Jered is supposed to bring the people who will take care of Lucas.

It's a home that looks like it was built in a bygone era, a forgotten time to most, but not all apparently. The four white pillars at the front of the mansion stand tall and proud, connecting each level of the home from the bottom of the porch on the first floor, through the second floor's porch, up to the overhanging roof. The home looks well-kept, even though it's old.

"Do you like to swim?" Lucas asks me. "There's a lake in the back."

"It's far too cold to go swimming," Malcolm informs Lucas as he gets off his horse. He then turns back around to reach up for his son.

"I know," Lucas says, placing his hands on Malcolm's shoulders as his dad plucks him out of the saddle, "but I thought we could bring Anna here next spring before it gets too hot to go swimming."

"I'm afraid I don't know how to swim," I say, almost regretting the fact for the first time in my life.

"My dad can teach you how to swim," Lucas says confidently. "He taught me how in no time at all."

"I don't really like the water either," I admit.

"Well, you could watch us at least," Lucas says, quickly thinking of an alternative. "We could still have fun. I bet the babies will love the water."

"Babies?" Malcolm says, looking completely lost. "What babies?"

"The ones you and Anna will have. Geesh, keep up, Dad."

I try to hide my smile but fail miserably at it and let out a little giggle.

Malcolm looks at me and raises an eyebrow. "That only encourages him."

"I know," I say. "I'm sorry. I just find everything he says to be cute."

"And it's *aaaalllll* true, too. You'll see," Lucas tells us with a firm nod of his head. "Come on, Anna. I want to show you my room."

Lucas comes up to me and takes my hand into his. Malcolm walks up to the porch and pulls out a fake floorboard where an old-fashioned key is hidden. He unlocks the front door and Lucas runs inside, obviously excited to be back in this particular home he shares with his father.

Malcolm gently touches me on the arm to hold me back a second.

He looks into the house to make sure Lucas isn't within hearing range.

"Please don't encourage this fantasy world he's built about us all living together in Cirrus. I don't want him to be too disappointed when it doesn't happen."

"How do you do that?" I ask, feeling the happiness Lucas has brought back into my life being twisted away by Malcolm's words.

"Do what?" Malcolm asks. "Be realistic? He's my son, and I don't want to see him get hurt because his expectations don't get met."

"No," I whisper, because my throat suddenly feels tight by me forcing myself not to cry. "How can you twist my heart so easily with just a few words?"

Malcolm lets go of my arm. "I don't want either one of you to think something is going to happen when it isn't."

"And there goes another twist," I say, looking away from Malcolm before he can see the tears welling in my eyes.

I walk over the threshold and enter the home. I see Lucas standing at the foot of a staircase leading to the second floor, staring at me. I have a bad feeling he heard our conversation because he looks sad all of a sudden. He holds out his hand to me as if offering me the love his father can't, or won't, give.

I go to him and take his hand as a tear rolls down one of my cheeks. I quickly wipe it away, but it's too late. Lucas has seen it.

"Don't cry," he whispers to me. "Everything will be all right. You'll see."

I try to smile at him but can't quite force my lips to do something that my heart isn't feeling.

"Come on, Anna," Lucas says, tugging on my hand. "I want to show you my room."

Lucas takes me upstairs to his room and shows me all of his toys. He's so proud of everything he owns, and I can tell he takes care of each little thing, not taking for granted what he has like most children his age would. Yet Lucas's soul feels like an old one.

The depth of compassion and love he harbors for those in his life is so transparent in his looks and smiles. I wonder how a six-year-old can look so young yet carry the soul of someone so wise.

"Can I show you something without you telling my dad about it?" Lucas asks unexpectedly while we're building a castle with his wooden blocks.

"As long as it isn't something that's a danger to you," I reply.

Lucas smiles and stands up from the floor to walk over to one of the nightstands by his bed. He pulls out some papers and walks back over to hand them to me.

I take the white sheets of paper and notice they're all drawings of me.

I look up at Lucas, and he smiles.

"See," he says, "I told you I saw you in my vision."

My eyes begin to well again with tears because I'm torn between wanting to believe Lucas's vision and knowing that his father is doing everything he can to make sure it never comes to pass.

"It's a nice dream, Lucas," I tell him, handing back the drawings, "but that's all it is—a dream."

"No," Lucas says decisively. "It's not a dream. It's our future. I know it is."

I smile wanly at him and return my attention to the building blocks. I know if I don't, I might become upset in front of Lucas, and that's the last thing I want to do.

Lucas returns his drawings to the nightstand and comes back to sit with me on the floor.

"Anna," he says a little later, "have you ever thought about wooing my dad?"

I look up at Lucas. "How on earth does a six-year-old even know what 'wooing' means?"

Lucas shrugs. "Saw it in a movie once about a guy trying to get this girl to like him. It worked for him. I don't see why it wouldn't work for you."

I sit back and think about what Lucas just said.

"What exactly did this guy do to woo the girl he loved?"

Lucas sits and thinks before saying, "Well, he found out what she liked and then did things to make her happy."

"What does your dad like to do?" I ask.

"He loves to build things," Lucas says. "He has a workshop out back and stays in there a lot when we come to this house."

"Anything else?"

"He likes to cook. He said a friend of his showed him how to do it a long time ago, and it just sort of stuck with him. Oh, and he loves to play chess. He's always trying to teach me, but I just don't like it. Takes way too long to play. I like checkers better."

"I'm not very good at chess," I confess.

"That's perfect," Lucas says enthusiastically, "because my dad loves to win!"

I giggle.

"Lucas," we hear Malcolm say from the doorway, "it's time you went to bed. It's getting late."

Lucas groans but doesn't argue. He stands up and goes to his chest of drawers from which he pulls out a set of pajamas.

I stand up.

"Where is my room?" I ask Malcolm.

Malcolm tilts his head to the side, indicating I should follow him.

"Night, Anna," Lucas says, walking up to me before I leave the room and giving me a tight hug around the waist.

I bend down and kiss the top of his head. "Good night, Lucas. Sweet dreams."

He lets me go and continues to take his clothes off to change.

I follow Malcolm down the hallway to another bedroom. He

flips on the light in the room for me, and I see that it's a fairly large one with a good-sized bed and matching furniture.

"I brought up the satchel Jered gave you," Malcolm tells me, nodding to indicate that it's sitting on the bed. "If there's anything he forgot, just let me know. I might have something that will do."

"Thanks," I tell him, walking into the room.

"We'll be here for at least a couple of days," Malcolm tells me. "So try to get some rest while we're here. There's really nothing else to do."

"Okay," I say, "I will."

Malcolm just stands in the doorway, looking reluctant to leave.

"My room is at the end of the hallway," he tells me, "in case you need me for anything."

"Okay."

Still, Malcolm doesn't act like he's going to leave.

"Was there anything else you wanted?" I ask, needing him to either come in or go, because his reluctance to leave me is just fueling a hope that may cause me more pain in the end.

"No," he says, taking a step back from the door. "Good night, Anna."

"Good night, Malcolm."

Malcolm walks away, and I close the door, listening to his foot-falls as he walks away from me.

I walk over to the satchel on the bed and open it.

Jered bought me a couple of changes of clothes, some toiletries, and another pair of boots. I look in the satchel again but can't seem to find anything to sleep in. I don't particularly want to sleep in my leather outfit for another night. So I step out of my room to seek out Malcolm to see if he has a spare shirt I can borrow.

I hear voices coming from Lucas's room and make my way over there.

"Why don't you like her, Dad?" I hear Lucas ask.

I stop in mid-stride, curious to find out the answer to that question myself.

"I like her just fine," Malcolm answers, sounding amused by the question. "Why would you think I don't like Anna?"

"Because I heard what you said to her about not getting my hopes up."

"Oh," Malcolm says, obviously thinking our conversation had stayed private.

"Please, don't screw this up for us, Dad," I hear Lucas beg Malcolm. "She's everything we need to make us into a real family. I love her, and I think you do, too."

I lift my hand to my heart and close my eyes because I know I won't be able to stop the tears this time. I turn around and go back to my room, not worrying about a nightshirt anymore. After I quietly close the door behind me, I lean my back up against it and let my sorrow flow unhindered.

If Malcolm would just accept the love I have for him, our lives would be like the dreamworld Lucas saw in his vision. We could have a life only a few people get to share with one another. But I'm at a loss as to how to make that happen.

I'm not sure how long I stand there crying, but eventually I hear a soft knock on the other side of the door.

"Yes?" I ask, wiping at the tears on my face.

"I wasn't sure if Jered packed you anything to sleep in," I hear Malcolm say from the hallway. "I brought you something in case you need it."

I curse softly under my breath because the last thing I want is for Malcolm to see me crying. The best thing I can do to hide the fact is turn off the light in the room before I open the door.

I don't open the door fully, and I only allow half my face to be seen, angling the door in such a way that Malcolm can't see it fully.

Malcolm stands in the hallway, only wearing a pair of white silk pajama pants, and I wonder if he realizes what seeing him like that does to me. He hands me what looks like the matching shirt to the pants he has on. I take the shirt.

"Thank you," I tell him, moving to close the door when he places his hand on it to stop me.

"Are you okay?" he asks, his voice full of concern.

"I'm fine," I tell him, moving to close the door again, but Malcolm stops me once more.

"No, you're not," he says matter-of-factly. "I can feel it."

I just look at him, wondering how he can deny the fact that we belong together when he can stand there and feel my pain.

"Then do something about it if you care so much," I tell him, not trying to hide my aggravation as I force the door closed.

I stand there with only the closed door separating us, waiting for him to leave, but he doesn't for a long time.

I reach for the doorknob, about to wrench the door open to see what he will do, but before I can, I hear him walk away, and the sound of a door closing down the hallway tells me where he's gone.

I walk back to my bed and undress, slipping on the shirt Malcolm gave me. I climb into the bed and instantly feel cradled in its softness, realizing just how tired I am. It doesn't take long before exhaustion completely washes over my body and I have no lasting memory of even falling to sleep.

Sometime in the middle of the night, I feel something warm wiggle against me. The sensation wakes me immediately, and I find Lucas crawling into bed with me.

"Are you okay?" I ask him, assuming something must have spooked him during the night and he's simply seeking sanctuary.

"I know I won't get to spend a lot of time with you before I have to leave," he tells me. "We probably won't see each other again until you and Dad finish your mission and we can all be a family."

"Lucas," I say, a warning in my voice, "please don't get your hopes up. Your dad's made it pretty clear he doesn't want to have anything to do with me after we complete our mission."

"You can change his mind," Lucas says, full of confidence. "Tomorrow we're gonna start Operation Family."

Dear Lord, could this kid get any cuter? Is it possible for me to love him any more than I do right this moment? I don't think so.

"What exactly do you have in mind?" I ask him, feeling completely amused by the notion.

Lucas snuggles in next to me, and I wrap my arms around him.

"Lots," he tells me, closing his eyes and sighing in contentment. "Just you watch, we'll get Dad to smarten up."

I rest my chin against the top of Lucas's and smile. I hope my little partner in crime is a miracle worker in disguise, because I think that's what we'll need ...

... a miracle.

CHAPTER 22

I wake up the next morning and find Lucas gone from my bed. I immediately sit up and notice that the door to my room is cracked open. In the quiet of the morning, I can hear him giggling somewhere in the house. The deep rumble of Malcolm's laughter joins Lucas's and travels into my room, piquing my interest about what the two of them are up to.

I quickly slip off my nightshirt and slip on some of the clothes Jered bought me. The clothing is simple and something downworlders must wear. He bought me a soft, dark pink knit sweater and a pair of blue jeans. The boots are black leather and simple, but hardy enough to get me through any type of weather.

I walk down the stairs to the first floor and follow the sound of their voices until I come to a bright and airy kitchen.

Lucas is standing on a stool by an old-fashioned stove with a spatula in his hands. Malcolm, dressed in a pair of jeans and a white button-down shirt, looks on in a supervisory role as Lucas flips something cooking in the pan in front of him with the spatula.

Lucas laughs and lifts his arms in the air, shouting, "I did it!"

Malcolm chuckles at Lucas's enthusiasm and looks over at me when he realizes I'm standing there.

The laughter in his eyes fades when he sees me, and I'm instantly saddened that just looking at me can accomplish such a task.

I avert my gaze from them and look out the windows on the back side of the house.

"Is that snow?" I ask in amazement. "Real snow?"

"It must have started sometime during the night," Malcolm answers.

I can't help but smile and rush out the double doors that lead from the kitchen to a veranda on the back of the house. I walk down the steps from the porch to the backyard, which faces the lake. I hold out my hand and let the flakes of snow land there. They don't melt instantly like the artificial snow in Cirrus did, but they do eventually liquefy. I hold my face up to the gently falling snow and let it kiss my skin.

"You're going to get sick just standing out here in what you have on," I hear Malcolm say behind me.

He runs one of his hands down my right arm until he reaches the crook of my elbow and then gently tugs.

"Come inside the house, Anna. You can play in the snow later."

I turn to look at Malcolm and see amusement in his eyes as he looks at me.

"Is that a promise?" I ask him, not wanting to leave the snow just yet.

"Yes," he says, almost smiling. "I promise you and Lucas can play in the snow later. Now, come on. The breakfast he made for you will get cold."

I follow Malcolm into the house and find Lucas setting a plate full of pancakes on the kitchen island across from the stove.

"I hope you like pancakes," Lucas says to me. "It's probably not as fancy as what you eat in Cirrus, but they're my favorite."

"They smell wonderful," I tell Lucas as I sit on a stool at the island.

Lucas is very attentive and makes sure I have plenty of butter and syrup for my pancakes. Malcolm even pours me a glass of fresh milk.

"Were you here recently?" I ask Malcolm. "Is that why you have fresh food in the house?"

"No, we haven't been here since the summer," Malcolm tells me. "But we have a preserver."

I know what he's talking about because we have them in Cirrus. It is a device used to preserve perishables to keep them from spoiling for extended periods of time.

"I thought that type of technology was outlawed here."

"It is. I procured mine through Bartholomew's services."

"So even overlords aren't allowed technology from Cirrus?"

"No, we're not. I have a hard time believing the royal family would put me in jail for owning a few things, especially considering how much money I make for them."

"What will happen to your business while you're an accused traitor to the crown?" I ask.

"I'm sure Levi will give my job to someone he can control. In the long run it doesn't really matter, because you will be the ruler of Cirrus soon enough and straighten out the mess this world is in."

"Yes, I will," I say confidently. "I'll prove to the other cloud cities that it's time we stopped keeping the down-world in the dark. Once they see us succeed, I have no doubt they'll follow our lead."

"I expect you'll accomplish your goals," Malcolm says. "I'll do everything I can to make your dream come true."

"Does that mean you'll make *my* dreams come true, too?" Lucas says hopefully, grinning his gap-toothed grin at Malcolm.

Malcolm ruffles his son's hair and declares, "You are completely incorrigible."

"I don't even know what 'incorrigible' means," Lucas confesses.

"It means you're spoiled rotten," Malcolm tells him. "Now go make me some pancakes, too."

While we eat breakfast, Lucas tells me his itinerary for us for the day, which starts out with us making a snowman. I begin to wonder if Lucas has completely forgotten Operation Family, since most of his other ideas only include me and him.

After he wolfs down his pancakes, Lucas sets his plate in the sink and says, "I'm gonna go get my coat!"

He rushes out of the kitchen, and I can hear his little feet as they pound up the stairs.

"Your leather jacket is probably the best thing to wear outside," Malcolm tells me. "It'll keep you warmer than anything I have for you to wear."

"Are you going to come outside and play with us?" I ask Malcolm, hoping he will so we can spend some quality time together.

"I have a project I'm working on in the workshop," he tells me. "I would like to finish it before we have to leave."

I'm more than mildly disappointed but don't say anything. I get up from my stool and place my dirty dish in the sink on top of Lucas's.

Just as I'm leaving the room to go upstairs and grab my jacket, Malcolm says, "Lucas said you and he were going to prepare supper tonight."

This statement brings me up short, but I don't tip my hat and let the surprise show on my face.

"Did Millie teach you how to cook?" he asks.

"Not exactly," I say, leaving the answer as ambiguous as it sounds.

But Malcolm's no fool.

"Have you ever cooked a meal in your life?" he asks me, a hint of a smile on his face.

"Not exactly," I say again, unable to hide a smile of my own.

Malcolm turns to face me fully and crosses his arms over his chest.

"Well, this should be interesting to see," he says dubiously. "Very interesting."

"You say that like you expect me to fail."

"I haven't known a female in your family who could cook an edible meal in the last thousand years. So, yes, I actually do expect you to fail ... miserably."

I place my hands on my hips. "That sounds like a challenge, Overlord Devereaux. Would you like to put a wager on your low expectations of my culinary skills?"

Malcolm narrows his eyes at me. "What kind of wager?"

"If I can cook a meal that is completely edible, you have to do something for me."

"And what exactly would this something be?" he asks, his interest aroused.

My mind races with the possibilities of such a wager, but I settle on something simple.

"A kiss," I tell him, watching for his reaction.

He doesn't give much away, and I can't read his expression to let me know how he feels about my request.

"What do I get if I win?" he asks.

"What do you want?" I ask in return, holding my breath because I feel like I might have made a big mistake in this little contest of ours. What if he asks that I stop trying to make him face his feelings for me? I think he knows me well enough by now to realize I would stay true to such a promise, no matter the pain it would cause me.

"If I win," Malcolm says slowly, "you have to play a game of chess with me."

Inwardly, I sigh in relief.

"Deal," I say, turning my back to him to walk away. For some reason, I look over my shoulder as I turn the corner of the hallway toward the stairs. I find Malcolm watching me with a thoughtful expression on his face. It's a look that gives me hope. I just pray it isn't a fool's hope.

Just as Lucas and I are about to walk out the double doors of the kitchen to the backyard, I hear Malcolm call my name.

I turn around to see him walking toward us carrying some knitted items in his hands.

"You should wear these," Malcolm says, setting the items on the kitchen table, picking up the scarf first, which he wraps around my neck for me. "The jacket will keep your chest warm, but the rest of you might feel the effects of the cold."

He reaches back and lifts my hair up over the back of the scarf so it can flow freely. He then picks up a pair of black leather gloves and holds them out one at a time for me to slip my hands into.

"They're big," he notes, "but they should at least keep your hands warm."

The last accessory is a black knit cap that he pulls over my head a little too far down, making it cover my face to my nose.

"Sorry." He chuckles as he folds it back up in the front to make it possible for me to see again.

Malcolm makes sure the sides are covering my ears, and I watch his expression turn thoughtful once again. His hands linger on either side of my head as he looks down at me. His hands slide down gently over my cheeks, cupping my face in a tender caress before falling back to his sides.

"You two have fun out there," he tells us but keeps his eyes steadily on me. "Don't get too cold."

Lucas tugs on one of my hands, and I reluctantly follow him out to the backyard.

First on Lucas's agenda is for us to make a snowman. I begin to ball up some snow to make the base, but Lucas says, "No, I don't want to make it here. I want to make it over there."

He points a short distance away. So I abandon my efforts and go to the spot where he wants us to work. We're working on patting down the snow on the belly portion of the snowman when Malcolm walks out of the house, only wearing a thin black jacket over his clothes. He makes his way to the workshop, which is closer to the shoreline. I watch him walk through the snow toward the building, but he doesn't seem to sense me staring at him. He walks into the rather large structure and flips on the light inside.

A window on the side of the workshop we're facing lets me see Malcolm stop dead center of it and look at something on his work-table there. He looks up and meets my gaze.

"Well, aren't you a devious little boy," I say to Lucas with a smile, now understanding why he was so exacting about where we built our snowman.

Lucas shrugs his shoulders and smiles cheekily.

"Like I said last night," he tells me, "Operation Family is now in full effect."

"Yes, your father told me about my offer to cook dinner for us tonight, something I don't remember promising at all. I really wish you had talked about that little part of your strategy with me first, Lucas."

"The fastest way to a man's heart is through his stomach," Lucas says like a recitation.

"Where did you learn that little gem?"

"Read it in a book," he tells me.

"A book?" I ask in surprise. "You can read?"

"I've been reading since I was three years old," he tells me proudly.

I stop patting the snow on our snowman and look at Lucas.

"Are you a genius?" I ask him.

"I'm pretty smart," he says immodestly. "My dad says I'm the smartest person he knows."

I smile. "That, my little matchmaker, I don't doubt for a moment."

"Then trust in my crazy genius!" Lucas says with maniacal laughter.

I reach down and grab a handful of snow, quickly forming it into a ball and throwing it at my crazy genius's head.

Lucas looks at me in surprise.

"Hmm," I say, "I thought a crazy genius would have seen that one coming."

Lucas's eyes squint up at me as he fakes a mad face.

"Oh, you really shouldn't have done that," he says ominously.

We both reach down for more snow at the same time.

I feel sure the fight that commences should go down in the history book of snowball fights. I end up laughing so hard I become blinded by tears and grab my little hellion around the waist before he can finish his next snowball. We tumble onto the ground together, still laughing.

"I surrender!" I tell him as we both lie in the snow.

"Hey, Anna!" Lucas says excitedly, sitting up to look at me. "Have you ever made a snow angel?"

I shake my head. "No, how do you make one?"

"Just stay on your back," he tells me, standing up. "Now put your arms out to your sides and spread your legs apart."

I do as Lucas instructs, but apparently I'm not doing it right. He helps position my arms and legs at the angles he deems proper.

"Now wave your arms and legs back and forth," he tells me.

I do as he says and feel completely silly, waving my legs and arms against the snow. But at this angle, the sun is shining directly onto my face, and I luxuriate in its warmth.

In Cirrus, the dome protecting us doesn't allow the natural heat from the sun to penetrate through to us. The contrast between the heat of the sun and the coldness of the snow is strangely comforting. I stop moving my legs and close my eyes, basking in the strange sensation.

"I'm gonna go make us some hot cocoa, Anna. You stay here," Lucas says to me.

I immediately open my eyes. "Is that safe?" I ask him. "Do you need me to come in and supervise?"

"Crazy geniuses don't need help making cocoa!" Lucas assures me. "I do it all the time. No worries, Anna."

Lucas scampers off toward the house, and I lie back down in the snow to enjoy the sunlight on my face.

"Where is he off to?" I hear Malcolm ask.

I open my eyes and see him looming over me, watching Lucas run up to the house.

"He said he was going to make us some hot cocoa. Is that safe for a boy his age to be doing all by himself?" I ask, shielding my eyes from the sun with one hand while I look up at Malcolm. "He told me he does it all the time, and I didn't sense a lie."

Malcolm looks down at me. "I think you've probably figured out by now that Lucas has an above average intellect."

"Yes," I admit. "I've noticed."

"You, on the other hand, greatly disappoint me," Malcolm says, but his voice has a note of jest in it, not seriousness.

"How so?" I ask, curious to see where this leads.

Malcolm proceeds to hold up one of his hands over my face with a snowball in it. Before I can react, he drops it.

"Far too easy, Anna." Malcolm laughs.

I instantly sit up, sputtering for breath and wiping the snow from my eyes.

"Run," I tell Malcolm in as menacing a voice as I can muster.

"And why, pray tell, should I do that?"

"Because you're about to lose a war you have no chance of winning."

"Really?" Malcolm says, sounding completely amused by my threat.

Before I know it, he drops another snowball on me, which lands directly on top of my head.

I decide two can fight dirty.

I grab two handfuls of snow and begin to make a ball. I see Malcolm bend over to start making his own ball, but before his hands can even touch the snow at his feet, I sweep one leg toward both of his and knock him to the ground and onto his back. Before he can recover, I quickly get to my feet and straddle his waist to keep him down on the ground.

Malcolm peers up at me, looking amused at finding himself in such a compromising position.

"Why, Empress Annalisse, who knew you liked to play so dirty?"

I smile down at him, patting my ball firmly between my hands.

"Why, Overlord Devereaux, who knew you could be bested by a woman so easily?"

Next thing I know, Malcolm grabs the back of my thighs and rolls me over onto my back in a blink of an eye, with him positioned on top of me between my legs.

"Did you ever consider the possibility," he says, leaning forward and bracing his hands on either side of my head as he brings his face down to mine with only inches separating us, "that it was part of my strategy all along?"

"Did you ever consider," I say back, having a hard time remembering my plan because the closeness of his lips is making it hard for me to keep a coherent thought in my head, "that this was part of mine?"

I reach between us and grab the waistband of Malcolm's pants, pulling them down just far enough to stuff my snowball into them.

Malcolm leaps off me, softly cursing me underneath his breath. I laugh as I take my opening and make a mad dash toward the safety of the house, but I soon hear the crunch of Malcolm's boots close behind me.

I'm only a short five feet from the steps leading up to the veranda and sanctuary when I feel Malcolm grab the back of my jacket and yank me backwards until I'm flush against him.

"Well, you do play dirty," Malcolm says against my ear, wrapping his arms around my waist, "but so do I."

With no time to react, he crams a snowball of his own up underneath my sweater, causing me to squirm against him, but he doesn't let me go. He keeps his arms firmly around me while he laughs.

I suddenly don't mind the snow against my belly even as it melts against my skin.

Malcolm is holding me and laughing. What more could I possibly want?

I begin to laugh, too, as the water begins to trickle down my pants.

Malcolm's hold on me loosens, and I take the opportunity to turn around in his arms and face him.

The smile on his face makes my heart flutter with happiness and, as selfish as it might be, I don't want this moment to end. I wish we could just forget about the world around us and what needs to be done so we can keep our focus on one another. I like seeing this playful, happy side to Malcolm. It's a part of him I haven't seen before, and all I want to do is keep him this way.

Unfortunately the outside world isn't something I can keep out, and I see the smile fade from Malcolm's lips as it begins to intrude into the moment.

"You should probably change your clothes," he tells me. "I probably should, too, if I'm ever planning to have children again."

I can't help the laugh that escapes with my breath.

"Sorry about that," I tell him. "Kind of."

Malcolm raises an eyebrow at me. "I wouldn't be. It was a good move because it was totally unexpected. I never would have thought you to be the type of woman to stuff her hand down the front of a man's trousers."

"I didn't go that far down," I defend.

"No," Malcolm agrees, a devilish twinkle in his eyes, "not nearly far enough."

I feel myself begin to blush and hear Malcolm chuckle.

He drops his arms away from me.

"You should go change clothes, and I should probably check on Lucas."

I nod, turning to walk up the steps when Malcolm grabs hold of one of my hands to stop me. I turn back to face him and wait for him to say something.

He simply looks at me and doesn't say a word.

I don't speak either, because I don't think he took my hand to tell me anything. I get the feeling he's like me and just doesn't want the moment to end yet.

Finally he lets my hand go. I hesitate, waiting to see if he wants to say something, but he never does.

"I'll be back down in a few minutes," I tell him.

He nods his head but still doesn't say anything.

When I walk into the kitchen, I see Lucas sitting at the kitchen table with three mugs of cocoa in front of him.

"Have fun?" he asks me, looking awfully pleased with himself.

"Yes," I tell him, realizing Lucas *is* a crazy genius. "Although I'm completely wet now."

"Really?" Malcolm says, like this simple statement intrigues him for some reason.

"Soaking wet," I admit to him freely.

Malcolm's grin grows wider, but he doesn't say anything else.

I'm totally confused but don't question his odd reaction.

It's not until I'm walking up the stairs to my room and taking off my gloves that I suddenly realize what Malcolm was actually thinking about when I said I was soaking wet. I feel my cheeks burn from embarrassment, but a small light of hope flickers inside my breast that maybe, just maybe, the wall surrounding Malcolm's heart is melting enough for me to find a way in.

I go up to my room and quickly change out of my wet clothes. If Malcolm is ready to let me in, I don't want to waste the opportunity.

CHAPTER 23

When I go back downstairs, I see that Lucas has talked Malcolm into playing a game of checkers with him while they sip their steaming hot cocoa. Malcolm is sitting at the head of the table. I sit on the other side of him, opposite Lucas.

The two of them look so serious, as they study the board between them, that I can't help but smile. Knowing Malcolm is smart but having to think so hard to play a game of checkers against a six-year-old tickles my heart.

As they both concentrate on their separate strategies, I look at them and understand why Lucas so desperately wants us to become a real family. It just feels right. I grew up in a home with only my papa and always felt that was enough, but now, feeling the way I do about Lucas, I wonder what it would have been like if my mother had survived my birth and been able to raise me herself.

I never felt the absence of a mother's love because my papa always lavished me with his. Yet I begin to wonder how different my life would have been if my mother and Lucifer had raised me.

Or would Lucifer have even stuck around to be a real father to me? He obviously didn't want to have anything to do with me after I was born. Maybe he would have abandoned both my mother and me even if she had lived. I just didn't have any way of knowing because I didn't know much about my biological father. I didn't know the real reason he left me after my mother's death any more than I knew the real reason Malcolm asked my papa to take me to Cirrus right after my birth.

However, I wouldn't change a thing about my life. Andre Greco was the most attentive father I could have ever asked for. He loved me enough to trade in his immortality, just so he wouldn't have to go through the pain of losing me to death. I had two parents who gave up everything for me. One gave her mortal life, so that I could have a chance at one, and the other gave up his right to live forever and live as a human.

I look over at Lucas and know that if we ever found ourselves in a life-and-death situation, I would choose his life over mine without having to think twice about it.

During the game, Malcolm diverts his attention away from the board and looks over at me. A small smile lifts one corner of his mouth, and for the first time since meeting him, I see an emotion within the depth of his gaze as he looks at me that brings much needed warmth to my heart. He looks ... content.

I know then that Lucas' Operation Family is having the desired effect on one Malcolm Xavier Devereaux.

The game ends about thirty minutes later, with Malcolm winning. I have a hunch Lucas might have let him win.

This day *was* designed to make and keep Malcolm happy, after all. And Lucas did say that Malcolm liked to win.

Malcolm stands from the table and says to Lucas, "Why don't you put your coat on and come to the workshop to help me with my project?"

He then looks over at me. "I think it might be time for you to begin our bet."

I look to Lucas. "I thought Lucas and I were going to make supper together."

Malcolm smiles. "That was before we made our wager. I don't think it's a true bet if you don't try to prepare supper by yourself, do you?"

Lucas looks startled, like he thinks this is a monumentally bad idea and turns his gaze to me. "Have you ever cooked?"

"No," I say hesitantly, "but I'm sure I can figure it out."

"All of the meats and perishables are in the preserver," Malcolm tells me. "There are some canned items in the cabinets. I'm sure you can find something to make."

"Like I said," I tell him confidently, "I'll figure it out."

Malcolm puts on his thin black jacket and takes ahold of Lucas by the shoulders.

"Come on, Lucas. I have a feeling it might be safer for us outside."

I feel my forehead crinkle at the remark.

"You don't think she's gonna burn the house down, do you?" Lucas asks, looking up at his dad in worry, like it's a real possibility.

"With her family's history for cooking, I wouldn't rule it out."

"Oh, please," I say with a roll of my eyes. "I'm not going to burn the house down!"

Malcolm doesn't look convinced. "Well, if you do, then I definitely win the bet."

"What's the bet?" Lucas asks.

"None of your business," Malcolm tells him, ruffling his hair. "Come on. Let's go to the workshop. I think Anna is going to need the next couple of hours to figure things out."

As they walk out of the house, I just shake my head at them, thinking Malcolm is being a bit ridiculous. Even the lowliest of servants in Cirrus knows how to cook. How hard could it possibly be?

I rummage through the items in the preserver and settle on a cut of frozen meat that looks a lot like a roast. Millie always made the best roast beef, and I at least know what it should look like once it's fully cooked. I find a deep roasting pan in one of the cabinets and set the meat inside it. Also in the preserver I find some potatoes, carrots, and onions. I locate a cutting board, and a knife, and slice up the vegetables to a paper-thin width.

I shake my head, not quite understanding why Malcolm thought this would be such an impossible task for me to accomplish. I just hope he doesn't try to back out of his part of the wager when I win.

I find some dried herbs and seasoning salts in the cupboard and sprinkle them on the meat. I turn the oven on and try to guess what temperature the meat will need to cook at, wishing I had read at least one cookbook in my life. Although cooking in Cirrus is definitely faster than here. We have ovens that cook food almost instantaneously. I decide to set the temperature to four hundred degrees, thinking this should be plenty hot to cook the meat.

After this is done, I begin to wonder what I should do with the rest of my time. Not having anything else better to occupy me, I put my jacket on and go out to the workshop to see what the boys are up to.

When I open the door and step inside, Malcolm and Lucas look up at me in surprise.

"Done already?" Malcolm asks.

"It's cooking," I say, completely confident in what I've prepared.

Malcolm sets down the small hammer in his hand. "What exactly are you cooking?"

"A roast."

Malcolm raises his eyebrows. "In the oven?"

I nod my head. "Yes."

"At what temperature?"

"Four hundred degrees."

Malcolm looks at an old-fashioned clock on the wall, as if he's making a note of the time.

"Wanna help, Anna?" Lucas asks me.

I walk over to where they are and look at the wooden house they are standing in front of on the workshop table.

"Is it a playhouse?" I ask.

"No, it's a birdhouse," Lucas tells me.

"Lucas likes to watch the birds when we're here," Malcolm says. "I built him a small one, but apparently that wasn't enough for Little Lord Fauntleroy. He wanted them to have a mansion instead."

The birdhouse they are working on looks like a miniature replica of Malcolm's home. It stands at least three feet tall and two feet wide. It even has the front and back porch built onto it. I notice the small birdhouse that they mentioned sitting on a corner of the worktable.

"What are you going to do with the small one?" I ask.

"Really haven't thought about it," Malcolm says with a shrug.

"It looks like it needs to be painted."

"Do you know how to paint?" Lucas asks me.

I shrug. "I don't know. I've never tried."

"Caylin was an excellent artist," Malcolm tells me. "Maybe you inherited some of her skill."

"It might be fun to try," I say, walking over to the birdhouse.

Malcolm finds me a stool, some small paintbrushes, and some paints. While he and Lucas continue to work on the large birdhouse, I study the small one and try to envision what I want to see. I soon figure it out and start to work.

I become so engrossed in what I'm doing that I don't notice the passage of time. I'm faintly aware of what Malcolm and Lucas are doing but don't really pay them much attention either. It's not until I feel someone beside me that I look up from my project to meet Malcolm's amused gaze.

"Having fun?" he asks me.

I let out a small laugh. "Is it that obvious?"

Malcolm grins at me and looks at the house. "You have a natural talent. I thought you might. Most of the girls retained Caylin's aptitude for painting."

"I never knew I could do it," I say, surprised by how good I am at it.

Lucas comes over and stands by Malcolm to see the front of the birdhouse, which is all I've finished so far.

"Looks kind of girly," he comments, scrunching up his little nose at it.

I study the house and have to admit that it does look a bit girly with the flowers I've painted.

"Well, I'm a girl," I say, thinking it perfectly logical that the house should look girly because of this fact.

"Come on," Malcolm tells us, "we should probably make sure the house is still standing."

"Why wouldn't it be?" I ask, getting up from my stool and placing the paintbrush in my hand into a cup of water Malcolm got for me to wash the brushes in.

"It's been close to three hours since you came out here," he tells me.

"Three hours!"

I rush out of the workshop and into the house before either Malcolm or Lucas have a chance to react.

The kitchen is a little smoky but not nearly as horrible as I feared it would be. I go to the oven and grab a towel from the counter to pull the roast out of the oven. The outside of it looks dry and burnt, and the thinly sliced vegetables surrounding it are dehydrated to a crisp. I know my only saving grace is to see if I'm able to salvage some of the meat on the inside. I quickly find a knife and begin to cut the roast, but the knife doesn't make it all the way through the meat. The core of it is still frozen solid.

I sigh because I know I'm completely defeated and have lost my chance at being kissed by Malcolm. I can't deny my extreme disappointment. I would have liked a kiss from Malcolm. And I have a feeling he wouldn't have voiced any complaints about it either.

"So," I hear Malcolm say as he and Lucas come into the kitchen, "how good are you at chess?"

"About as good as I am at cooking," I admit with a sigh. "It should be a very short game."

Malcolm tries to hold in his laughter but finally gives into it and laughs so hard he starts to cry.

I don't mind. I don't even mind losing the bet that much since I at least get to hear Malcolm's laughter again. In a way, I feel like I *have* won. His mirth becomes totally infectious, and Lucas and I soon join in.

Since my plans for supper are completely ruined, Malcolm makes a quick meal of sandwiches for us to eat.

All the activity from the day seems to have made Lucas extremely sleepy. After we eat, he crawls up into my lap while Malcolm is washing the dishes in the sink. Lucas kisses me on the cheek and whispers in my ear, "I think Operation Family was a success."

I smile down at him as he lays his head on my chest and closes his eyes.

"Anna, would you sing to me again?" he requests.

I begin to sing the same lullaby as before and find that it lulls him fast to sleep. I cradle him in my arms and stand up.

"Could you fix his bed for me?" I whisper to Malcolm, not wanting to unintentionally wake Lucas.

Malcolm nods and precedes me out of the kitchen, up to Lucas's room.

After Malcolm has the covers of Lucas's bed drawn down, I lay Lucas on the mattress and slip off his shoes for him. Malcolm covers his son with the sheet and quilt. He leans down and kisses Lucas on the forehead before we both leave the room.

"Ready for that game of chess?" Malcolm asks me as we descend the staircase.

"Like I said," I tell him, "it will probably be a short game. I've never been very good at it."

"That's all right," Malcolm says with a shrug and sly grin. "I like to win anyway."

I have to smile because his words are almost a mirror of his son's from the previous night.

When Malcolm reaches the bottom of the staircase, he turns around to face me and holds out his hand for me to take.

"I don't think I've shown you my study," he says to me. "I have my chessboard set up in there."

I slip my hand into Malcolm's and let him lead me to his study, which turns out to be a room just off the foyer.

The room is homey with tall bookshelves lining all four walls.

I look at all the leather-bound volumes in amazement.

"Are all of these real?" I ask, never having seen so many books made with paper before.

"Yes, we still produce them here on the surface," Malcolm tells me, letting go of my hand to walk over to the fireplace to start a fire.

The smell of the room is overwhelming, but in a good way. I love the mingled scents of leather, wood, and paper. It just seems so much like Malcolm that I instantly feel comfortable in it. In a short time, Malcolm has a roaring fire going to take the chill out of the air, and I see that he has his chessboard set up in front of the fireplace with two brown leather wingback chairs on either side of the table it sits on.

I raise an eyebrow at the board as I sit down in one of the chairs.

"Another contraband item?" I ask, having seen this particular type of chessboard before.

Malcolm grins. "I like chess, and this is the best board money can buy."

Malcolm runs his hand across the board, and holographic images of real people dressed as their particular chess pieces appear on their designated squares. I'm given the white pieces to play, while Malcolm is black.

"White always makes the first move," Malcolm says.

I tap one of my pawns on the head, gaining his attention, and touch the square I want him to move to.

As promised, the game is short and sweet, and Malcolm wins in fewer than twenty moves.

"You really weren't kidding," Malcolm says. "You're awful at this game."

I shrug, completely unapologetic. "Told you."

Malcolm sweeps his hand across the board, automatically resetting the pieces into place.

"Two out of three?" he asks.

"Sounds like fun," I say, just happy to have him come up with such a suggestion, like he wants to keep me near and spend time with him.

When Malcolm wins the next game just as easily, he sighs heavily.

"I'm going to have to teach you how to play this game properly," he tells me, standing from his chair. "I think I have a book you can read that explains some strategy. It should help you a great deal."

I watch as Malcolm goes to one of the bookshelves and begins to scan the shelf in front of him for the volume. As I watch him standing there, I can't help but feel a heated impulse to go to him. I see no reason not to give into the force that is driving me to him. Malcolm was made for me, after all. God said so.

I stand from my chair and walk up behind Malcolm. He's holding the book now and is looking inside it with his head bowed, flipping through the pages like he's looking for some passage in particular.

When I reach him, I tentatively place the palm of my hands on his shoulders near the base of his neck. He flinches slightly, but I get the feeling it's just because he wasn't expecting my touch, not because it's unpleasant to him. He doesn't say anything, and he doesn't try to move away. I take that as my cue to continue.

I glide my hands across his broad shoulders and then down the sides of his back, feeling his muscles tense slightly beneath my hands as they travel over him. He slowly places the book back in its place and grabs the edge of the shelf with both hands, leaning his forehead against it while bending one leg at the knee. I let my hands travel around the sides of his waist until I feel the firm ripples of his stomach through his shirt. I glide my hands over his taut belly until they come to rest against the firmness of his chest.

"Anna," he sighs, closing his eyes, "what are you doing to me?"

"What I've wanted to do to you for quite some time now," I tell him, letting my hands slide back down from his chest and return to the small of his back.

Malcolm turns around to face me and leans his back against the bookcase, halfway sitting on the lowest shelf. His eyes hold a need for me that I've longed to see from him, causing hope to flare inside my chest like a red-hot beacon. I take a step toward Malcolm.

He grabs me by the waist and has my back up against the bookshelf in an instant. He puts one knee between my legs and gently lays his forehead against mine, closing his eyes and breathing heavily.

I raise a hand to his face, tenderly cupping his cheek and marveling at the sensation of his warm breath against my lips. I take a chance and lean in to touch his lips with mine, but he instantly pulls his head back before they have a chance to meet.

I look into his now-open eyes and see an intense war of emotions playing out within their depths.

I have a feeling this is the moment that will determine our fate with one another. It's time for me to lay open my heart to him, completely naked and vulnerable, to see if he will accept everything I am offering or reject me and the future we can have together.

"I love you," I tell him, finally saying the words that have been living inside my heart for so long now. "I've been in love with you since the first moment I saw you. I always told Auggie that when I finally met the person I was supposed to be with, I would feel the earth beneath my feet move and my heart quake just from being near him. I felt those two things happen the moment I saw you, Malcolm. I didn't need God to tell me we were meant to be together because I already knew that. And I don't think you can stand here in front of me and keep denying the connection we have to one another anymore. This is me willingly giving you all that I am. Accept my love for you. Accept everything that I'm offering you so we can both finally find happiness."

Malcolm closes his eyes again, and I see his Adam's apple move up and down as he swallows hard. He begins to shake his head slowly and mutters, "I can't. I can't."

"Yes, you can," I urge, knowing that if I don't change his mind this night, he's lost to me forever.

Malcolm continues to shake his head. "I'm so sorry, Anna. I just can't. I don't think I'll ever be able to give you what you need. I'll never be able to provide you the happiness you deserve. You need to forget about me, about us."

His words provide the final twist to my already fragile heart, breaking it completely in two.

"I guess I was a fool to let myself hope you could love me like I love you," I tell him, not attempting to hide my tears from him because there's no point. He has to know how much pain he's causing me. It's not like I can conceal my sorrow from the man whose soul is tethered to mine. "Today was like a dream come true for me, Malcolm. I saw the person you could be if you would just open up your heart to me. That's the person I want to share my life with. That's the person who makes me feel whole. If you can't be that man for me, then I guess you're right. I guess I have no choice but to try to forget the man you could be. I may be strong, but my heart's just too fragile to keep going back and forth between the man you were today and the man you were yesterday. I can't survive this kind of pain any longer. I can't keep hoping you'll pick me to live in the present with instead of choosing to live in the past with Lilly's ghost haunting your dreams. My heart can't take any more of your uncertainty."

Malcolm looks into my eyes and says nothing for what feels like forever.

Finally he says, "I'm sorry."

My heart feels like it's made out of glass and Malcolm's words are a hammer against it, shattering it to pieces inside my chest, scattering the remains to the four corners of the earth, forever lost. I only know of one way to repair it enough, just to continue on and retain at least a small portion of my sanity.

"Then I have to let you go," I say, taking a deep, shuddering breath. "I release you from our bond, Malcolm. I hope that makes you happy."

I gently push Malcolm away, and he doesn't resist.

I walk out of the room but have no idea where I'm going because all I feel is blinding pain.

On impulse, I go to the kitchen and grab my jacket from my chair at the table and walk out of the house. I head straight for the workshop because I need something to take my mind off of what just happened. I turn the light on in the building when I get there and go sit down in front of the small birdhouse I was painting earlier. I sit there and stare at it for a long time, my mind completely dazed and confused.

I suddenly hate everything about the small birdhouse sitting in front of me. The stupid happy flowers are just a reminder that my life will never truly be a happy one. The beautiful fantasy world Lucas conjured up had me fooled into believing it was something I could actually have. He would never be my son, and I would never get to know the children he said he saw me and Malcolm having in his vision.

I pick the house up with one hand and throw it against a wall of the workshop, shattering it into pieces.

I let out a small sob and bury my face in my hands, crying so hard I feel like my heart is about to burst out of my chest from the agony I feel.

Every hope, every dream I ever had about a life with Malcolm slowly floats away with each tear I shed. I know my life will never feel complete, and I'll have to live with this aching emptiness inside my chest for the rest of my days.

I begin to wonder if someone can actually die from a broken heart and selfishly wish for such a sweet release.

CHAPTER 24

(Malcolm's Point of View)

I can't even make myself watch her leave because it's hard enough to feel the pain she's in. It's a pain I know I've caused her by not being able to fully give her my heart or be the man she truly deserves. I want to be that man, but something deep inside my soul holds me back, like a rusty old anchor that wants to break but is simply too strong, or too stubborn, to let go.

I never wanted this. I never wanted to fall in love with Anna, and I consider it a cruel joke my father has played on us both.

When Anna was first born, I didn't want anything to do with her. I didn't even want to see her. The love child of Lucifer wasn't even something I wanted living underneath the same roof as me. I considered her an abomination of everything we had worked so hard for during the last thousand years. She was my greatest failure, and that's why I had Andre get her out of my house almost as soon as she came into this world.

I had no intention of ever seeing her in person. She was a

reminder of how I failed to keep my last promise to Lilly, a promise I had no intention of ever breaking.

Amalie, the most stubborn of all the descendants, chose Lucifer to fall in love with of all people. Now I realize their union was meant to be. At the time, my anger at her insistence that Lucifer was her soul mate did nothing but fuel a rage that had been building inside of me for a thousand years. Lucifer's constant goading of me down through the centuries to give into my pain and freely hand him my soul in exchange for an end to my suffering tarnished my heart and almost drove me insane.

He played his part well as the great tempter, offering to lift the curse his hellhound placed on me with its bite. And for a thousand years I stoutly refused his propositions, even though there were times I almost gave in. There were times I *wanted* to give in. It was only the strength of my promise to Lilly that kept me strong. When Amalie defied my orders to stay away from Lucifer, I felt part of my resolve begin to crumble. I had failed Lilly. What was the point of fighting fate?

However, the pain I've endured because of that curse is nothing compared to the pain I feel now with Anna's sorrow coursing through my veins like molten lava.

I turn away from the bookshelf and hurriedly march out of the room. I head straight for the front door and walk out into the night, welcoming the cold, biting wind that now blows, cooling my skin but doing nothing to ease the ache in my heart.

I hike through the forest until I come to her house.

I walk up the steps to the back porch of a place I once considered my home, too. It was Lilly and Brand's home, but they always made me feel like a part of their family. For years I never quite understood why Brand put up with me being around them so much. I finally figured out that he knew Lilly needed me in her life almost as much as she needed him. She may not have loved me like she did him, but a part of her needed the friendship and comfort I offered. Just like I knew she belonged with Brand, Brand knew that my heart was pledged to Lilly and that I would help keep her safe no matter the personal cost.

I don't come to this place much anymore. The memories of the people I love are hidden around every corner, like echoes of a happier time. I look to the boathouse where Caylin's art studio used to be and can still see her smiling at me. I look to the castle swing set and see a pigtailed, three-year-old Mae sliding down the rainbow slide, laughing. Everywhere I look, I see phantoms of those I have loved but who had to leave this life, and me, behind.

For years, I yearned for the day when I could be made human and finally end an existence that had no more meaning.

Then I felt Anna.

The night I sensed her pain was unlike anything I had ever experienced before. Mason tried to explain to me how it felt when he would feel Jess's pain through the connection of their souls, but even his description didn't prepare me for what I felt that night. I don't even think it can be adequately described to another person. It's something you have to experience for yourself. The moment I felt her pain, I knew I had to go to her, and without even having to think about it, I went.

When I saw her lying on the veranda of her home, writhing in pain, I actually had to take a moment to rationalize what I was seeing at first. Caylin had told us about knowing who she was supposed to pick to watch over the princes and her descendants because they glowed to her eyes. At the time, she said it was a sign of their devotion. I never quite understood what she was talking about, but in that moment, standing over Anna, I finally did.

When I looked at Anna, she held a luminescent glow around her that not even the sun itself could match. Then, when I held her in my arms that night, I felt a peace settle over my heart unlike anything I had ever felt before. It was almost the same type of peace I felt the first time I met Lilly, but far stronger ... everlasting.

However, I couldn't admit any of this to Anna. Hell, I couldn't even admit it to myself. When she looked at me for the first time, I knew she loved me. It was so plainly written on her face that I couldn't believe it at first. I had to stand up and turn away from her gaze because I didn't feel worthy of her love. She looked so beautiful, like a true angel of mercy who was opening her heart to me, of all people, a sinner of the worst kind.

When she came to my room that night after the ball, I had been thinking about all of the events in my life that helped forge me into who I am. I thought about all the people I had loved and lost. I thought about Lilly and wondered what she would think about me falling in love with one of her descendants. Would she be ashamed of me? Would she be happy?

Most of all, I thought about Anna. I felt so different when she was near—almost at peace with myself but always having this nagging doubt that I didn't deserve someone like her loving me. When she phased to my room that night, I instantly felt her presence. Her touch made me yearn to grab her and never let her go. As she stood in front of me in just her thin nightgown, I felt my body stir with need for her, but I held myself back because I didn't truly believe she was mine to have. Why would my father gift a man like me with a woman who was so pure, so beautiful, and so loving?

When I phased to her bedroom to help her learn how to phase on her own, I sat on her bed, waiting for her to follow me. All I could think about as I sat there was making her mine and laying claim not only to her heart but to her body as well. I wanted to complete the connection between us and tenderly lavish every inch of her soft flesh with all the love I had pent up inside me. I almost gave in when she asked me to stay with her. Any doubt I might have had that she desired me in the same way instantly vanished. But I held myself back. I wasn't ready to fully commit to her then because I still felt a need to keep my love for Lilly alive and remain faithful to one of the truest loves I've ever felt.

Then Anna entered my dreamworld—a place I kept rich with all of my memories of Lilly. When I realized what she'd done, I hated her for it. I hated the fact that she had trespassed on, what was to me, hallowed ground. No one, not even Lilly, had ever been privy to my true thoughts and feelings like that. No one knows the depth of pain that I've lived with since Lilly's passing. I've always been one to keep my emotions buried deep inside my heart, and I certainly never had any intentions of sharing them with Anna. I felt violated afterwards and let my anger get the best of me. I tried to become indifferent to her but found it an impossible act to keep up.

Even though I knew she loved me and would give me everything I ever wanted if I asked, I kept myself distanced from her as best I could. I didn't want to give her false hope. I didn't want to cause her unneeded pain because I felt sure I could never be the type of man someone so pure of heart and so strong-willed deserved. I tried so hard to let her know that there could be no future for us. But she just wouldn't give up. Stubbornness is one trait I wish she hadn't inherited.

Then today, I felt like maybe I could accept the love she seemed so determined to give me. Maybe I could be the man she needed and offer her a place inside my heart. Perhaps there was room enough in there for me to hold onto my love for Lilly while accepting what I felt for Anna. But I think I've just loved Lilly for far too long. I'm not sure I can let her go. I'm not sure I have it in me to want to let her go.

"Malcolm," I hear a familiar, disappointed voice say behind me, "what are you doing?"

I squeeze my eyes shut tight and bow my head, feeling the presence of my dearest so close to me after all these years.

"You pick *now* to come to me?" I ask, not trying to hide my hurt. "Why now, Lilly? I've begged for you to talk to me for so long. Why are you picking this night of all nights to answer my prayer?"

"Because you need me," she answers, her ever-present compassion for me in her voice. "And you need to hear me tell you that it's time for you to let me go."

As I turn around to face the woman who helped me find myself again all those years ago, I sigh heavily and brace my heart for what it's about to go through.

"I don't know if I can let you go," I tell her. "I've loved you for so long. I don't think I know how to stop."

"You don't have to stop," she tells me. "You can always love me like I've always loved you: as a friend. Malcolm, this is your time to live a life that you've always deserved but always thought you didn't. Anna loves you more than anyone else ever will. Her love for you isn't something that just happened. She's loved you for a very, very long time."

"We've only known each other for a few days," I say, trying to make sense of what Lilly is saying but not able to.

"Do you remember that time Caylin and I went to Heaven to see Utha Mae?"

I nod. "Yes, of course I do."

"We met Anna while we were there," she tells me. "She told me then that I shouldn't worry about you, because when she was finally able to come to Earth, she would take good care of you. I believed her then, and I believe her now. You've seen the evidence of her devotion to you with your own eyes, even before either of you spoke a word to one another. Anna loved you before she ever came into this world. She is the one you were always meant to be with, Malcolm. If anyone was a cheap substitute here, it was me. I was simply someone who showed you that you *could* love again. Anna's love is the one you've been waiting your whole life for. Her love for you is the truest you will ever feel. She's offering all of herself to you. That was something I could never do because you and I were never soul mates."

"I'm tired, Lilly," I confess, feeling the strain of the last thousand years all at once. "This life hasn't been an easy one. I've wanted to give up so many times."

"I know it hasn't been an easy life for you," Lilly says sympathetically. "But if you would just follow what your heart is telling you to do, you would have the life you've always wanted—the life I've always wanted for you. Anna's love for you is unconditional and so pure I can practically see its light from Heaven. You were made for her, Malcolm. Stop pushing her away and accept the happiness she's offering you. She is everything you've ever wanted and everything you never even imagined you needed. Stop fighting what you feel and just love her."

I walk up to Lilly and tentatively stretch out my hand to touch her cheek. I need to know she's real and not just a figment of my wishful thinking.

She closes her eyes and smiles at me when my hand cups the side of her face.

"How are you here?" I ask her. "How are you so real?"

Lilly opens her eyes.

"It's my gift," she answers. "I was able to travel from Earth to Heaven when I was alive. Now I can travel between Heaven and Earth in my second life."

I let my hand fall back to my side.

"All these years you could have come to me, but you didn't. Why, Lilly? Why did you leave me all alone for so long?"

"I didn't want to interfere with your destiny. Now your stubbornness is causing both you and Anna so much pain that I had to come. Someone had to try to knock some sense into that thick skull of yours."

I chuckle and shake my head. "You're the only one who has ever been able to do that."

"I know," Lilly says with a smile. "That's exactly why I'm here now."

We fall silent, and I feel a need to say, "I'm sorry. I'm sorry I failed you."

Lilly tilts her head at me. "Failed me? You haven't failed me at all, Malcolm. If anything, you've exceeded my expectations."

"But I let the relationship between Amalie and Lucifer happen."

"If you hadn't, we wouldn't have Anna now. It was all meant to be, Malcolm. You should know better than anyone that your father works in mysterious ways. You didn't fail me; never think that. And you didn't fail the mission God set you on either. If anything, the pieces are finally falling into place because of you. I couldn't be prouder."

I feel a weight lift off my heart with Lilly's words. My head feels clearer than it has in centuries.

I feel a sharp, twisting pain inside my chest and know Anna needs me.

"I have to go," I tell Lilly.

Lilly walks up to me and kisses me on the cheek.

"Go to her, Malcolm," she urges, smiling at me. "Go be with the woman you love."

I hug Lilly fiercely.

"Thank you," I tell her.

"Go!" she says, laughing. "Go before she changes her mind!"

I pull back and look at Lilly.

"Would she?" I ask, never having really considered the possibility until now.

"I don't think she could even if she wanted to," Lilly answers. "But why take the chance?"

I nod in total agreement as I turn away from my past and run toward my future.

CHAPTER 25

(Anna's Point of View)

My whole body feels bereft of life, like Malcolm's rejection of me has ripped out my beating heart and left an immense void inside my chest that can never be filled. Telling Malcolm that I was letting him go is the hardest thing I've ever done. I just wish my soul would stop crying out for him and gift me just a small moment of peace for my sacrifice. Yet it still wants to hold onto hope, no matter how tenuous it might be that Malcolm will realize neither of us can be whole without the other. However, I can't live my remaining days waiting for the impossible to happen.

I told Jered that I loved Malcolm enough to let him go if that was what would make him happy. And I have ... at least he'll think that I have. I'm not sure I'll ever be able to truly make my heart believe it.

I wonder if Malcolm can sense the pain I feel right now. If he does, I know I can never truly hide how I feel from him. I wish I could just break the tie that binds us to one another because it makes concealing my love from him virtually impossible. Maybe that's what God intended all along. Maybe He doesn't want me to hide my feelings from Malcolm for some inexplicable reason.

I don't know. I can't seem to think straight. All I can do is try to mend my heart enough to where it doesn't call out to Malcolm's in the middle of the night when the pain I feel over his loss consumes me. I need to harden my heart. I need to build my own wall like Malcolm has and not feel anything for anyone. But how do you perform such a miracle of numb oblivion?

The door to the workshop suddenly crashes open, causing me to jump involuntarily.

Malcolm steps over the threshold, instantly meeting my gaze, and I hear myself gasp at the unexpectedness of his appearance.

Malcolm is glowing like the sun itself is shining down upon him, just like my papa, Will, Jered, and the other Watchers do to my eyes. Papa told me it was a sign of their devotion, but this is the first time I've seen it around Malcolm. I don't fully understand why his devotion to me is showing up now, after I willingly let him go. It just doesn't make any sense.

I wipe the tears from my eyes because I don't want him to feel guilty over not being able to love me like I do him. I don't need, or want, his pity.

He walks up to me with quick strides.

"Anna," he says, a desperate plea in his voice, "forgive me."

I look up at him as he comes to stand beside me. He reaches out and cups my face between his hands, using the pads of his thumbs to brush away tears that refuse to stop.

The look in his eyes instantly tells me the story of his life—the pain he's suffered, the loss of loved ones—but they also show a yearning for me to better understand him, to listen to what he has to say, because it's been a long time coming.

"I love you, too," he declares, and I start to cry harder because I know he's telling the truth. "I knew you were my soul mate the moment yours called out to mine that night. I've just been too obstinate to accept it. But I know now that you and I have always been meant for one another. I want the future Lucas has seen for us. I want us to be a family. I want you to have my babies, and I want the privilege of calling you my wife, my lover, and my friend. Please, tell me I'm not too late. Please tell me that you haven't let me go from your heart just yet."

There's a part of me that wonders if I'm dreaming and another part of me that knows there's only one way to find out.

I stand up from the stool and wrap my arms around Malcolm's neck.

"You're not too late," I tell him, searching his eyes, making sure that it's truly him standing in front of me and not just a figment that my broken heart has conjured up. "You could never be too late."

I bury my fingers in Malcolm's hair.

"Kiss me, Malcolm," I beg. "I need to know this isn't just a dream."

"This is the best dream of them all," Malcolm says, smiling down at me, "because it's real."

Malcolm leans his head down to mine. His mouth is so close I can feel his next words vibrate against the tender flesh of my lips.

"This is only one of many kisses we'll share in our lives," he says to me like a promise. "I will always cherish it, because with this one, simple kiss, I pledge not only my heart and my body to you but also that part of my soul that has belonged to you since the beginning of time. I will stay by your side no matter what happens, and I will do everything within my power to give you the life you deserve. I won't take your love for me for granted ever again. I promise you that."

Malcolm barely touches his lips to mine as he breathes, "I love you, Anna."

I wrap my arms tighter around his neck as our lips fully join and find that Malcolm's mouth is a perfect match to my own.

Malcolm groans deep inside his chest. He drops his hands away from my face to pick me up and sit me on the worktable, so that our faces are level with one another. I wrap my legs around his hips, wanting all of him closer. I keep my lips locked to his and twine my fingers deeper into his silky mane. I suddenly feel as though I can't breathe. But I don't care about breathing. I can breathe later. Right now, the man I love is kissing me, and that's all that matters.

I feel Malcolm lean into me farther, deepening the kiss with the first, delicious taste of his tongue against mine. I tighten my hold on his head, not wanting him to back away too soon. I need the taste of him in my mouth, and I instantly know I want so much more. My whole body feels like it's been lit on fire from want, and there's only one way to ease the aching void within me.

I tear at the shirt he's wearing and hear the buttons pop off, bouncing against things in the room, but I don't care. All I can think about, all that I want, is Malcolm. I need to feel him against me, and his clothes are simply getting in my way.

I feel Malcolm's hands begin to work the zipper of my jacket down, but he stops unzipping midway.

Suddenly he pulls away from me, acting like he's trying to take in a breath that never seems to reach his lungs. His brow furrows in confusion at what's happening, and his eyes grow wide with alarm. I grab at him just as he falls unconscious and gently lay him down on the floor of the workshop.

"Malcolm!" I yell at him, but receive no response. "Malcolm!" I yell again, shaking his shoulders, trying to make him wake up.

I continue to desperately try to wake him, but nothing I do seems to work.

Minutes pass, and then I hear, "Well, that certainly took longer than I expected."

I look up to see Levi, masquerading in the body of my best friend, staring down at me with a goading, lecherous smile on his face.

I stand to my feet and see that he's not alone. Five Cirrun guards are standing behind him.

"What did you do to Malcolm?" I demand, feeling the flames of hate ignite in the pit of my soul.

Levi laughs. "I didn't do anything. It was all your doing, my little dove."

"Me?" I ask, completely puzzled. "What did I do?"

"You kissed him, wife. That's all you had to do."

"You're not making any sense," I say.

Levi smiles at me knowingly. "Didn't you ever wonder what those shots Empress Catherine made you take were for?"

A vision of the green liquid Millie and Eliza injected into my arms each week flits through my mind. I look down at Malcolm and feel my world begin to fall apart.

"I don't understand," I say with a shake of my head.

"Apparently Empress Catherine didn't trust your down-worlder hormones very much. Those shots were to make sure you stayed true to her son before and after marriage. Any man who didn't match the genetic profiles of either Augustus or your father was to be instantly poisoned by your sweet kiss. It was her insurance policy that you didn't get knocked up by anyone but her son."

I look down at Malcolm and feel warm tears spill from my eyes.

"Is he. ..." I can't even make myself ask the question for fear of what the answer might be.

"Dead?" Levi finishes for me. "No, unfortunately he can't die that easily. Plus, the poison in your system is probably at its lowest level since you haven't had an injection for almost a week. He'll simply remain knocked out for a while."

"How did you find us?"

"Oh, Empress Catherine thought of every contingency. I have to admit even I didn't know she could be so ingenious. Not only did she pump you full of poison, but she also placed trackers in your body to activate when the poison was released. I guess she wanted to make sure you couldn't hide from her after betraying your vows to her son. I figured it would only be a matter of time before you and Malcolm became physical with one another. Though I have to admit, I didn't think it would take *this* long. He must be losing his touch. I thought for sure he would have tried to bed you before now."

It all made sense. It was exactly something Auggie's mother would do to either ensure my purity or seek out a reason to dissolve the marriage contract between me and Auggie so she could remain in power.

Levi walks over to a toolbox on the worktable and picks up a small saw.

"You know, with Malcolm conveniently knocked out and looking so absolutely pathetic, I think I'll do something I've been wanting to do to him for years."

Levi makes to walk over to Malcolm, but I phase in front of him to stop his progress.

"Don't you dare touch him," I growl.

Levi smiles at me tight-lipped. Before I know it, he stabs me in the shoulder with a silver dagger, causing me to scream out in pain.

"A little souvenir from Amon," Levi says, pushing his face in front of mine while he twists the dagger deeper into my flesh. "It will keep you from phasing until I decide to remove it. Guards!

Please hold the empress back for a moment while I attend to her lover."

All five of the guards phase over and grab me. It takes their combined strength to hold me back from Levi. Before I can stop him, Levi grabs a fistful of Malcolm's hair and starts to cut it off with the jagged edge of the saw's blade. He repeats the process until all of Malcolm's long locks are shortened.

"Finally!" Levi says in triumph, throwing the last handful of Malcolm's hair onto the floor. "I've wanted to get rid of that mangy mess since he showed up on this godforsaken planet with it. I feel sure he'll thank me for the haircut after he wakes up. However, he may curse you, my little dove, for his capture. I hope that kiss was worth what I'm about to put him through."

"What are you going to do to him?" I ask, feeling a hatred buried so deep inside me that I never knew it existed until that moment.

"I'm going to make him wish you had never been born," Levi says, like the answer should have been obvious. "I may not be able to kill him, but that doesn't mean torturing him won't be fun."

"What do you want?" I ask, knowing Levi must have a price I can pay to save Malcolm from his hands.

"Offering yourself to me, are you?" Levi asks, sounding intrigued. "Actually, I've been thinking about that. I think I do have something I want from you. It's something only you can accomplish for me, and no, it's not having my child. It's something far more beneficial to me. But we'll get to that later."

Levi looks at one of the guards. "Go search the house. If you find anyone in there, take them to Cirrus. I'll deal with them later."

I don't say anything about Lucas, praying he has time to hide himself from the guard but not having too much hope for such a miracle.

"You," Levi says to another guard, "take this big oaf to a prison cell until I can find some time to play with him."

The guard bends down and touches Malcolm on the shoulder, phasing the love of my life away from me.

"And last but certainly not least, please escort my wife to the palace where she can wait for my return."

"What are you going to do?" I ask.

Levi produces his lightning whip in his hand. "I'm going to burn this place to the ground. I need to send a message to those who would defy me that this is what happens when you rebel against the emperor."

I stare at Levi and ask, "How can an angel from Heaven be such a monster on Earth?"

Levi laughs.

"Ask your real father the next time you see him. Lucifer's the one who made me into what I am today," Levi says with mock pride. "Now, go! Go back home so you can wait for your husband's return like a dutiful little wife."

Just before the guards phase me, I look into Levi's eyes and silently promise him that he will pay for any real harm he does to Malcolm or Lucas.

As Auggie so wisely said not so long ago about me and the love of my life, *"God help anyone who tries to come between the two of you. ... You would tear them to pieces if it meant protecting someone you love."*

I realize in that moment that not even God Himself will be able to protect Levi from the fury of my wrath.

I am Empress Annalisse Desiraye Greco Amador, daughter of Andre Greco, soul mate of Overlord Malcolm Xavier Devereaux, last descendant of Lilly Rayne Cole, and the only child of Lucifer, the first and most powerful archangel ever created.

I will protect those I care for with my life.
And I will get back the man I love, no matter what I have to do.

THE END

AUTHOR'S NOTE

Thank you so much for reading **Malcolm**, the first book in **The Redemption Series.** If you have enjoyed this book please take a moment to leave a review. To leave a review please visit:
Malcolm http://mybook.to/Malcolm1

Thank you in advance for leaving a review for the book.
Sincerely,
S.J. West.

NEXT IN THE WATCHERS UNIVERSE

  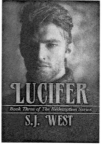 

THE REDEMPTION SERIES

ANNA,
REDEMPTION SERIES BOOK 2

Levi uses Anna's love for those she cares about to further his own agenda. He forces her to do something for him that not even Lucifer was able to accomplish in a thousand years of scheming.

While Anna attempts to work through her feelings for Lucifer, she becomes increasingly confused by his actions. One moment he seems to want to form a connection with her, and the next he does something which could tear them permanently apart.

As Anna and Malcolm grow closer, he opens up even more to her about his past and his hopes for the future. Drawing strength from her love for Malcolm and her ever growing extended family, Anna meets the trials and tribulations presented to her as a new set of threats emerge and threaten to ruin the happiness she's found.

Exclusively on Amazon, Free on KU!
http://mybook.to/Anna2

ABOUT THE AUTHOR

Once upon a time, a little girl was born on a cold winter morning in the heart of Seoul, Korea. She was brought to America by her parents and raised in the Deep South where the words ma'am and y'all became an integrated part of her lexicon. She wrote her first novel at the age of eight and continued writing on and off during her teenage years. In college she studied biology and chemistry and finally combined the two by earning a master's degree in biochemistry.

After that she moved to Yankee land where she lived for four years working in a laboratory at Cornell University. Homesickness and snow aversion forced her back South where she lives in the land, which spawned Jim Henson, Elvis Presley, Oprah Winfrey, John Grisham and B.B. King.

After finding her Prince Charming, she gave birth to a wondrous baby girl and they all lived happily ever after.

As always, you can learn about the progress on my books, get news about new releases, new projects and participate on amazing give-aways by signing up for my newsletter:

FB Book Page: @ReadTheWatchersTrilogy
FB Author Page: https://www.facebook.com/sandra.west.585112

Website: www.sjwest.com
Amazon: author.to/SJWest-Amazon
Goodreads: https://www.goodreads.com/author/show/6561395.S_J_West
Bookbub: https://www.bookbub.com/authors/s-j-west
Newsletter Sign-up: http://eepurl.com/bQsosX
Instagram: @authorsjwest
Twitter: @SJWest2013

If you'd like to contact the author, you can email her to: sandrawest481@gmail.com

Made in the USA
Monee, IL
22 May 2022

96890070R10177